Chase the Sun

Charles Ray

North Potomac, MD

For more information on new release and other writing-related news, check out the author's web site at http://charlesray-author.com/. Independent authors thrive when readers know about and buy their books. That's done by word of mouth, and reviews. If you liked this book, take the time to do even a short review, to let others know.

Cover design by the author

Printed in the United States of America

DEDICATION

If you like a good story, this book is dedicated to you

.

Chapter 1

August 1812, Lost Island in the Bahama Island Chain

After leaving *Mama Lillie's* on Cat Island and boarding *The Vixen* for the voyage to Lost Island, Colin Worth stood next to Elizabeth on the quarterdeck, watching quietly as she shouted orders to the men in the riggings, getting them to adjust the sails to take full advantage of the prevailing winds. He was rehearsing in his mind just what he would say to her when they arrived at her villa, which served as a haven when she and her crew were not prowling the mid-Atlantic in search of fat merchant vessels to plunder.

He was beginning to experience doubts about his mission. It had all seemed so simple when Captain Llewelyn Morris, sitting in his cramped office at naval headquarters in Charleston, South Carolina, explained it to him. Return to the Caribbean and make contact with one of the most notorious pirate captains in the area, Elizabeth Parker, master of *The Vixen*, and organize her and her crew to create diversions in the Caribbean, thus, giving the American forces, land and sea, to prosecute the war in the North Atlantic, the Great Lakes, and the northwestern frontier, without having to worry about a major attack from the Gulf of Mexico, or up through Florida.

The devil, though, is always in the details. True, they had successfully played cat and mouse with vessels of the American and British navies for months when Colin was recuperating after being thrown off his ship, *Intrepid*, by the mentally unbalanced captain, Beauregard Dangerfield. Stranded in the Atlantic in a small boat, without food or water, Colin had been rescued by *The Vixen*, and after a rocky beginning to their relationship, had made friends with the pirate crew, and begun a tentative romance with Elizabeth. After some time had passed, he made his way back to Charleston just in time to testify at the court martial of Dangerfield for dereliction of duty, resulting in the man being relieved of his command and cashiered from the navy, and Colin being given command of *Intrepid*.

In June 1812, when the United States declared war on Great Britain in retaliation for the English kidnapping men from American vessels, and English officers stirring up the Indian tribes on the western border, Colin had been summoned to Morris's office in Charleston. His mission, as described by Morris, was to use the pirates to occupy the English fleet in the Bahamas and keep them from being able to mount a major offensive in the south, to be 'mosquitos biting at the English in the Caribbean.' While it sounded good as a theory, he also knew that a well-timed, well-placed slap could kill a mosquito, and the English, with their fleet present in most of the world's oceans, had a lot of swatters.

It was, however, too late to back out. The fate of his country hung in the balance. Even though he personally thought it beyond foolish for the United States to be the aggressor by declaring war, he had a sworn duty to carry out the mission he'd been assigned. For better or worse, he would, by Jove, carry it out, or die trying. The thing that worried him most, though, was that Elizabeth could also die.

The way she had reacted to his proposal, it hadn't seemed that this worried her.

"Will this adventure you are suggesting involve taking a lot of fat merchant vessels or sending English warships to the bottom?" she had asked.

He had to tell her that, while it might involve just that, the primary objective was to divert the English fleet away from the American shores. He then suggested they wait until arrival at her home on Lost Island to discuss the details.

And, she'd taken him at his word, not saying another word about it for the entire voyage.

The Vixen's anchorage at Lost Island was a small cove that cut into the island in a crescent shape. Just deep enough for the ship to sail into it without its keel scraping the bottom, it was reached through an inlet just wide enough for one vessel, flanked by black rock walls that were overgrown with tropical vines; barely visible to the uninitiated, even from up close.

The vessel's return was greeted by the blowing of conch shells and a crowd of cheering adults and children on the beach as the crew lowered boats and rowed to shore.

Colin's presence, sitting next to Elizabeth in the first boat, caused a murmur of excitement. Several of the old women in the crowd put their heads together, speaking with their hands masking their mouths, and the younger men gazed at him with envy in their eyes. While Colin and Elizabeth had made a valiant effort to keep their relationship private, the community of Lost Island was small, and information, like water soaked up into a sponge, spread quickly.

He silently endured the many pats on the back and shoulders, the sly grins, and winks on the walk from the beach to Elizabeth's house.

After they mounted the steps to the wrap-around verandah, Elizabeth stopped and turned to face the crowd that had gathered in her front yard. She raised her hands, and the murmuring of the crowd finally died down.

"My people," she said. "It's good to be home. And, as you see, our friend Colin Worth has returned with me. Please prepare a welcome celebration for him this evening here in my front yard, and we will eat, drink, sing, and dance the night away."

A deafening cheer erupted. Children danced and did cartwheels. Old men stamped their feet and smiled, and women hugged each other. Colin smiled, remembering how much the people of Lost Island loved their celebrations.

"I assume we will have the chance to discuss my plan before the celebration," he said quietly.

"Of course. M'nondo, Diego," she said to the two men standing to her other side. "Get out the best brandy and prepare the dining room for a quick conference."

M'nondo, the dark skin of his bare skull glistening like polished rock, smiled at Colin.

"You plan to get him drunk before the party?" he asked. He nudged her shoulder.

"Of course not," she replied. "Just a little private celebration of his return before the place is overrun with people."

Diego Garcia, first mate of *The Vixen*, and once Colin's rival for Elizabeth's affections, had a serious look on his face. Even though he and Colin had settled their differences, and it had been made clear that Elizabeth did not share his feelings, he still carried a torch for her.

4

"Captain, should I get out the maps?" he asked in a stiffly formal tone.

She looked at him, her left eyebrow raised. "Of course, Diego. Spread them on the dining table, will you? Colin and I will be in directly."

He saluted, spun on his heel and entered the mansion. M'nondo, a wry expression on his face, looked at Colin.

"He did not expect you back so soon," he said. "I think he still lives on hope."

Colin shrugged.

"If things go as I expect they will, he'll soon be too busy to concern himself with anything but being alive at the end of each day."

M'nondo's smile widened.

"Ah, so you were being truthful, you do plan to offer us great adventure."

Elizabeth, who had been watching the three men out of the corners of her eyes, turned, hands on hips, and shot a mock glare at M'nondo. "*Kofi*, the brandy will not pour itself." She tossed her head, causing her fiery red hair to cross in front of her clear blue eyes.

Her use of the Fante term for 'Friday,' her pet name for him since they were children, took all the sting out of her words. Companions since she'd been taken by the pirate, John Cleague, from the ship bearing her parents to Boston, where her father was to be the new British consul, they had become siblings in all but blood.

"Yes, *Esi*," he said. Calling her 'Sunday,' a name he'd given her because it had been on a Sunday when Captain Cleague had assigned him to be her guard and companion, let her know he understood she was joking. He bowed. "My sister's wish is my command."

Straightening, he winked at Colin and went into the house.

One last wave at the crowd, and Elizabeth turned her attention to Colin. The way she looked at him made him feel weak in the knees, and even though he was a full five inches taller than she, he felt as if he was looking up at her.

"Well, Colin, shall we go inside. You can tell me all about this grand plan of yours."

She took his arm as they entered the grand entry hall of her residence, which also served as the headquarters for their piracy operations. People were busy in the hall, and it was hard for Colin to tell which ship's crew were and which were villagers, for everyone lent a hand to moving chairs and tables to the center of the room. He knew that as soon as they'd assembled what they needed, they would then move them outside and arrange them across the lawn. The tables would soon be laden with all manner of foods and drink, and chairs would be placed conveniently for Elizabeth and her ship's officers, but primarily for the elderly and infirm. A place would be left clear in the center of the area for dancing. Colin knew that he would get no sleep his first night back on Lost Island.

In the large dining room, with its long table set in the center under an ornate crystal chandelier, M'nondo and Garcia had already arranged things for Colin's briefing. A large map of the Caribbean, the Gulf of Mexico, and the southern coast of the United States was spread out on the table, held down at the corners by four large bottles of brandy. Empty brandy snifters sat in front of four chairs, one at the head of the table, two on the left side, and one on the right.

Colin went to the single chair on the right, leaving the chair at the head of the table for Elizabeth. With a nod, she acknowledged her position. Colin nodded at the two men sitting across from him.

"Okay, gentlemen, you want adventure? I think I have just what you seek."

"What is it you wish us to do?" Elizabeth asked.

"Our mission here will be to divert the English navy away from American shores. The American navy is able to handle the English in the North Atlantic and Great Lakes, hopefully, but if they bring in large numbers of additional troops, especially in the south in places like New Orleans, our army is no match for them."

"You are saying that after winning your independence from the *Ingles*, you could lose it?" Garcia looked at Colin, his expression a mixture of skepticism and amazement.

"I doubt they would try to recolonize us," Colin said. "But, if they defeat us, their terms would probably bankrupt us. We would then be ripe for picking by any greedy European power with an eye on our territory."

"Like I just said, *amigo*, you just won your independence less than forty years ago, and you could lose it because of this stupid war."

"Well, yes, I suppose that's true. I hadn't thought of it quite like that."

"Okay," M'nondo said. "So, we are to make sure the English are unable to invade from the south. That is a tall order, my friend."

"That it is." Collin nodded. "At least we won't have to worry about Florida. The Spanish are unlikely to allow the English to bring troops ashore there. But, if they come ashore at Mobile or New Orleans in any significant numbers, and cut off our southern seaports, we'll be in big trouble."

Garcia laughed. "Is no big problem, *amigo*," he said. "We just have to sink a few of their ships, and they'll be running around like the chicken with no head."

"I wouldn't take such a light view of it, Diego." Colin put his hand, palm down, on the Atlantic Ocean. "The English have the biggest, and most powerful navy in the world. Our spies in London tell us they have over 140,000 men in the English fleet, and 30,000 of those men are armed marines. And, even with that many men, they can't fully man their ships. Think about that. That's a lot of ships, with a lot of firepower. They wouldn't need but a few of their ships of the line to obliterate us if they decided to do so."

Elizabeth, who had been sitting quietly watching their conversation, leaned forward.

"Colin is right," she said. "If the English decide to come after us, we would be easily defeated."

"That's why we have to be constantly on the move," Colin said.

She cocked her head to the side and tapped her finger on the hard wood of the table top, making a clicking sound.

"You are right, that is necessary. But, it is not enough. The English are likely to be on the lookout for us after the first raid or two, and should they ever trace us here to Lost Island, my people would be in danger. I cannot have that."

Colin looked back at her, crestfallen. She had so readily agreed to help, and now seemed to be changing her mind.

"Yes, there are risks, but—"

She waved a hand, cutting him off. "So, the first thing we must do," she said. "Is relocate our headquarters. I am thinking that Skull Island would be perfect. With the jungle separating us from the inhabitants, should the English track us by some miracle, the local people wouldn't have to suffer."

His mouth dropped open, and then snapped shut. It took him a few seconds to regain his composure.

"That's an excellent idea. We should move right away."

Waving a finger in the air in front of his face, she said, "Not until after our welcome banquet."

Chapter 2

August 1812, Skull Island

The welcome banquet had gone on until well after midnight, with much drinking and dancing when the food was gone.

Colin only had a vague recollection of events, or of being pulled away from a group of young women, all insisting he dance with him, and being hustled, still fully dressed, under the bed covers in the large bedroom adjacent to Elizabeth's.

The next morning, far too early for Colin and the headache he was suffering, Elizabeth banged on his door, rousing him to help move the equipment and supplies to the beach to be loaded aboard *The Vixen* for their journey to Skull Island.

After a quick breakfast of hot rolls and coffee, they boarded and set sail. Even after a second cup of steaming hot coffee, though, Colin's head still felt as if someone was inside it banging on drums. He stood behind Elizabeth on the quarterdeck, his rump pressed against the polished wood rail, hoping she and the rest of the crew would not notice his distressed condition.

No one spoke to him for the entire voyage. It was only after they'd dropped anchor in the sheltered lagoon at Skull Island where they'd surprised and attacked *Intrepid,* when it was under Dangerfield's command, and were being rowed to shore, that Elizabeth turned to him with a strange smile on her face.

"Are you going to be able to do a full briefing for the crew today after we set up camp, or should I just let you sleep it off, and we can do it after breakfast tomorrow?"

His headache was mostly gone, and now that he was on land, and away from the pitching and swaying of *Vixen's* deck, he felt almost human again. He looked at her indignantly. "What gives you the idea that I'd not be able to do it today?"

"Oh, come now, dear Colin," she said. "You were probably in too much distress to hear yourself, but I clearly heard you groan each time we hit a swell. I think, mayhap, your stomach was back home too long, and you became unaccustomed to our strong drink."

He shrugged. Nothing got past her, he thought. "I guess I was a bit under the weather. I'm fine now, though. Let's get a temporary camp set up, and I'll explain the mission to the crew. Then, we can start construction of a more suitable headquarters."

She put a hand on his shoulder. "Are you sure? You don't have to pretend with me, you know."

"No, I'm fine, truly. And, the quicker the men are briefed, the quicker we can start planning implementation of my plan."

She looked skeptical but nodded and patted his cheek.

Elizabeth jumped from the boar as soon as the prow touched the wet sand of the beach. Colin was close behind her.

Few signs of *Intrepid's* presence remained, a few charred boards scattered about the beach.

Colin and Elizabeth stood beneath a towering palm and watched as the crew unloaded the first bundles of equipment brought from the ship and began setting up camp.

As a crewman carrying a large easel passed, she called out to him. "Edward, please set that easel up over there." She pointed. "Commander Worth will need it when he talks to us."

The man bowed and hastened to comply, setting the easel up in front of a large boulder at the edge of the thick jungle that ringed the lagoon.

Colin took the rolled map of the Caribbean area from his haversack, and, using wooden dowels, affixed it to the easel.

"Are you able to see the map clearly from over there?" he asked Elizabeth.

"Of course, but the map is not needed," she said. "My crew and I know these waters like a bitch knows her pups. I daresay we know a few places that you will not find on your map."

Colin smiled. That, he knew to be true. The map would stay, though, because, unlike the pirates of *The Vixen*, his knowledge of the local seas was limited.

"Okay, I'm ready whenever you are," he said, turning and facing the clearing, his arms folded across his chest. He watched as the crew, with the practiced moves borne out of years of experience shuttling pilfered cargo from captured merchant ships, from ship to ship, and ship to shore, transferred the supplies to the beach, stacked boxes neatly, and got a cook fire going.

When things were arranged to Elizabeth's satisfaction, she had the men assemble in the clearing facing Colin and his map.

"All right, me hearties," she said. "Colin will now tell us what mischief his masters in Washington want us to get up to."

Her comment was responded to with laughs and whistles. Knowing what he did about what they were being asked to do, Colin didn't feel much like laughing. He knew, though, that he would have to maintain a firm and calm demeanor in front of them.

He waited until the noise subsided, and then swept the gathering with his steely gaze.

"Captain." He nodded toward Elizabeth, who stood to his left, beside the front row of men sitting on the sand. "Comrades," he said. "We are being asked to provide a distraction for the English here in the Caribbean, to enable the American forces to deal with the threat from the east and north without having to worry about an attack from the south."

One of the men in the front row raised his hand and waved it in the air. Colin nodded in his direction.

"So, you be wantin' us to raid English merchant shippin'. Ain't much different than what we been doin' all along."

"That is only a part of it." Colin smiled at the look of surprise that blossomed on the man's face. "In addition to merchant shipping, we'll be going after some of the smaller, more vulnerable warships."

Looks of surprises turned to frowns. A burly, bald man in the back row, stood and glared at Colin.

"There ain't no loot to be had from no English warship," he said.

"True, there is no gold or silver to be taken from warships but think of the weapons and ammunition we would get if we were able to capture one of the small sloops. In addition, such an act would certainly get the attention of the English."

The man rubbed a work-hardened hand over his bald pate. "It would that, for sure. They'd be scouring the sea lookin' for us."

"Precisely," Colin said, making a chopping motion with his hand. "And, every ship out looking for us means one less attacking American ships or ports."

A murmuring arose from the assembled pirates. More than one angry scowl was directed at Colin. He felt that he was losing their support.

M'nondo stood, stepped forward, and turned to face his comrades. "What Colin says makes sense," he said. "But, it is no different than it would be otherwise. Every time we take a merchant ship, the English send warships to look for us. Now, though, we would make them pay for such an act by destroying some of the hunters. I, for one, would not mind owning one of those rifles the English marines use."

The bald man didn't look convinced. "It ain't gonna be easy for us, though. We be fightin' the whole English fleet in these seas."

Elizabeth moved to stand beside M'nondo.

"You knew that life would not be easy when you became a pirate," she said. "However, I will not order any man here to take part in this mission. Any who wish not to participate, are free to leave. I will have *The Vixen* take you back to Lost Island, and you can stay with the women, children, and old people."

"I didn't say I wasn't gonna do it," the bald man said. "I was just pointin' out the problems, is all."

"I take it, then, that you are all in this." She put her hands on her hips and faced them, her expression steely.

"Aye, cap'n, we're all in," a gap-toothed older man in the front row said. "You just tell us what you want us to do."

"Very well, then." She turned to Colin. "Now, Colin, will you continue with your briefing?"

"Thank you, captain," Colin said. "First, I must acknowledge that this will not be an easy mission. I believe, however, that we can do it in such a way to minimize our danger and inflict maximum damage on the English.

He turned back to the map.

"With hundreds of islands, many unknown to their captains and crews, we have no shortage of hiding places. We have a fast and capable vessel, that has already proved that it can hold its own against a heavily-armed vessel. Don't forget; we took on *Intrepid* and defeated her. We can use the same tactics against the English. In addition, I propose that we set up a network of spies and informants in the islands to keep us apprised of ship movements. That way, we can stay one step ahead of our enemy. A series of quick raids in scattered locations around the islands should sufficiently confuse them, that they won't have a clue to our location, will also afford us additional protection."

"We still be able to take loot, though, right?" a pirate asked.

"Most assuredly. In fact, raiding their supply vessels will be our first priority."

The bald man stood. "Well, when do we get started?"

Colin let out the breath that he'd been holding and smiled. Thanks to Elizabeth and M'nondo, he now had a small, but highly efficient fighting force, and could take the war to the English in a way they wouldn't be expecting. It would still be a dangerous undertaking, but there was that small glimmer of hope that they might actually succeed.

Chapter 3

Once the briefing was concluded, work on building a permanent base of operation began in earnest. Small trees were felled and stripped of bark to construct rudimentary cabins at the edge of the jungle. The first building completed, larger than the rest, was to be the central command headquarters and lodging for Elizabeth, Colin, M'nondo, and Garcia. Farther into the jungle, small huts were constructed to hold supplies and armaments.

The ship's cook prepared midday and evening meals while the rest of the crew worked. The midday meal was eaten at whatever work site the man was involved in, but as the sun sank into the west, everyone gathered in the clearing in front of the big cabin for the evening meal.

Elizabeth sat between Colin and M'nondo at a small makeshift table constructed by one of the men who was skilled in woodworking. Although intended originally to hold maps and charts, Colin had insisted that Elizabeth, as captain, should not eat sitting unladylike on the bare ground like the rest of the crew.

"But, I am wearing pants," she said. "There is no danger that anyone will see anything. Not, mind you, that I have anything under my clothing to see that all of them have not already seen before."

Colin looked away, red-faced at her brazen attitude. "It's not that," he insisted. "It's just more befitting your status as captain."

"Very well. Even though I don't believe in this nonsense of the captain having to be remote from the crew, I'll sit here. But, only because I know you just hate sitting on the ground when you eat." She laughed, making a sweet, musical sound to Colin's ears.

He knew, though, that she was more correct than not. He had never been fond of eating while sitting on the dirty ground.

"It is why I joined the navy instead of the army. Those soldiers spend far too much time sitting on the ground—or, walking on it for that matter."

M'nondo poured a generous portion of the fiery red rum into Colin's cup. "It makes it much easier to pour drinks," he said.

Colin raised h is cup and took a sip, grimacing as the first bit of the fiery liquor crossed his tongue, but then smiling as the inside of his mouth became accustomed to the hot, sweet flavor of the cane liquor. "I'll drink to that," he said. "This reminds me of my early days as a young subaltern. Sitting around one of the taverns near the wharf, sipping rum or ale and telling stories."

"I would love to hear some of them," Elizabeth said.

"I would rather hear about your life."

She shrugged. "I have been a pirate for all of my adult life, and the childhood that I remember was spent either on Captain Sprague's ship, or on Lost Island."

"I've never understood how you came to be part of Sprague's band," he said. "Where did you come from before Sprague?"

"I . . . I don't know. I don't remember." She looked at M'nondo. "Do you know where I come from *Kofi*?"

The big man turned away from her, a mournful look in his dark brown eyes.

"You do know, don't you?" Colin speared him with a sharp look. "I would love to hear her story."

M'nondo shook his head. "Her story is not mine to tell."

"But, *Kofi*, I would like to hear it as well." Elizabeth put her hand on his wrist.

"Are you sure?"

"Yes. I think it is time that I knew just who I am."

He took a long swallow of rum and wiped his mouth with the back of his hand.

"Very well, *Esi*, I will tell you what I know."

He began his tale with the lookout aboard *The Vixen* spotting the English galleon, *City of Dover*, off the coast of the United States, about 200 miles east of Boston, where the vessel was bound. He described the way the pirate ship had come up behind the galleon in the predawn dimness, and then surprised her with a broadside of cannon shot, followed by a boarding party that caught the English crew, most of whom were asleep, completely off guard.

Tears welled up in Elizabeth's eyes when he described the slaughter of the parents she barely remembered. Colin put a hand over her hands. He could feel them trembling.

"P-papa Jack killed my mother and father?"

M'nondo shook his head. "Not him personally," he said. "I am not sure who it was. When we boarded, the rest of the crew began to wake up, and they fought us. Our men fought back, and in the confusion, your mother and father were killed."

"Why was I not killed also?"

"Old Captain Teague was so impressed with your spunk, he decided to keep you." He took another drink. "I think at first, you were like a pet to him, but pretty quick, he came to really like you. You became a daughter to him."

She closed her eyes. "So, that is why my name is Parker, not Teague. I have a very vague memory of a man and a woman, but I am unable to remember much about them."

"When you jumped from behind those crates on the deck and challenged us, Captain Teague asked you who you were, and you said Elizabeth Parker. You were a sight to see, a scrawny little girl screaming and biting." He rubbed his shoulder. "Where you bit me, it took two weeks to heal. Anyway, the captain thought it was amusing, so he decided not to kill you. He put me in charge of taking care of you. It was hard at first. You refused to eat, bit me every time I let my guard down, and cried yourself to sleep every night. But, pretty soon, you calmed down, and after six months, I think you must have forgot your parents, because you never asked about them again."

She put a hand over her eyes. "I think I must have," she said. "I have these vague memories sometimes, but they never last long. I can't even remember their names."

"I do not know, either. We burned the log book and records with the ship. All I know is, based on the condition of the cabin they were staying in, he must have been an important Englishman."

Colin looked at her, with his face wrinkled in concern. "So, you're English. That could present a problem to our mission."

She let her hand drop into her lap and looked back at him. Her expression was unreadable.

"Why is that?"

"We Americans are in a war with your people," he said. "I hesitate to put you in that situation. If I'd known this before, I would have refused it."

"And, my dear Colin, just what do you mean by that? Who are *my* people?"

"The English, of course."

"Hm." She pinched the bridge of her nose. "I suppose, if you mean where I was born, then, yes, I am English. But, I have spent most of my life here in the islands. *These* are my people. I might have been born in England, but I am not English. I am from Lost Island, which is part of the Bahamas chain of islands. I very much doubt that the English would claim me. It is more likely that they would hang me if I stepped forward to claim citizenship. You forget, my dear; I am a pirate."

Colin smiled. "So, you have no problem attacking English ships?"

She turned and smiled at M'nondo. "*Kofi*, would you please tell him what we have been doing for the past many years."

"We have probably taken more English ships than any other nationality, except maybe American." He pointed at Colin. "You forget, Colin, the English and Americans are the biggest traders in these waters, even with the French and Spanish territories. I imagine that hangman's nooses await us in all four of those countries."

"I hadn't thought about it that way," Colin said. "I can say this, though. After taking on this mission, I believe I can get pardons for all of you in the United States." He leaned forward, his hands on the table. "That would be something to look forward to, don't you think?"

Elizabeth laid a hand on top of his. "Thinking over much about the future is not something pirates do. For now, let us concentrate on getting your mission done successfully.

Chapter 4

September 1812, The Navy Board, Somerset House, London

Vice Admiral Sir Stanley Kensington, his blue tailcoat in an uncharacteristically casual manner, sat on the edge of his high-backed chair, his elbows resting on the surface of the wide teak desk. He stared across the desk at the unimpressive looking man sitting in a small chair facing his desk. He was not in the best of moods. The First Lord of the Admiralty had given him a most unpleasant task, one that he felt was unworthy of his status and position, and certainly not something that a gentleman should engage in. But, it had been made clear to him that, if he wished to add the third star with a promotion to admiral, or even, if the fates were kind, a third star with anchor and crown of fleet admiral, he would not only take the job, but he would succeed.

It meant, though, that he had to hold his nose, and consort with the likes of Liam Macintosh. Kensington had little use for Scots in general, and he disliked this particular Scot in particular. The man embodied everything Kensington disliked about the working classes, from his plain attire to his crude manner of speaking. Grudgingly, though, he had to concede, these very qualities made him ideal for the mission Kensington was about to give him.

"Do you have any idea why I have summoned you here, Macintosh?" His voice dripped with condescension.

If Macintosh was aware of this, from his expression, he didn't notice.

"Aye, guv," he said. "You be wantin' me to go to the colonies in the Caribbean and spread a wee bit of mischief."

Kensington snorted. "That is a bit simplistic, sir," he said. "Your mission will entail more than a mere bit of mischief making. How familiar are you with the situation in the Bahamas?"

"Not very much, sir. I just know that the fleet there is spread thin, and in addition to lookin' out for the bloody Yanks, it has to contend with pirates who're spread over the region like flies in a fish market."

Even though he winced at the man's coarse language, Kensington had to admit that his summary of the situation was basically accurate.

"Yes, the fleet there is small at the moment, while we concentrate on hitting the Americans in the northern lakes area. But, there are plans to reinforce the south for a push from the Gulf, up to the port of New Orleans, to cut off supplies from the south and open up a second front."

"Aye, I've heard of this plan. How am I to support it?"

This was the part that Kensington had the most doubts about. If the bloody Scot failed, he thought, the entire southern strategy could collapse.

"According to an agent we have in Boston, the Americans have sent a *provocateur* to the Bahamas to stir up trouble with the pirates," Kensington said.

"Your primary mission is to identify and eliminate him, then you are to identify all pirates and any others who have worked with him and turn them over to our people in the governor's office."

"By eliminate the Yank spy, I assume you mean I'm to kill him? What about the pirates? Wouldna it be easier to just eliminate them—or, at least, their captains—as well?"

Kensington, a look of disgust on his patrician face, shook his head. "No, it sends a better signal to the pirates if we allow the authorities to deal with them. This American agent, however, is another matter entirely. When you find him, before you . . . dispose of him, you must learn everything from him. I suspect he will know the American plans for the south. Such information would be most valuable."

Kensington shuddered at the look of eager anticipation on Macintosh's face. The man was practically salivating. "Aye, guv, now, that sounds just fine to me. I can take my time with him. When I'm done, not only will he be beggin' to die and be done with it, he will have told me everything he knows."

"Very well, then. Your contact will be the governor-general's secretary in Nassau. You are to keep him informed of your activities as much as possible. You are to go to Southampton immediately, where the sloop, *H.M.S. Exeter*, awaits to transport you to Nassau. Before you leave, do you have any questions?"

"Nay, I have'na anything to ask. I'm packed and ready to travel, and I'll let you know as soon as I arrive in Nassau."

Macintosh stood and proffered a work-hardened hand. Kensington stared at it for a heartbeat, reluctant to even touch the man. But, he realized that his future depended upon this rumpled, disreputable Scot, and that, in order to succeed, he needed to maintain his loyalty. He took a deep breath and clasped the offered hand, wincing at the feel of the calluses, and feeling a strong urge to immediately wash his hand with the strongest soap he could find.

"I wish you Godspeed, Mr. Macintosh, and success in your mission."

"Aye, I be thankin' ye guvnor, but I'll be goin' up against a bloody colonial. It's hardly a fair match. The bloody divul's as good as dead."

Something in the man's tone chilled Kensington's blood. The man seemed to be looking forward to committing murder with relish. As he watched him saunter out of the office, he sat back and sighed.

"You stupid Americans," he muttered to himself. "Why in heaven's name did you have to declare war on us, forcing me to have to soil myself by consorting with the likes of this? You have just opened the doors to hell, and the devil himself is coming out to greet you."

Chapter 5

September 1812, Aboard *The Vixen,* east of Bermuda

Three and a half weeks without shaving had resulted in a lush growth of Colin's beard, which, along with the rough garb he wore, gave him the appearance of the pirates who were now his crew mates.

The Vixen had been underway for most of the day, searching the seas east of Bermuda's main island for prey; hoping to intercept a merchant ship carrying supplies for the British army that was slowly being built up in the islands for a southern attack. He stood in the bow, peering over the rail at the slate gray swells of the Atlantic, and breathing in the salt-tinged air blowing across the deck as the ship sailed a northerly course.

They were now two weeks into their search, and had, so far, come up empty, but had, the day before, heard rumors of a supply ship inbound from England. The informant hadn't been able to tell them whether or not it contained military supplies, but even if it was only a commercial cargo, taking it would get the attention of the authorities in Nassau.

The time at sea, with the deck swaying beneath his feet, had given him more time to think than he'd had in many months, and his thoughts troubled him. He found that he liked the life he was now leading. While pirate crews were not as orderly in dress as the men aboard *Intrepid*, they were every bit as disciplined. And, in many ways, because they all knew that everyone beyond their shipmates would be against them, there was an even greater sense of camaraderie than existed within the navy crew; men who, at the end of a voyage, could walk freely in port, or return home to their families without fearing that the authorities were on their tail. He could see himself staying here—mainly because *here* was where Elizabeth was—enjoying the companionship of this hardy, uncompromising band of cutthroats, anyone of whom would put his life at risk for one of his friends. Here, there were no complicated regulations to worry about. You did your job, you stood by your comrades, and you kept your ship ready to sail. It was the life he dreamed about as a boy, and now, it was his for the taking. But, he had, upon accepting a commission in the American navy, taken an oath, and he'd also been taught never to betray a solemn promise.

His thoughts, the damp caress of ocean spray on his face, and his focus on spotting English ships, caused him to miss the sound of boots clomping across the deck toward him. The pressure of a hand on his shoulder caused him to start. He whipped around, a look of surprise on his face.

"You looked like you were a thousand leagues away," M'nondo said.

"I don't I could see three thousand miles, even in my dreams," Colin said. "But, you're probably right. With nothing to see on the horizon but sea and sky, I guess I was doing a bit of wool gathering."

"You were thinking about how much you love the life out here on the open sea."

"Uh, yes, but how did you know?"

"I have seen that expression before. I remember when I was a child, hearing my father talk about those who chase the sun."

"Chase the sun? What does that mean?"

"Some of our tribes lived near the great sea; what you call the Atlantic Ocean. I remember when I was small, wondering where the sun went when it sank into the sea. Some, though, did more than wonder. They made large boats of the trunks of palm trees, with fronds for sails, and put out to sea. My father said that they were chasing the sun to see where its home was. There were others who traveled in the opposite direction, hoping to find the place where the sun sprang from the earth each morning."

Colin smiled. "Ah, I see. We, too, have those who chase the sun. Men who wander into the wilderness to see what's there. In a way, I suppose that's what I've been doing for most of my life; chasing the sun."

"But, the sun is wily." M'nondo chuckled. "He can never be caught."

Shrugging, Colin said, "So, the chase goes on."

"Ships off the port bow," the lookout atop the main mast shouted.

The deck erupted in a flurry of activity. Those assigned to the six cannons ran to their stations, two men with long-barreled muskets climbed into the riggings where they would act as sharpshooters, while others readied their pistols and sabers for boarding action. All of this was accomplished without a command from the captain. Elizabeth stood next to the helmsman, her eyes focused on the ocean to the northeast.

"How many, and how far?" she shouted up at the lookout.

"Two, a small sloop, and a galleon," he replied. "I put 'em at about three miles. They be on a east by southeast course."

Upon hearing the lookout's warning, Colin and M'nondo had dashed the length of the deck and mounted the quarterdeck. They were standing next to Elizabeth when the lookout responded to her question.

"That means they're likely heading for Nassau," Colin said.

"Are they English?" Elizabeth called up to the lookout.

"Looks like an English flag flyin' from the quarterdeck of the galleon, captain."

She turned and looked at Colin. "Do you think we can take them both?"

"We probably could, but it's not worth the risk."

"Maybe we can separate them," M'nondo said.

Colin stared at the two ships, separated from each other by three lengths of the galleon, which followed the faster sloop as best it could. A plan began to form in his mind.

"That's not a bad idea," he said. "Perhaps if we can frighten the sloop into fleeing, the galleon might be ripe for the picking."

Elizabeth snapped her fingers. "Ah ha. I think I see where you're going with this." To the helmsman she said, "Set a course as if you plan to cut across the bow of the sloop."

"Aye, captain," was the replay.

The ship dipped and swayed as the bow swung left.

"Set the sails for full speed," she shouted. "And, ready the cannons on the port side."

Colin could see that she had figured out what he wanted to do. They would make for the faster sloop at full speed. Outgunned and outmanned, the smaller vessel would probably attempt to increase speed to escape, leaving the lumbering galleon to them.

And, just as he'd anticipated, the sloop began a change of course toward the west, heeling sharply as it did, but, *The Vixen* was fast for a ship of its size, and the gap between the two vessels was quickly narrowing.

Just as they came within the limits of cannon range, the bow of *The Vixen* pointed at the forepart of the sloop, Colin turned to ask Elizabeth to execute the turning maneuver he had in mind. But, she was anticipating him.

"Hard to starboard, helm," she said. "Port cannons, prepare to fire."

The two ships were matched stern of the sloop aligned with the tip of *The Vixen's* bowsprit, both gliding over the surface of the ocean at rapid speed, when the three port cannons fired, so close together, it sounded like one great 'boom'. Flames gushed from the mouths, and white smoke billowed across the deck. Colin watched as the three white-hot lead balls arced across the distance separating the two ships. All three impacted; one smashed the port rail amidships, and the other two left gaping holes in the hull a few feet above the water line. The cannon crews on the sloop's port sides had ducked when *The Vixen's* cannons fired, and by the time they'd recovered, their target was already well past them and heading toward the oncoming galleon.

Colin stared over the stern rail as the sloop continued its journey, satisfied that it wouldn't turn back to help its large, but vulnerable comrade.

"Well," he said. "That worked well. Now, let's go get that fat bastard."

Their maneuver to frighten off the sloop had taken them three miles away from the galleon, and sailing against the wind, it took them two hours to get back to within range for the cannons.

Through Elizabeth's looking glass, Colin could read the ship's name, done in ornate letters on plates attached to the bow, *Balmoral*. He could also see a wide-eyed young man in the garb of an English merchant seaman staring at him from the crow's nest atop the main mast.

"She's a merchant," he said as he lowered the glass. "So, she'll be easy prey."

Elizabeth smiled and nodded. "Prepare for boarding," she said in a commanding tone.

The swishing sound of knives and sabers being unsheathed drowned out the whisper of wind across the deck. The sharpshooters in the rigging readied their muskets. Cannon crews were loaded and primed. *The Vixen* was about to pounce.

Balmoral began an evasive maneuver, veering to starboard, putting the ship on an easterly course. Elizabeth gave orders to set *The Vixen* on a diagonal intercept course. The ship's bow dipped as it swung to port, rose high in the air, and then the wind filled the sails and the ship shot forward, knifing through the water like a dolphin.

As the gap between them narrowed, *Balmoral* made a sharper turn to starboard, heeling over so far, spars on the mainmast cut the water. But, the larger ship, riding low in the water, was no match for *The Vixen*.

"I don't know what her cargo is," Colin said. "But, the way she's riding, it must be heavy."

Standing beside Colin now, M'nondo squinted at the ship. "She will be easy to take," he said. "How do you want to do it?"

"If the captain approves, I'd like to send some cannon shots into their hull to let them know we mean business. After that, we board, remove what we can easily carry, put the crew into their boats, and burn and scuttle the ship. If possible, I'd like to avoid injuring or killing any of the crew."

"Why would you worry about hurting them?" Elizabeth asked.

"If they know they can survive our boarding, word will get around, and hopefully fewer of them will put up any resistance."

"But, if they fight back?" M'nondo smiled at him.

"It's on their heads," Colin said.

"Very well," Elizabeth said. "We'll do it your way. Which cannons do you wish to fire first?"

Colin wet an index finger and held it up to check the wind. "The way the sea's running, it'll be easier to make the first turn to starboard," he said. "So, port cannons first, then starboard."

Elizabeth nodded. "Got it. Helmsman, prepare to change course to four degrees starboard on my command."

The maneuver Colin, Elizabeth, and M'nondo had discussed before their patrols began, M'nondo had christened the python.

It was a simple maneuver but required precision timing on the part of both the helm and the men at the cannons.

Colin positioned himself just down from the quarterdeck. From that position, he could see over the rails, had a clear view of both starboard and port cannons, and was within hearing of Elizabeth as she gave instructions to the helmsman. M'nondo stood at his side, prepared to act as a runner, relaying instructions to gunners, and course adjustments to the quarterdeck.

As he got a good view of the galleon, now turned into the wind on a westerly heading, he waved up at Elizabeth.

"Change course, now," he shouted.

She repeated the order to the helmsman. Colin braced himself as the deck tilted, keeping his eyes on the target, just out of cannon range.

"Go to the port cannons, M'nondo," he said. "Have them prepared to fire on my signal."

M'nondo trotted off and positioned himself behind the second cannon.

Colin's head swiveled continuously, keeping an eye on the ship they were approaching and on M'nondo. He didn't want the first cannon salvo to mortally damage the ship, so, as soon as he judged they were just inside the effective range of the small cannons, he raised his hand and brought it down in a sharp chopping motion. M'nondo slapped the back of the gunner in front of him and yelled 'Fire!' at the same time.

As soon as the flame and smoke gushed from the mouths of the cannons, Colin and M'nondo were moving to starboard, and the helmsman, following Elizabeth's orders, was swinging the ship's course to port. Colin looked over his shoulder and saw that all three shots had hit their mark, two in the forepart of the hull, just above the water line, and one had torn through the foremast, ripping spars and sails, and sending the men on the galleon's deck diving for cover from the falling debris.

"Starboard cannons prepare to fire," M'nondo shouted over the cheering that had erupted on *The Vixen's* deck.

Colin watched as the galleon came into view on the starboard side. It appeared to have lost some of its speed and was riding even lower in the water. They were close enough now to enable him to see men on the deck of the ship, many of them holding rifles. He was the barrel of a small cannon poking through a port in the ship's side.

"Marksmen, fire at that cannon," he shouted up to the riflemen in the rigging.

His command was answered with the 'pop' of musket fire, as the sharpshooters fired, reloaded, and fired again as fast as they could. The cannon disappeared from the port, and the men on the deck dived behind barrels and boxes lashed to the deck.

When he judged that the main part of the galleon was within the shot pattern of the three starboard cannons, he signaled to M'nondo, and was answered with another boom as all three cannons fired at the same time.

A gray mist floated a few inches above the deck planking, and the reek of burned powder filled the air. All three shots hit the galleon just below the railings, making three jagged holes.

Colin looked up at Elizabeth. "I think she's ready to be boarded."

"Helmsman, bring us alongside, to her starboard," she said.

"Boarding party, assemble on me," Colin said. "Port cannons prepare to fire . . . if necessary."

With Garcia leading them, twenty-five men, armed with cutlasses and short-barreled flintlocks, rushed across the deck and stood expectantly in front of Colin. Their eyes glowed with excitement.

"Prepared to board on your order, Colin," Garcia said. The swarthy first mate looked more excited than anyone.

"Okay, Diego. Now, you men remember, we're not to kill anyone unless it's absolutely unavoidable. We want these men to get to Nassau to tell their story."

Garcia smiled wolfishly. "Aye, we understand. This will not only strike fear into the hearts of every English sailor in the Caribbean, but it will be sure to get the attention of their navy. You are a devious one, Colin."

Colin smiled. Garcia's unhappiness at Colin's return had faded over the days they were thrown together in the cramped confines of the ship, and their old camaraderie had come back.

The crew, having done this very thing for many years, moved with practiced efficiency. As the boarding party assembled on the port side, forward of the cannons, other men dropped bags filled with sand over the rail. Attached to ropes, they lay against the hull, and would act as cushions when *The Vixen* came alongside the other ship, which Colin could see now was *H.M.S. Whitechapel*. Not a merchant after all, but a military transport. He wondered why the crew were not in uniform but filed that anomaly away to focus on the immediate task of taking the ship with minimum casualties on either side.

After the bumpers were in place, four other men, with large iron grappling hooks attached to ropes, move up to the rail.

When the two ships were about five feet apart, and *The Vixen's* helmsman had matched *Whitechapel's* speed, the four men threw their grappling hoods across the gap. The hooks snagged on the rail, and the four, the largest and strongest of the crew, began hauling on them, their muscles bulging, and their brows slick with sweat.

When a dull thump and a shudder of the deck informed them that the two ships had made contact, the four men made the ropes fast.

On *Whitechapel*, men with muskets and swords rushed onto the deck, but a few well-placed shots into the wood at their feet from the sharpshooters in *The Vixen's* rigging, three marksmen near the bow, and another on the quarterdeck, and the sight of a bearded Colin and twenty-six men waving cutlasses and brandishing pistols, pouring over the rail, caused them to drop their weapons and raise their hands.

Rounding up the crew was a matter of minutes. The captain, a graying man with muttonchop whiskers, strode to the front of his captured crew. He stood with his feet spread wide and his chest puffed out. Even out of uniform, to Colin he reeked of navy.

"Now, see here, my good man," he said. "We are a peaceful vessel on His Majesty's business. I must insist that you get off my ship and allow us to proceed."

Colin couldn't hold back his smile. The arrogance of the English upper class never ceased to amaze him. Here, the man was completely at the mercy of, as far as he knew, a bloodthirsty band of corsairs, and he still had the temerity to demand what he assumed was his right as a member of the English elite. He bowed slightly.

"My apologies, captain," he said. "But, I regret to inform you that you have it in reverse. It is you, and your crew, who must get off the ship, and allow *us* to proceed."

The English captain's face turned dark red, and his eyes blazed. "What? Is it your intention to maroon us at sea? That is entirely unacceptable, my good man."

"I'm not your good man, captain. And, the alternative is that we leave all of you aboard when we sink her."

"Y-you wouldn't dare!"

Some of the arrogance began to crumble, and murmuring started in the men assembled behind him. One of the men, a tall redhead, stepped forward to stand just behind the captain.

"S-sir, we be not far from landfall at Nassau. We can be there in two, maybe three days."

Still not totally subdued, the captain glared at the man before turning back to Colin. "You cannot put all of us into boats for that many days without food or water." There was a slight note of pleading in his voice.

Pleased to see that he was on the verge of capitulation, Colin bowed again.

"Of course not. You may take as much food and water as your boats will hold. You will, of course, have to leave all weapons, except your swords, behind."

Looks of relief blossomed on the faces of the men, but the captain still had a sneering look on his face.

"When we reach Nassau, this *will* be reported, and the entirety of His Majesty's navy in this region will hunt you down."

"Oh, I have no doubts of that, sir," Colin said. "Hunting is one thing but finding us is another matter." He turned to five of his boarding party. "You men, escort the captain and crew to the boats. Let them load food and water, but make sure they pile their weapons on the deck before they board themselves. Then, lower them away." To the captain, he said, "I would suggest you begin rowing as fast as you can, and don't look back. My sharpshooters will make you regret it if you do."

The five men began pushing the English with the barrels of their muskets, herding them to the long boats lashed to the rails on either side of the galleon's upper deck.

"You want me to check the cargo in the hold?" Garcia asked.

"Yes. Take ten men and remove anything that's easy to carry. The rest of you, check the staterooms and any other spaces. Let's see what this big fish has to offer."

He moved up to the quarterdeck, from where he could see the entire ship. While the captain and crew were shepherded into boats and unceremoniously lowered into the heaving waves, Garcia and his crew of scavengers were grabbing every crate or barrel that could be lifted and tossing them across the narrow gap between the vessels to the deck of *The Vixen*, where the crew that hadn't participated in the boarding, stowed them below deck. Their loot included all of the ship's rations, consisting of beef, pork, bread, butter, cheese, oatmeal, suet, vinegar, beer, and rum, except for a small amount of beef, bread, pork, cheese, and water, which he had put in each of the boats with the exiled crew, much to their surprise.

He waved at Elizabeth, who stood proudly on her ship's quarterdeck, watching the disgruntled English captain and crew row as fast as they could toward the southeast. The Atlantic is an unpredictable ocean at the best times, and hurricane season, when the cyclonic winds develop off the west coast of Africa, pick up heat and energy crossing the middle passage, and slam into the east coasts of North and South America with hellish ferocity, was fast approaching. If the four boats, which rode low in the water because they were carrying the maximum number of people possible, hit one of the squalls that were precursors to hurricanes, they would be swamped, and nothing would save their occupants. Not that this bothered her. They were the enemy. If the tables had been turned, she and her crew wouldn't have been put in boats and allowed to leave. They would have been put in irons, crammed below decks, and taken ashore at Nassau for a date with the gallows. She knew why Colin had decided to try and spare the entire crew of this, their first prize, and it made sense. There would be more stories told of the day's events than there were men to tell them. Some would even be true, but, true or not, it would get the attention of the English in Nassau—maybe even in London—and, without doubt, ships would be diverted to hunt for them.

But, before they were done, people would die. Maybe, she knew, even some of her crew. The thought of death didn't bother her. Death comes to all, she often thought, and when it came for her, she would face it defiantly, fighting until the very end.

By the time the boats were too small to see details, Colin and the men had finished stripping *Whitechapel* of everything they could carry, and their loot included a number of new muskets, shot, and powder, as well as the ceremonial silver and china from the captain's cabin. All in all, not bad. The wait had been worthwhile.

When the last man, carrying a sack of dried beef, leapt across to *The Vixen's* deck, Colin and Garcia began tipping over the barrels of tar stowed under the quarter deck across the main deck and railings, leaving only a small clear space that they would use to cross back to safety. Satisfied with their work, they mounted the rails and jumped to *The Vixen's* deck.

"Remove the grappling hooks," Colin said. "And, get me some torches."

When six of the flaming rods were brought out, he gave one to M'nondo, one to Garcia, and one each to Cacao Rodriquez and Martine Devereux, the two men who had rescued him from the boat in which Captain Dangerfield had placed him. Then, he took the final two to the quarterdeck, and handed one to Elizabeth.

"I thought you'd like the honor of helping send this beast to the bottom, captain," he said.

She smiled as she took the proffered flame. "You know I would."

When they'd moved about five feet away from *Whitechapel*, Colin shouted, "Now!", and three his torch at the ship's deck. Elizabeth copied him, and the four men standing on the main deck threw theirs as well. When the flaming torches hit the deck, six blossoms of flame erupted, and quickly spread across the surface, joining up and shooting high in the air. The sails ignited, and powder that they'd somehow missed in their scavenging, exploded with a roar, and a gush of orange flame and white smoke from beneath the front of the quarterdeck.

In seconds, the ship was engulfed in flames that burned so hot, even fifty feet away, Colin could feel the heat on his exposed skin.

"Helmsman," Elizabeth said. "Make your best speed getting some distance between us and that vessel. I wouldn't want the wind to blow sparks across into our sails."

As if responding to her fears, and taunting her, the wind changed direction, and a great cloud of blinking sparks floated toward them, only to dissipate a few feet from the flaming wreck.

When *The Vixen* was a quarter mile away, Elizabeth ordered 'heave to,' and the sails were set to bring her to a stop, with the bow of *Whitechapel* abeam of *The Vixen*. From there, everyone on board had a good view of the doomed vessel.

A great orange blossom appeared in the thick smoke surrounding the ship, followed a second later by a dull boom. The bow and stern dipped, and *Whitechapel* split in two at her midsection like a brittle twig breaking.

"We must have overlooked a store of powder somewhere aboard her," Colin said, as the two halves slipped beneath the water, leaving behind nothing but a greasy slick, a wispy haze, and the soothing sound of the wind and sea.

Elizabeth clapped him on the shoulder. "Just as well," she said. "Now, we can make for home and store our booty."

"Aye, aye, captain. And, after that, perhaps we can make a side trip to Cat Island. I need to talk to Mama Lillie."

The air was filled with the sound of lusty sea chanties as they got underway.

Chapter 6

Government House, Nassau, Bahamas

Liam Macintosh looked with barely concealed disdain at the popinjay seated behind the desk in a nondescript office in the bowels of Government House on Duke Street in Nassau.

After a narrow escape from the pirate attack, the sloop, *H.M.S. Zephyr*, had made the best possible speed getting to Nassau, careful to avoid straying into waters where American naval vessels might be lurking. A native of the Scottish Highlands, Macintosh was not fond of the sea, and almost being sent to the bottom of the ocean by some bloodthirsty brigand didn't change his feeling. In addition, being forced to share the confined space of the sloop with the bunch of bloody plonkers that made up the crew. The officers hadn't been much better, either. Despite their upper-class pretensions, when they thought no one was looking, they engaged in the same boorish behavior as their men, and at times even worse.

When his feet were solidly on the cobblestones of the wharf at Nassau, he felt like kneeling and kissing the ground. But, of course, he hadn't done that. He'd adjusted the six-inch dirk he wore strapped, hilt down, to his left forearm, making sure that the long sleeve covered it well, and flagged down a rickety looking carriage pulled by a spavined donkey and driven by an ancient, withered black man to take him to Government House.

He'd been impressed by his first look at the place. Unlike the rest of the buildings of the city, mostly constructed with wood, Government House was an imposing stuccoed coral rock structure, done in classical European style, with high columns flanking the front entrance, which looked out over the city and harbor. It had been built in 1783, inspired by American loyalists from that country's south, who had fled to the islands after the bloody Americans gained their independence from England. The relentless attention of salt-laden ocean breezes had changed the white stone to a pearl gray, which, to Macintosh, only made it look more imposing.

A soldier in dress uniform, a shiny bayonet on his musket, stood guard at the door. When Macintosh identified himself and asked for directions to the governor-general's office, the man told him to talk to the clerk just inside the entrance. That worthy, a middle-aged man with thinning brown hair and a rat-like expression on his face, had directed him to a cramped office in the rear of the building's ground floor, where he was greeted by Alwyn Brice, who identified himself as one of the governor-general's assistants.

He had a narrow face, a nose that looked like a hawk's beak, which he tilted his head and stared at Macintosh over, and greased light brown hair that was plastered to his skull. His eyes, yellowish amber and oval-shaped, reinforced the bird-of-prey impression created by his nose. His thin lips were pursed as he looked up at Macintosh, with an expression like a hawk sizing up a field mouse.

"I was told to report to the governor-general," he said. "I be here on a vital mission."

Brice sniffed as if smelling something unpleasant. "I am well aware of your mission, Mr. Macintosh. But, acting governor-general Merriwether will be departing in less than three months, and Mr. Cameron will be resuming the office. He feels that he should not become involved in such a matter under those circumstances, so he assigned it to me. Mr. Cameron arrives in December, and if he decides to take personal responsibility, that will be his prerogative to do. In the meantime, I assure you that I am perfectly competent to handle this."

Macintosh was not assured, but he had no choice. It was the obnoxious little rat, Brice, or nothing. While he preferred working alone, it was always good to have a place to go when you needed resources that couldn't be carried around on your person.

"Very well," he said. "Do ye have any specific instructions for me?"

"Not at the moment. But, I would appreciate your views on the pirate attack upon your vessel."

Macintosh's mouth opened slowly, and his brows twitched. How in bloody hell did the man know about that? They had been in dock less than four hours. It made him feel like the rankest amateur, but he asked a foolish question. "How is it you come to be knowin' about that?"

"Sirrah, Nassau is a small town. Rumors here spread with the speed of a wild fire on the savannah in dry season. No doubt, one of the sailors aboard your vessel talked to one of the doxies who hang about the piers; she told her pimp, and so it goes. One of our local staff mentioned it to me not ten minutes before you arrived."

"Well now, I'll have to be keepin' that in mind." The local gossip mill could be both an asset and a liability. He would need to get a quick handle on it. "As to the attack, it was strange. This vessel, painted all black, with white sails, making it look really intimidatin', come at us out of the fog, a sudden like. Her master was skillful, I'll give him that. As fast as we was, he still managed to get off a good shot that near crippled us. If not for that fat merchantman that convoyed with us, I'm not so sure we'd of gotten away."

"A merchant vessel? Do you recall the name?"

"Aye, t'was *Whitechapel*. Must've been loaded, 'cause she rode mighty low in the water."

Brice's face turned ashen. "That, my good man, was not a merchant vessel. *H.M.S. Whitechapel* was one of His Majesty's vessels that had been converted to look like a private ship. It is part of the plan you are here to support."

"I think it *was* part of the plan, but no more. My guess is it's either been towed to some foreign harbor to be sold, or it's been scuttled. What was it carrying that was so important, or that required such secrecy?"

"I'm not sure you need to know that, sir."

"Now, look, laddie." Macintosh's face turned light red. "I'm here on the orders of the Admiralty, and if I'm to do the job they sent me to do, I need to know everything about everything. Now, what was on that bloody ship that was so important?"

Brice sat back in his chair, his chin quivering, as if he'd been struck. His face went whiter.

"W-well, if you must," he said. "*Whitechapel* was transporting the first tranche of arms and supplies for a planned invasion of New Orleans. There will be at least ten more ships, with men and supplies, scheduled over the next six months."

"Aye, so that explains tryin' to make it look like a private vessel. Couldna have the Yanks cottoning on to the plan too early." Macintosh rubbed the stubble on his jaw. "Well, I see what my first task will be. I'll have to find these bloody pirates and put 'em out of business."

"And, just how do you plan to do that?"

"Well, now, laddie, I'm not sure you'll be wantin' to know that. You just be ready to supply with whatever I might need and have whatever passes for a constabulary on this island ready to move at a moment's notice."

"You seem pretty sure of yourself, Mr. Macintosh."

"It's what I get paid to do, and I'd be tellin' a lie if I said I don't do it well. Your pirates are as good as dead."

Charles Ray

Chapter 7

Mama Lillie's Café, Cat Island

Three days after they'd taken the arms and supplies looted from *Whitechapel*, and carefully stored them in sheds hidden in the jungle on Skull Island, Colin, Elizabeth, and M'nondo sailed a small skiff to Cat Island. After anchoring the skiff in a secluded cove at the north end of the island, they paid a local farmer to give them a ride into town in his oxcart.

Mama Lillie, her large form covered by a deep violet dress, with a yellow scarf wrapped around her head, greeted them at the door.

"Ah, m*es enfants*, it has been too long since you come to visit your *mama*. Come into the back room where I have the special lunch prepared for you," she said, as she wrapped Elizabeth in a smothering hug.

"But, Mama Lillie," Colin said, ducking as she grabbed his shoulders and pulled him in for a wet kiss on the cheeks. "It's well past the midday meal hour."

"I know, *cher*, but I also know that you have had a long boat ride, and you probably did not eat properly since morning, *non*?"

"That's true, *maman*," Elizabeth said. "And, if that special lunch is some of your gumbo, I will have two bowls."

Lillie tapped the side of her head with a meaty, brown forefinger. "This one, she is *tres* smart, is she not. How you know I have gumbo, child?"

'Because, it's what I've been thinking about since the last time we were here. You know I love your gumbo more than almost anything."

"Actually," Colin said. "If you're serving gumbo, I suppose it really doesn't matter what time it is, because it's my favorite as well."

"Well, you three come on, and I'll serve you up three bowls."

She led them through the beaded curtains beside the counter, and into a small antechamber that contained a small round table and six chairs. Through a door to the side they could see into the kitchen, where a large iron pot sat on the stove. The tangy, sweet smell of gumbo hung in the air.

The three of them sat, and Lillie went into the kitchen. She came back a few minutes later with a wooden tray with three large bowls of steaming gumbo, which she sat in front of them. Beside each bowl, she placed a wooden spoon.

Without hesitation, they began scooping the seafood mélange into their mouths. Lillie sat at the table, her hands in her lap, and smiled indulgently as they ate.

After a second bowl for each, they sat back and rubbed their stomachs. Elizabeth let out an unladylike belch, which caused the others to laugh so hard the shed tears.

"Do not laugh at the child," Lillie scolded. "In some cultures, belching after a meal is a sign of how much you enjoyed it."

"Well, in that case," said Colin. He let out a belch that sounded like the roar of a bullfrog. "I loved it."

M'nondo, not to be outdone, sucked in air, then opened his mouth, and let go with a sound like thick paper being ripped.

"I loved it even more," he said.

"Now, that you two are through playing like silly schoolboys," Lillie said. "Let us get down to business, *non*."

Colin and M'nondo changed from silly smiles to serious looks. Elizabeth looked at them and stuck out her tongue.

"Now, who's being silly," Colin said.

"He is right, *cherie*, a lady does not do such things." Lillie slapped her lightly on the back of her hand. "Now, pay attention, for I have many things to tell you.

She adjusted the scarf on her head, and leaned forward, her elbows on the table.

"First, there is the rumor that the *anglais* will be using these islands as a, how do you say it, staging base, for some kind of big military operation."

"This big operation, will it be land or sea forces?" Colin asked.

"I am told, *mon cher*, that they plan to bring in the muskets and cannon, and much shot and powder."

"So, a land operation. If they're staging from here, it must be the plan to attack New Orleans. Have your sources heard anything about when this operation might take place?"

Lillie shook her head. "No, *cher*. I do not think *les anglais* have move any people yet. I am told they are just beginning to bring the supplies here to the islands, but they have run into a problem."

"What kind of problem?"

"One of their supply ships was attacked by pirates a few days ago," she said.

"Ah," Colin said. "So, the crew did make it?"

Lillie smiled. "When I heard this news, I thought it must be you. +*Mais non*, this news did not come from the crew of the supply ship. They have not been heard from. There was another ship, a smaller one, that got away when the pirates attacked. It is from this ship that the news came."

Colin looked pensive. Even though he knew that his companions were not concerned about the fate of *Whitechapel's* crew, he was not one to idly take a life, and it was important to his plan that the story of their raid be told by those who experienced it. He sincerely hoped that they would make landfall safely. Letting the sloop go, though, had paid off. Already, the story of their daring raid would be circulating around the islands.

"I'm pretty sure the crew will be arriving in Nassau in due course," he said. "Of course, the loss of that supply ship will have put a bit of a hitch in their invasion plan."

"No doubt it will," Lillie said. "But, you must never underestimate *les anglais*. They are slippery like the eel. I was also told that there was a special passenger on the small ship."

"Special passenger? Special in what way?"

"Ah, I have your attention, do I not? There was a small man on the small ship, not dressed like a sailor, but the officers of the ship treated him with much deference and respect. When he got off the ship, he went straight away to Government House."

"So, London has sent some big nabob out to help plan the invasion. No matter."

"Colin, *cher*, I do not know this nabob word, but I assume you mean *un homme* who is *tres important*."

"A nabob's a kind of boss, Mama Lillie. I assume that if the British want to keep this invasion under wraps, they would sneak their people in."

"True, but the man who will command the attack is already here, or in Nassau, at least. Major General Edward Packenham will be the commander of the forces. They have not made a public announcement, but, they talk about it in their clubs and offices, paying no mind to the many black workers who clean and fetch for them."

Colin smiled. He knew all too well how the menials, even in America, often became like the furniture; only noticed if out of place or missing, but when present, and doing what they were intended to do, completely invisible, which made them the perfect spies.

"So, if this new arrival is not important to the invasion, who is he, and why should we even care?"

"Colin, I did not say that he was not important, now did I?" Lillie waved a finger at him. "Do not put the words in my mouth, *cher*. In fact, this man must be important. He got off the boat, and went straight to Government House, where he met with Alwyn Brice, the chief secretary to the Governor General himself."

Colin sat back, his eyes half closed. "I see. You might be right. No, I think you *are* right. Did your informers find out who he was?"

"No, only that he speaks the English with a strange accent. Not like the other *anglais* here in the islands."

"Maybe he was German."

"No, not German. They recognize the way Germans speak the English. He was *anglais* but, at the same time, not *anglais. Tu comprends?*"

"Yes, I believe I do. He was probably either Scottish or Irish. Both speak English that is very different from what we are accustomed to hearing. If I could hear him speak, I could tell you."

"I do not think you want to get to close to him. He is very dangerous. He tries to hide it, but my friend, the driver of the cart that took him to Government House, said he wears a long dagger under his left sleeve."

"Hm, not something you would expect from a gentleman, or even a military man. It might be dangerous, but I have a feeling we need to know more about this man. Anything else of importance?"

"Well, one last thing," she said. "The English, I hear, are planning to have warships escort merchant vessels in large convoys. I fear that will make it more difficult for you to attack them."

Colin frowned in concentration for a few seconds. "Perhaps, perhaps not. Actually, if they run in a pack, it might be even easier to give them a bloody nose."

Elizabeth looked at him, surprise on her face. "You're not thinking of attacking a convoy, are you. Even two warships would be more than we could easily handle or get away from."

"No, I'm not thinking of attacking, at least, not in the way you're thinking. I plan on putting a fox in the henhouse." Everyone around the table looked at him in confusion. "It's really simple. The next ship we take, instead of sinking it, we will keep it. Then, when we see a convoy, we'll slip it into the pack. I don't imagine anyone will notice until it's too late. We'll attack them from within, but with *The Vixen* standing off, in sight, but out of effective range. When the first shot is fired, and they see you, I'll bet the warships immediately give chase. We can then use the decoy to create havoc from within the convoy."

M'nondo laid a hand on Colin's arm. "Colin, my friend, are you sure you were not a pirate in a previous life? You come up with the most devious plans. But, you know, I think it just might work a time or two."

"It only has to work once. After that, they will be slowed down as they double check every ship in their convoy. We can than alert the American navy and let them have some of the fun."

"Well," Elizabeth said. "Let the fun begin."

Chapter 8

October 1812, Skull Island

Over the next several days, they had prowled the ocean to the north and west of Skull Island, and a few days before the first of October had lucked out and encountered a three-masted merchant vessel that was large enough to mount six cannons on each side. They rigged the cannons to look like cargo crates, but with a hinged front to each crate to allow them to be pushed forward to fire through the oversized scuppers.

After rigging the vessel, which they had rechristened *Avenger*, Colin, Elizabeth, M'nondo, and Garcia met in the big house for a strategy session.

As the servant, the wife of one of the pirates who had volunteered to join them to care for Elizabeth, poured rum into the flagons in front of each of them, Garcia looked morosely across the table at Colin.

"You look like you have a bee in your bonnet, Diego," Colin said. "What's troubling you?"

Diego took a long swallow of his rum, grimacing as the fiery liquid slid down his throat. "I really do not know, *mi amigo*. I am hearing that the English are planning something big, but no one knows what it is."

"We do. It's their plan to invade the United States from the south."

"No, not that. That is the worse kept secret in the islands. This is something different. It is to take place here in the islands. All I have been able to learn is that one of my sources heard an English officer talking about many bodies swinging from the gallows."

"They are probably talking about us," M'nondo said. "While we have only done a small amount of damage, they must know about it, and are trying to find us."

Colin shook his head. "We know that. After all, it was our plan. But, I can't imagine they know enough to plan any kind of serious operation."

"Especially," Elizabeth said. "Not talking about hangings. That is an ominous sign."

"I agree." Colin nodded. "We need to find out what they're up to. In fact, I think that should take precedence over our raids for now."

"What if that is exactly what they want us to do," M'nondo said.

Colin looked at him. The big man had a serious look on his face. "Explain," he said.

"Think about it, my friend. Even though we are only one ship, they don't know where we will strike, making us an unknown factor that could disrupt their plans. By spreading a story like this, if we stop raiding, either out of fear, or as you proposed, to find out what is going on, we are no longer an irritant."

It was the longest speech Colin had ever heard from the usually stoic man, and, it made sense.

"You're right. We won't stop raiding. But, we still try and discover what they're up to."

"I suppose I could ask my friends to dig a bit deeper," Garcia said.

"You know, it might not be a bad idea for you to be on the scene to make sure they do just that."

Garcia looked suspiciously at Colin. "You mean, not go on the raids?"

Colin sensed the unease. "Just until we sort out this rumor. Don't worry, you'll still get your fair share of any loot."

"It is not the loot. I am the first mate of *The Vixen*. Where she goes, I should go."

"And, there's not a finer first mate sailing the seas," Elizabeth said. "But, Colin's right. We need to keep the raids up, but we also need to know what is going on in Nassau. And, you are the best person to discover that."

Garcia stared down at his drink, seemingly lost in thought. Finally, he raised his head and looked around the table. He nodded.

"You are right, of course," he said. "But, there are many eyes and ears in Nassau. I will not be able to handle it alone. I would like to take one man with me."

"Certainly," Elizabeth said. "Who would you like to take?"

He thought for a few seconds. "I can handle those who speak English and Spanish, but, there are many French speakers in Nassau. I think, perhaps, Martine would be the best choice to deal with them." Martine Devereux, a mulatto from New Orleans, had been an itinerant gambler until a dispute with several men who had accused him of having cards up his sleeves forced him to flee to the Bahamas, where he signed on to Elizabeth's crew during one of the periods when she was hiring new men.

"I agree," she said. "When we finish here, go and find him. The two of you should prepare to leave at first light tomorrow."

"I think we're done," Colin said. "There is only the matter of deciding where we sail tomorrow in search of prey."

"Then, I will be off," Garcia said. He drained the last of his rum, wiped his lips with the back of his hand, and left.

"His job will be far more dangerous than ours," Colin said, after the door closed behind the first mate. "If he is caught, he will surely be hung."

"He knows and accepts the danger, as do we all," Elizabeth said. "Now, let us decide where tomorrow's hunting ground will be.

Chapter 9

November 1812, Presidential Residence, Washington, DC

Dolly Madison, her dark hair askew and her body-hugging shift awry, paused in her supervision of the servants who were polishing the silver, to greet the gaunt, balding man who entered the great dining hall of the presidential residence.

"Good afternoon, Mr. Gallatin," she said, holding out a slender hand toward the sweating man. "Is it hot outside today? Do forgive my unkempt state but keeping this place in order is quite taxing."

He took her hand in his gnarled one and bent low over it. Sweat glistened on his liver-spotted scalp. "Mrs. Madison," he said. "You look absolutely ravishing, even in work-stained garb." Despite his long time in the United States, Albert Gallatin still spoke with a strong French accent, which was the language spoken in the part of Switzerland where he grew up. "As for the weather, it is rather warm for November I suppose. Forgive my sweaty condition. I walked here from the Treasury Department, and while it is no far, I fear it taxes a man of my age and condition."

She smiled, flattered by his old-world customs, that forbade him from being vexed at her intemperate reference to his appearance. A natural hostess, her first inclination was to make him feel comfortable and at home. "Can I get one of the servants to fetch you a glass of lemonade. I do believe we have some freshly made."

"It would be most wonderful, madam, but I do not know if I have time before meeting with the president."

"Oh, I'm sure James would rather you were refreshed for the meeting. Now, you sit yourself down here and I'll have one of the girl's get you a glass." She turned and snapped her fingers at one of the women bent over the table brushing the pungent paste off the silver. "Sallie, go get Mr. Gallatin a glass of lemonade."

The girl dropped her rag, stood and scurried away.

Gallatin, seated in a chair near the high front windows, wiped at his sweaty forehead with a large handkerchief he'd taken from his jacket pocket. "You do keep this place immaculate, Mrs. Madison. You have made it one of the most coveted invitations in Washington City."

She smiled demurely but knew that he only spoke the truth. When she'd lived at Montpelier, Madison's home plantation, after Madison left the House of Representatives, she had entertained the local gentry, and, when Madison had been summoned to the new capital city of Washington in 1800 by newly-elected president Thomas Jefferson, to serve as his secretary of state, she had honed her hostess skills even more. She had instinctively known that social events were crucial to developing the necessary support for political policies, and was so good at what she did, Jefferson, a widower, often had her serve as his hostess at ceremonial events. While the official residence was being built, she had even worked with the architect to furnish it. When the Democratic-Republicans had nominated Madison to replace Jefferson in 1809, and he'd won the election, she renewed her decoration efforts in *her* new official residence. The social functions she hosted, contributed greatly to Madison's popularity, and by the time of his reelection in 1812, she'd become established as the preeminent hostess in the capitol.

"Well, after all," she said. "It is supposed to be the people's residence. That being the case, we must endeavor to make it as presentable as possible."

"I must say, madam, you have done a most remarkable and successful job. One must have some diversion in this miserable place. The swamps near Georgetown and Alexandria keep such moisture in the air, the summers are hotter than cities to the south, and the winters colder than those to the north. And, in summer, the mosquitos and other flying pests from the swamps make Washington City a war zone, and the people are losing."

She pouted in sympathy with him, for she too, especially in summer, when the combined heat and humidity was oppressive, felt that the Founding Fathers had made a mistake in accepting donations of land from Maryland and Virginia for the construction of a national capital city that was separate from the states. She knew well that the southern planters and some of the western farmers had resented the fact that the northern, Quaker-dominated city of Philadelphia had been the de facto national capital since independence, more for the city leaders' stance on the question of slavery than just about anything else. But, having the new capital surrounded by two slaveholding states, and situated in land that was almost unfit for human habitation, with conditions to terrible, the few European diplomats to the new American government described it as worse than Timbuktu, made no sense to her. While she'd been raised a Quaker—only being expelled from the Society of Friends after marrying Madison, a non-Quaker—and wasn't a strong supporter of the institution, she accepted without quarrel the enslaved house servants in the presidential residence, just as she'd accepted the enslaved workers at Madison's Montpelier plantation. Still, though, it would have made more sense, she thought, to compromise the two sides by having the capital in a more neutral location, say between Pennsylvania and Maryland, or Delaware and Maryland. But, no one was interested in the opinion of a mere woman on such weighty matters, despite the fact that she was probably smarter than most of those who had made such decisions.

"Yes, I do tend to stay indoors during the summer months," she said. "But, now, the weather is not so oppressive, so I get out occasionally."

The young maid returned with a tall crystal glass on a silver tray. She placed it on the table near the chair where Gallatin sat, and stood mutely awaiting further instructions.

"That will be all, Sallie," she said. "You may return to your duties."

The girl bowed slightly and returned to the other room.

"That is a large pile of silver they are working on there," Gallatin said. "They will be very late doing it all."

"But, they will stay at it until it's done."

"Do you not worry that if you keep them too late, they will the mayor's new curfew? A fine of twenty dollars, or six months in jail, is a harsh penalty for working hard for someone."

"Oh, they won't have that problem. Those girls there are slaves that James brought with us from Montpelier. They have quarters here."

Gallatin frowned. As a European, he had no doubts about the superiority of his race, but, he agreed with the Quakers on the wrongness of one person owning another. He wondered how a Quaker, or former Quaker in this case, could have such a nonchalant attitude about the institution.

He lifted the glass and took a long swallow of the refreshingly sweet, and cool beverage. Putting the glass down, he rose. "I think I have kept the president waiting long enough. Thank you most kindly, madam, for your hospitality." He bowed. "I assume he wishes to meet me in the usual place?"

She laughed. "Of course. For some reason, he loves that tiny little office. He says it's because he can turn around from his desk and see the rose garden outside his window. I think it's just because he can only squeeze a few people in that little room, and he hates large meetings."

"A strange attitude for someone who served so many terms in congress," Gallatin said. "Although, I do agree with him that such large meetings are a waste of everyone's time. Again, thank you, madam, and now I will take my leave."

He bowed again and made his way across the large room to the corridors that led him on a winding journey to the west side of the building. James Madison's office was a small space, to the west of the large room where Jefferson had held his meetings, just beyond the large semicircular hall where every president since John Adams had welcomed official visitors. It did indeed have a good view of the garden outside, although in November, there were no blossoms to see, and, as Dolly Madison had so aptly described it, it would only comfortably hold about eight people.

Madison, as was his usual practice, was seated behind his desk, his jacket draped over the back, and his shirt sleeves rolled up, leaning close to read one of the many documents piled to his left. He looked up as

Gallatin rapped on the door, a frown of annoyance on his oval face. "Who is it?" he asked.

"Mr. President, it is I, Albert Gallatin."

Madison's frown relaxed. "Ah, Albert, please, do come in."

As the door opened, Madison rose to greet his old friend and colleague. Gallatin looked at his proffered hand, and then down at his own. "I fear, Mr. President, that my hands are a bit damp with sweat. It is somewhat humid and hot outside, despite the time of year."

"Never fear, my old friend. I was raised on a plantation, so I'm accustomed to sweaty hands. They do not offend me in the least."

The two men clasped. Madison guided his visitor to a chair, wedged with a table and another chair, into the corner of the small office. When they were seated, facing each other, Madison leaned forward, his hands on his knees, and a look of concern on his face.

"I suppose you're wondering why I summoned you here today, Albert?"

"I assume, Mr. President, that you wish to discuss the financial situation. I must say, it is dire. Congress is reluctant to consider raising taxes to support the military effort, despite having approved the declaration of war against England, the northeastern states refuse to provide funds to pay soldiers, and even our own party is divided over the situation. I have, though, made contact with John Astor and other merchants, and they have expressed willingness to loan the government money. But, that is only an interim measure. At some point, we will have to find the funds to repay these loans."

Madison ran his hand over his brow. "Ah, yes. Even our own party is not unanimous in support for war. But for the southern and western states, we would be totally alone. But, it's not just the financial situation I wish to discuss with you. We are experiencing severe problems on the military front. General Hull failed in his attempt to invade Canada, and I fear his incompetence and timidity imperils our western front."

"Mr. President, as treasury secretary, I feel that I am not qualified to address military matters. That would be better taken up with those in cabinet with that responsibility."

Madison leaned forward and patted Gallatin's knee.

"You sell yourself short, Albert. You were my first choice for army secretary, and but for the machinations of some in congress, that's the job that you would hold, and I am confident that you have the ability to perform well. I have William Eusley and Paul Hamilton coming in later, but before they arrive, I would like your opinion on the military situation."

Eusley, the army secretary and Hamilton, secretary of the navy, were holdovers from the Jefferson Administration. Eusley, a doctor in private life, was proving himself completely incapable of managing the small army, or dealing with personalities like the mercurial general, Andrew Jackson, who was the overall commander of ground forces, and Hamilton was wedded to the construction and use of gunboats, rather than building a fleet of ocean-going warships, which Madison was convinced was the key to defeating the British fleet.

Gallatin hesitated, rubbing at his fleshy jaw.

"Well, if you insist, sir," he said. "I think that one of the major problems is that the cabinet is divided on this issue, with some siding with the northeastern merchants. Frankly, I think you need to clean house, and staff all cabinet positions with those who support you unequivocally."

"Ah, easier said than done, old friend. Congress seems intent on keeping me in check by ensuring that I don't do just that. Look at what happened when I nominated you for the post of army secretary."

"Yes, that is a problem. And, it is further compounded by the incompetence and lack of experience of the generals in the field. For all of his abrasive personality and rampant political ambitions, Andrew Jackson is the only field commander worth a farthing."

"Yes, I know that Jackson wants my job, but you're right. He is an able commander, so I have no choice but to keep him. And, as much as I would like to fire all the others, I have no one to replace them."

"If you could convince the governors to be more supportive, I'm sure good men would arise from the state militias."

"Yet another thorny issue," Madison said, sighing. "Even the southern and western governors give me problems there. The militias refuse to fight outside their states, and the governors refuse to order them to. The northeastern states, in addition to refusing to provide money to support the army, are also refusing to mobilize their militias, and many of them continue to engage in smuggling with Canada, violating the embargo on trade with Britain."

Gallatin sighed heavily. "That, sir, leaves us with only the navy to rely on."

"Fortunately, in that we're lucky. Most of the naval commanders are competent. Men like that young John Paul Jones are all that stands between us and catastrophe at the moment. But, they will need more heavy warships if they're to prevail against the largest and mightiest navy in the world."

Before Gallatin could reply to that dour assessment of the young country's chances against its former colonial master, there was a soft tap on the door.

"That," Madison said. "Sounds like the mousy tapping of William Eusley. Please come on in."

The door open, and two heads peeked in. Both men of around the same age as Gallatin, one diffident and looking as if he worried that a hooligan waited for him inside the room, the other brash, and full of bluster, hesitated at the entrance.

"Are we late, Mr. President?" Eusley asked, looking askance at Gallatin.

"No, William, Albert and I were just discussing some financial matters. You two gentlemen come on in and pull up chairs." Madison waved a hand negligently toward four chairs lined up along the wall just inside the door.

The two grabbed chairs and arranged them around the table, with Hamilton seating himself to one side of the president and Eusley the other.

"What was it you wished to meet with us about, Mr. President?" Hamilton asked.

Madison tilted his head back and his eyebrows twitched. Gallatin compressed his lips to keep from laughing. He could see from the demeanor of these two why the president was so frustrated. Neither of them seemed to have the slightest awareness of the gravity of the situation. How could then not know why the president would want to speak with them, he thought. And, as if reading his mind, Madison spoke, the sarcasm evident in his tone.

"The only thing I would want to talk to the two of you about these days, of course," he said. "The situation of the war, and how we are to extricate ourselves from the bog we've gotten into."

The two looked at each other. Hamilton nodded. Eusley turned to look at a point just above Madison's breastbone. "Well, Mr. President, we are, as you know, not doing well on the ground. General Hull's invasion of Canada was, to put it mildly, a colossal blunder. He is preparing for another attempt, but, with the state militias refusing to leave their home states to fight, he is limited in his forces.'

"He's also a bit limited in backbone," Madison said. "The man turned tail and ran at the first sign of resistance."

"B-but, sir, he was outnumbered," Eusley protested.

"We were outnumbered by the English during the revolution, but we beat them to a bloody stalemate, and forced their surrender. I fear that the general of today lack the fighting spirit of their predecessors."

"Well, there is General Jackson. He is doing well in the south."

"Oh, sure, fighting the Indians. I've still to see how he fares against English troops."

Hamilton cleared his throat. "At least our navy is doing well."

"They would," Madison said. "Do even better with more ships of the line."

"But, Mr. President, our budget will not support such construction. Besides, gunboats served us well against the barbarian pirates of Tripoli. I see no need to change course now."

"The *Barbary* pirates," Madison said, deliberately stressing the word. "Are not the English navy. Most of them were reluctant to fight out of sight of land. The damned English sail to the far corners of the earth, and do not hesitate to fight. And, they have thousands of fighting vessels. We need to be able to answer them in kind."

"I just don't think, sir, that we have a chance of convincing congress to appropriate funds for such an endeavor. I strongly advise that we stay the course for now. Let's see how our boys do against the British when they enter the lake area."

Madison shook his head. "If they fail, only God can help us, for there would be nothing stopping the English from pouring thousands of troops onto our soil. And," he said, looking pointedly at Eusley. "They have no shortage of competent generals."

"B-but, sir, it's not fair to make such a comparison," Eusley said. "The English have been at war with France for a long time now, so they've had the opportunity to test their men in battle, whereas, our last major conflict was in the Mediterranean, and, that involved only the navy really."

"If we had a professional army, like other strong nations," Gallatin said. "We would have no need for this conversation."

Eusley and Hamilton looked at him as if they were just noticing that he was in the room. Madison, though, smiled and nodded.

"I have come to the same conclusion," he said. "Depending upon the state militia in a time of national crisis has proven to be dangerous. We need a strong standing army, led by professionally trained officers."

One of his requests to congress, one that had not been acted on, was the construction of a national military academy to provide those professionally trained officers. It was, unfortunately, too late for that now.

"Where will congress get the money for that, sir," Hamilton asked. "And, to build the warships you wish the navy to have?"

"Where congress always gets money when it wants something," Madison said. "It can raise taxes. They are low now, but if we lose this war with the English, people will wish they'd paid more, because it will be a pittance compared to what they will have to pay then."

"It is a problem," Eusley said. "What would you have us do, Mr. President?"

Madison pointed at Eusley. "You, sir, can light a fire under your generals. Make them fight instead of run. Go to the governors and try and convince them to get their men to fight outside their damned home states, to fight for the whole country for once." His finger arced toward Hamilton. "And, you, sir, build me some ships with teeth, not these panty-waist gunboats. I understand you're creating a shipbuilding facility in New York, near the lakes?"

"Yes, Mr. President," Hamilton said. "But, I'm not at all sure it would accommodate the construction of really large vessels."

"Well, get sure. Find out and get back to me. Unless you two have more questions, you know what I want you to do, so get out there and do it."

Madison's tone was clearly dismissive. The two men, expressions on their faces like whipped dogs, stood and left.

"You were perhaps a bit too rough on them, sir," Gallatin said after they'd gone.

"I wasn't tough enough. If they don't improve, I'll be even tougher, I'll replace them. If they don't hold the English off in the north, we're in big trouble."

"What about the south, sir, can Jackson handle an invasion from there?"

"If we can keep them from resupplying their forces, I believe he can."

"But, with our small navy occupied defending our ports, and dealing with the English in the north, how will we do that?"

"That was one other thing I wanted to discuss with you, Albert."

He paused, looking at the door, as if trying to see if someone was listening on the other side.

"I don't think even Hamilton is aware of this, but some of the senior navy officers have a plan for blocking the English from resupplying any southern invasion force. A young navy officer has been sent to the Bahamas to organize a rear-guard action."

"And, just how will one officer accomplish that?"

"They didn't give me details. I guess they don't trust us politicians. Anyway, I was assured that this plan, carried out by this particular officer, will work."

"I pray, Mr. President, that they are correct."

"So, do I, Albert, so do I."

Chapter 10

The Navy Board, Somerset House, London

As a vice admiral in the royal navy, Sir Stanley Kensington, whenever he passed the guard standing beside the wide entrance to the impressive front to the Admiralty, received a stiffly-executed formal salute, which he usually returned with a tight smile and a casual wave. On this morning, however, as he looked through the entrance at the tall, austere looking buildings that actually housed those who kept His Majesty's fleets around the world operating at peak efficiency, he paid the guard no heed.

Ordinarily, he would have enjoyed a visit to the board room, with its vaulted ceilings, imposing windows, extensive collection of books and rolls of charts covering the world, but, he could not help but view the current summons to appear before the Admiralty Board with some trepidation.

Of late, news from the west side of the Atlantic Ocean had been decidedly mixed. The lords of the admiralty, however, seldom wasted their precious time discussing the good news, and, of the bad news, that for which he had responsibility was a fulsome portion. They would be demanding answers, and seeking to hold someone accountable, and Kensington's neck was, unfortunately, closest to the chopping block. Instead of being considered in the running for the prestigious position of First Naval Lord, he feared that he'd be lucky if he wasn't assigned to command some backwater port in one of the empire's more remote colonies.

He made his way to the building housing the board room, entered, and took the stairs and then walked down a long hallway until he reached the imposing, floor to ceiling double doors of the board room. A Royal Marine, his pike held tightly in his hand, and a no nonsense look on his face, stood beside the door. He recognized Kensington and came to rigid attention as he approached. Kensington nodded his acknowledgment, and the man opened the door.

The Right Honorable Robert Dundas, Second Viscount Melville, First Lord of the Admiralty, and Vice Admiral William Domett, First Naval Lord, and de facto commander of all operational ships and naval units, sat at opposite ends of the long, green-cloth-covered conference table. On the side facing the large fire place, the book cases, and the rows of rolled charts hanging on the wall, were the other senior members of the Admiralty board. Facing them was a single chair. Kensington had no doubt that the single chair was for him.

He bowed stiffly, first to Dundas, then to Domett, then to the others in order of their rank and title. They merely regarded him with lazy expressions, and a slight tilt of their heads, as he made his way to the lone chair, where he sat, with the bright light of the large windows almost blinding him.

So, he thought, it's to be an inquisition. I wonder if the condemned will get a last request.

After some shuffling of papers and clearing of throats, Dundas, in a voice honed with his service as a member of parliament for Liverpool, who had just replaced another Tory, Charles Phillip Yorke, the MP for St. Germans, as the First Lord, said, "Gentlemen, this meeting will come to order. I believe that Vice

Admiral Domett has an issue of utmost importance that he wishes to bring before the board."

He nodded down the table toward the impressive looking man, resplendent in his full-dress uniform, bedecked with braid and the many awards that had been bestowed upon him during his long and illustrious career.

Domett shot Kensington a sympathetic look and cleared his throat.

"We have experienced some serious setbacks in the Bahamas of late," he said. "Beginning with the loss of *Whitechapel* and her cargo, corsairs have been regularly interdicting our shipments, and the few ships we have in the area have been unable to identify or locate them."

Kensington's face reddened. He made a 'harumph' noise.

"Do you wish to say something, Admiral Kensington?" Dundas frowned at him.

"Yes, milord," Kensington said. "I would like, if I may, to put events in the Bahamas into perspective."

"Please." Dundas' voice dripped with sarcasm.

"It is true that pirates have been attacking our supply ships as they enter Bahamian waters, and also true that our navy in the area has been unable to find or apprehend them. In defense of the navy." He looked at Domett. "Most of our ships in North America are concentrating on defending Canada, or on blockading the coast, so there are precious few left to hunt for pirates in the Caribbean."

Domett nodded. "Admiral Kensington is correct on that point. I doubt that we have more than four ships around Nassau. Hardly enough to effectively patrol the thousands of square miles of water and hundreds of islands."

Dundas made a sniffing noise and glared at Domett. "Be that as it may, admiral, we simply cannot allow these barbarians to run rampant over His

Majesty's navy and merchant fleet like this." He turned his attention back to Kensington. "Now, Admiral Kensington, I understand that you have sent a chap to the islands to take this matter in hand?"

"I have, milord. A bit of a ruffian, an uncultured Scot, but I think he is just the type we need in that situation."

"What can you tell us about him, other than his antecedents?" Dundas' voice was so condescending, Kensington felt like picking up one of the map books stacked on the table and throwing it at him, but he kept his face impassive.

"Liam Macintosh is his name," he said. "An unlikely first name for a Scot, but that's what was on his papers. He has worked for us in the past, a rather sticky mess in India, and I am told that he resolved it, albeit a bit of blood was shed."

"As long as it's our enemies' blood, it is of no consequence," Dundas said. "What has he learned about these pirates?"

"Very little, I'm afraid, other than it appears to be one ship, *The Vixen*. His problem is that he has been unable to locate the pirate base. He has a plan, though, to smoke them out."

"Well, I hope he does it soon," Domett said. "Even though our forces on the ground have done quite well in Canada, they sent that coward, General Hull, and his men packing after firing only a few shots, I fear our navy, for all its might, will have a hard slog in the border lakes. The damned Americans know them like the backs of their hands, and they have a number of competent captains who have the experience of fighting the Barbary states under their belt. We need those supplies to get to the Bahamas so that we have our backup plan in place should things not go well in the north."

"I assure you, this situation will be handled." Kensington coughed. He looked around but noticed that the blooder pikers hadn't even had the courtesy to provide a pitcher of water, or tea. "In addition to our man in Nassau, I was recently contacted by a former American naval officer who has offered us his services."

There were murmurs around the table.

"An American," Dundas said. "Are you sure you can trust him?"

"Not everyone there supports this war," Kensington said. "Those in the northeastern states, what they call New England, depend upon us for trade, and, according to reports from our people in Canada, have refused to support Madison in this foolish war. In addition, this particular American has an ax to grind with the American navy. It seems that he was a former ship's captain, and was cashiered, so he wants to make them pay."

"Money and revenge attract more people than patriotism, I'm afraid," Domett said. "But, we use whatever weapons are at hand. We need to get this blood war over with as soon as possible. After so many years fighting the French, our men need a bit of rest."

"Not to mention, the treasurer is being drained dry," said Dundas. "Well, I suppose that will have to do. Thank you, Admiral Kensington, for coming here today and briefing us. You may go now."

For a heartbeat, Kensington almost lost his stiff, English upper lip. Bloody cheeky bastard, he thought, summon me here like I'm some lowly landsman, offer me no refreshment, and then dismiss me like I was a chambermaid. I understand this chap, Dangerfield, a bit better now. One can develop an intense dislike for certain of one's colleagues.

He said nothing, though. Merely stood, bowed slightly, and with his back stiff, departed.

Charles Ray

Chapter 11

December 1812, *The Vixen* and *Avenger*, in the Atlantic, south of Bermuda

Colin and Elizabeth had decided to take *Avenger* out to give the crew a chance to work out any kinks in his strategy. Colin was standing near the helm, looking out to starboard, where *The Vixen* rode the waves like a sleek black dolphin.

On *The Vixen*, with Garcia in Nassau working with his informants to ferret out whatever he could learn about the strange new arrival, Elizabeth had chosen the Colombian, Cacao Rodriguez, to be acting first mate, while Colin had argued vehemently, and finally wore both of them down, that M'nondo should be his second in command on *Avenger*. His reasoning was simple; M'nondo knew and was respected by every man in Elizabeth's band, he'd been sailing since Jack Teague found him floating in the Atlantic in a boat he'd stolen when he ran away from the plantation where he'd been newly brought as a slave, and, more importantly, Colin knew and trusted him.

M'nondo had been a bit sullen at first. He'd not been long apart from Elizabeth, who he considered as a younger sister, since Teague had assigned him to look after and guard her that fateful day when they attacked the ship that was carrying her and her parents to her father's new duty station as the British consul in Boston. But, once they were underway, standing on the quarterdeck next to Colin, with the salt-laden air caressing his face, his expression softened. He stood there, like Colin, looking at *The Vixen*, his lips turned up slightly.

"She is one beautiful ship, is she not," he said.

"Aye, she rides the waves like no other vessel I've ever seen. And, with that black hull, she does look deadly."

M'nondo's face took on a wistful look.

"But, you know, my friend," he said. "I wish that we could sail the seas without having to look deadly."

Colin laughed. "But, you've been a pirate most of your adult life. What would you do if you didn't have ships to raid?"

"I would chase the sun, Colin, my friend, I would just chase the sun."

Colin's eyes widened. "Funny you should say that. I'd never heard that expression before you said it, but I think it describes what I've been doing since I left home. Chasing the sun . . . now, that has a nice ring to it. Maybe when this war's over, we can do that."

"Ah, but as long as people are people, I fear war will never end."

Now, it was Colin's turn to look wistful. "I guess you're right about that. My own country is a good example. You'd think, after fighting and getting our independence from England, we'd focus on peacefully developing what we had. But, no; we started in right away stretching out into the rest of the land, fighting the Indians and taking their land, squabbling with Spain over Florida, and finally, buying the Louisiana Territory from old Napoleon when he needed gold to fight the English and try to take over Europe. Seems we're always fighting over something."

"Yes, those that have power will do anything to hold on to it, and those who don't have power, will do anything to get it. We live, my friend, in a mad world."

Colin shook himself.

"Ugh, such depressing thoughts. Let's focus on what we're here to do and get our minds off the doom and gloom."

"I am all for that." M'nondo smiled broadly. "What do you wish us to do, captain?"

"Have *Vixen* signaled that we will separate by a quarter mile and start a search for ships. Hopefully, we'll find one that's not part of a convoy."

M'nondo trotted off to give the instructions. After a few minutes, *The Vixen* began tacking to starboard until the two ships were the required distance apart, but still within sight of each other. M'nondo came back to the quarterdeck.

"The ships are about a quarter mile apart," he said. "Lookouts have been posted aloft. We are in the main shipping lane for vessels coming from England, so if there is one, we will find it."

An hour went by without anything in sight, but a school of six dolphins that swam along with *Avenger*, arching up out of the water and cutting back in, making small waves. The crew was so intent, though, that there wasn't the usual line of men hanging over the rails watching. Colin glanced every few seconds, however, a smile creasing his lower face. If only, he thought, people could learn to coexist together and enjoy their surroundings like the dolphins did. He'd heard once that dolphins and whales were as smart as humans. After years of watching them at sea, he'd come to the conclusion that what he'd heard was wrong; they were smarter.

Just when Colin was beginning to feel that the day would be a lost cause, there was a shout from the rigging, "Single ship off the port bow, at about half a mile."

The main deck became a beehive of activity. Signals were sent to *The Vixen*, and sails were trimmed to change to an intercept course. They had decided to execute a classic pincer movement, with both ships converging on the target from behind, and then, *The Vixen* would put on a burst of speed and pull ahead, presenting her beam—and, her cannons—to the target, while *Avenger* would come alongside with a boarding party. If the ship was as lightly armed as Colin suspected it would be, there would be no resistance, and taking her and her cargo would be easy.

He also knew, though, that no battle plan survived the first shot fired. He had drilled this simple truth into the crew time after time and could only hope that they remembered his instructions. If possible, they wanted to take the ship without firing a shot, but, for insurance, he had six sharpshooters posted in the riggings, and the cannons on the starboard side, loaded and ready. Only a fool would try and resist such overwhelming force.

Two hours later, as *Avenger* glided along the port side of the ship, Estancia, according to the lettering on her bow, it became apparent that her captain was no fool. Sails were folded and the ship glided to a stop. Men stood on the deck, their hands in plain sight, and not a weapon in evidence.

Looking aft, Colin saw the Spanish flag flying from a slanted pole, but the men assembled on the deck did not look Spanish to him. He moved next to M'nondo, and in a low voice said, "This ship has a Spanish name, and is flying a Spanish flag, but those men on the deck don't look Spanish to me."

"Nor to me," M'nondo said, nodding agreement.

"Signal *Vixen* and tell her we're stopping here for a while until we've had time for a careful examination. She'll have to screen for us."

M'nondo nodded and walked to the signalman. He then returned to Colin at the rail.

"Will you be going with the boarding party, captain?"

"Yes. You have the ship until I return."

Colin joined the boarding party at the rail.

"Keep alert, men," he said. "There's something not quite right about this vessel."

As a man, they nodded, acknowledging his warning without looking at him.

When the two ships were even, bags of sand tied to rope were dropped over the side of *Avenger* to act as cushions when the wave motion threw the two ships together, and Colin led the boarding crew over the rails and onto the deck of the captured ship. The assembled crew looked on but offered no resistance.

"Where's your captain?" Colin asked in a demanding voice.

A thin man with a mostly bald head, wearing an ornate jacket and a ceremonial sword, stepped forward and bowed.

"*Soy Capitan Alfonso Alvarez Concepción,*" he said. "*A quien estoy hablando?*"

Colin knew only a few basic words of Spanish, but to his untrained ears, the *Spanish* captain sounded like he was reading instead of speaking naturally.

"My apologies," he said. "But, I don't speak Spanish. Do you have anyone here who speaks English?" As he spoke, his eyes roamed, and he noticed that almost every man in the crew looked his way. It was clear to him that they all spoke English.

"*No hablo inglés,*" the captain said in an insistent tone.

"I take that to mean you won't talk to me. No matter." Colin turned to his men. "Two of you stay here and keep an eye on these men, the rest of you, search this ship from top to bottom."

As the boarding crew, minus two of the largest and meanest looking, who stayed with Colin, but kept their hostile gazes on the thoroughly cowed crew, went about the business of searching. From what Colin could see of what those working above decks did, ripping open boxes and smashing barrels, it would be in a complete shamble below decks when they were finished.

While he waited for them to finish, he decided to have a little fun with the so-called Spanish seamen. He walked up and laid a hand on the bigger of his two men guarding them. "What say we have ourselves a little fun with these sons of whores," he said.

Out of the corner of his eye he saw that several of them frowned, and almost all of them looked fearful.

"Sounds like it would be fun, cap'n," the man said. "Which one you want to do first?"

Colin turned and glared at the group. He smiled and pointed at one in the front, a frail looking boy not yet old enough to shave. "Let's take that one and see how he looks swinging from the yard arm," he said. At that, the boy went white and swayed.

"Well now, will you look at that. I think that young man understood what I said."

His man chuckled. "I b'lieve you be right, cap'n," he said. "You want me to hang 'im anyway?"

"No, please," the boy cried. "I'll do anything you want. Please don't hurt me."

"Shut yer mouth, lad," the ship's captain said. Then, realizing that he'd just broken his cover, he clamped his lips shut.

Colin bowed in his direction. "Thank you, captain. Now, would you favor me with your real name."

"I have nothing to say to you, sir," he said instead.

"Maybe we'll swing you from the yard arm instead of this young seaman."

"Do what you will with me, you scurrilous brigand. I'm telling you nothing."

Colin could see from the set of the man's jaw that he meant what he said. Willing to die for King and country. He could understand that, though, seeing as how he was risking his own life for his country, and in the man's place would probably have said the same thing. But, if he was a good captain, and everything

Colin could see indicated that he *was* a good captain, he would be concerned for the welfare of his men.

"I see," he said. "Okay, we'll go ahead and hang the lad. How would you like that?"

There was just a tiny flicker of indecision on the man's face, but it was quickly replaced with what Colin thought of as that icy English resolve. "You brigands are going to kill us anyway. The lad will at least will die bravely, like a . . . well, like a good sailor."

"That's just the thing, captain. We're not planning to kill you, at least, not the rest of you. But, if you don't tell me what you're up to, I *will* kill one or two."

A look of surprise creased the man's face. "If you are not planning on killing us, do you mind telling me just what your plans for us are?"

Colin was, at that moment, adjusting his plan as it unfolded. His original plan was to replicate his actions when they took *Whitechapel*; put the crew in boats and order them to row for the nearest land and take their chances if they were unlucky and landed on American soil. But, this crew was special. Englishmen pretending to be Spaniards signaled strange happenings, and he couldn't help but wonder if it was related to the strange goings on in Nassau, which Diego Garcia had still not puzzled out.

"We're taking you and your men prisoner, captain," he said. "What happens to you after that . . . well, we'll just have to see, won't we?"

The captain looked at the young man, deep sorrow in his expression.

"Sorry, lad," he said. "But, we all have our orders. I order each of you to remain quiet, regardless of what these pirates threaten you with. As for you, lad, just know that your name will be forever remembered for sacrificing yourself for King and Country."

There were tears on the boy's face, but he squared his shoulders and stared at Colin.

"Aye, captain," he said. To Colin, he said, "If you be hangin' me, let's get on with it."

Colin was impressed with the boy's grit. Even the hard-bitten man standing next to him smiled at the boy.

"Oh, hell," Colin said. "Hanging you won't gain me anything. We're taking you all prisoner. As soon as we've finished searching your ship, we'll secure you, and sail you to your place of imprisonment."

It was just as well he was taking them instead of putting them in boats, he thought. It was over 1,000 miles to the nearest land, and that was in North Carolina, where they would, if they could make that distance in the small ship's boats, be imprisoned by American authorities, probably for the duration of the war.

"Captain Wo-, er captain," a voice called from one of the hatchways leading below decks. "We found something here you got to see."

Colin left the crew under the watchful eyes of his men and walked to the hatch. The pirate who'd called him, a mulatto who'd been born in a small village just outside Nassau, was holding a large leather satchel that was sealed with an iron lock.

"What is it, Henri?"

"We found this in the captain's cabin. It's one strange one. I never seen a valise with a lock on it before."

Colin looked closer. The lock had the seal of the English king etched in its surface.

"This is no ordinary valise, Henri," he said. "I think what we have here is a treasure trove of official English documents." He couldn't hold back a smile. This training mission had turned into a stunning success. Not only did he have a group of prisoners who were probably privy to many English secrets, but the documents, in addition to probably containing valuable information, could be used to pry more information from the tightlipped captain.

"All right, men," Colin said in a loud voice. "We can finish the search of this ship at base. Signal *The Vixen* to come alongside. We'll divide the prisoners up between her and *Avenger,* then put a skeleton crew on this ship and sail home."

Charles Ray

Chapter 12

January 1813, Skull Island

They took a circuitous route south to Skull Island to avoid English warships, arriving back at their base on the second day of the new year.

Colin had the captured ship's officers locked in one of the empty shacks at the edge of the jungle and posted two guards armed with muskets. The rest of the crew were housed in two sheds with four guards. He, Elizabeth, and M'nondo then went to the main building, where he broke the lock on the satchel and dumped its contents onto the table in the center of the room they used for their planning sessions.

He picked up one of the packets, a large, thick envelope, wrapped with a red ribbon, and sealed with was and the insignia of the British Naval Office. He ripped the ribbon off, opened the envelope, and extracted its contents. The document he withdrew was a ten-page list of naval supplies, ships, and men who would be transferred from the Mediterranean to the Caribbean to support operations against the Americans. He handed it to Elizabeth.

"You can see by this, they're planning a pretty big southern operation."

"If there was ever any doubt, this removes it," she said. "I guess that means it's even more important that we disrupt them here in the islands."

"It certainly does." Colin nodded in agreement. "But, there's more going on that we need to know about."

She looked at him, a question in her eyes, but instead of asking it, she gently laid her hand on his wrist.

"You know, Colin, my sweet, you worry too much."

He patted her hand and smiled. "And, you, my darling, don't worry enough. There's an English agent in Nassau working against us, and until we identify him, we'll be constantly looking over our shoulders wondering where he is and what he's doing."

"We *are* pirates, Colin Worth," she said. "We spend all our lives looking over our shoulders."

He laughed. "Fair point. Still, though, look at this document," he said. "It is absolutely nonsense, but it was in a bag of official documents." He put the document he'd been looking at down so she could see it.

On expensive looking paper, the letter was written in a delicate hand, almost like a woman's, Colin thought, and in flowery language that was typical of the classically educated, even in America.

My Dearest Cousin:

I do hope that this letter finds you in a much better mood than

was apparent in your last letter to me. It was with deep regret that I

read about your experience upon arriving. Please communicate your

condition to me at your earliest convenience, as our cousin from the

colony—or rather, I should say, former colony, has just arrived, and

wishes to travel to meet with you.

Things here are going well. I have been assured by mother

and father that the gifts for our family there will be placed on the

first available vessel. Do let me know if they arrive safely.

I hope to hear from you soonest.

Your faithful cousin Stanley

"Well, what do you make of it?" he asked when she'd finished reading it.

"A letter from Cousin Stanley to his unnamed cousin in Nassau," she said. "What is there to make of it."

"Doesn't it strike you as strange that it was in envelope without an address on the outside? How was the captain of that vessel we captured to know where or to whom to deliver it?"

"Oh, I see. Yes, that is strange. Unless, of course, the captain is a family friend, and knows this cousin."

Colin nodded. "While I will concede that is a possibility, I actually think not. This, however, is one of the first things I will ask the captain tomorrow when I question him."

"You think this is some kind of coded message between spies?"

"Yes, as a matter of fact, I do," he said. "This letter that was also in an unmarked envelope tends to support that theory."

He put another sheet on the table. Elizabeth smiled, but when she looked more closely at what was written on it, her smile faded, and her eyes went wide.

OPERATION FERRET

Ingredients for the pudding are being gathered

They must be stirred in carefully

When the pastry is done we shall prepare seafood

Do not forgot the spices

"What does this mean?" she asked.

"It's clearly some kind of code. I will endeavor to decipher it, as I will with Cousin Stanley's letter. I have a feeling that both of these missives contain vital information, if not for us, for Washington."

She shook her head. "Good luck with that. This makes absolutely no sense to me."

"That's the objective. Only the recipient, who has the key to the code, can make sense of it. It's not the most sophisticated code I've ever seen, but effective nonetheless."

"Will you be at this all night?" She tilted her head at him, with her rosy lips turned up in a half-smile.

Colin smiled back. "No, I have something much more important I wish to do tonight."

Chapter 13

March 1813, Mamie Lillie's, Cat Island

For the rest of January and February, *The Vixen* and *Avenger* prowled the waters north and east of the Bahamas, bagging five more unwary merchant vessels. In each case, they put the crews in the ship's boats and sent them rowing, and then sent the vessels to the ocean bottom after looting everything of value.

Colin had spent many an hour with the two letters, but had been unable to decipher them, and despite a rigorous, and at times threatening, interview session with the captain of the ship, Oscar Wainwright, the man persisted in his statement that he knew nothing about the contents of the satchel, and had only been instructed to take it to the governor general's residence immediately upon arrival in Nassau, and surrender it to Mr. Alwyn Brice, the governor general's chief secretary. That, at least, told Colin who the spymaster in Nassau was, and he'd passed the information to Garcia, who was still trying to uncover the identity of the spy sent from England.

They'd kept the English crew, interrogating the officers daily, until Colin was satisfied that they had no useful information. He and Elizabeth had agreed that holding them indefinitely would be a logistical nightmare, so on this day in early March, they'd blindfolded them, led them to the deck of *Avenger*, where they were ordered to sit quietly until told to move, and sailed to a remote, sparsely inhabited island to the east of Cat Island, where they were rowed ashore and left. Just before Colin left, the captain approached him.

"You never told me your name, sir," he said. "And that is as may be, but I have something to say before you take your leave."

Colin smiled at the man's formal way of talking even after nearly two months of being an unofficial prisoner of war.

"Say your piece, captain," he said.

"You, sir, might be a pirate, but you are also a gentleman. If we meet again, it will be my duty to send you to whatever hell awaits you, but, know this; it will be done with the greatest respect."

Colin bowed slightly. "The sentiment is reciprocated, captain."

Before the stunned man could react, Colin turned and went back to the boat waiting to take him back to *Avenger*.

Back on board, he gave instructions to sail for Cat Island.

"Why are we going there?" Elizabeth asked.

"I need to talk to Mama Lillie," he said. "And, there are a few other things I need to do before we go back to Skull Island."

She shrugged, and Colin smiled. There were things he couldn't share with even her. Not because he didn't trust her, but because the less she knew, the safer she would be in the event they were captured.

He had, for instance, insisted that she remain on the quarterdeck during their raids, and not, as had been her practice in the past, accompany the boarding party. He didn't want word to spread that there was a woman with the pirates, and there was no way anyone would think she was a man, even though she wore pants. Unlike a few of the other women who had become pirates in the region, like Anne Bonney Mary

Read, who had sailed with Calico Jack Rackam around 1717 or 1720. Both dressed as men whenever they fought. Elizabeth, on the other hand, wore pants, but they looked nothing a man's pants. Rather than being baggy to disguise her femininity, they hugged every curve, and accented it. Should someone from one of the crews that they put in boats happen to see and comment on a beautiful woman among the pirates who raided them, the authorities would know immediately that it was Elizabeth Parker, and that could put the residents of Lost Island in jeopardy.

It had chafed Elizabeth at first, but in time, she'd come to see the wisdom of his action, so, whenever he clammed up and kept things from her, she just made a little sniffing sound and changed the subject or kept quiet.

She kept quiet until they'd anchored in one of the hidden coves at Cat Island, said nothing during the short boat ride to the beach, and kept her mouth shut during the ride in a donkey cart into town to Mama Lillie's place. She uttered her first words when they pushed through the door into the café.

"Maman, we've come for some of your gumbo," she said.

Lillie came through the beaded curtain that separated the kitchen from the rest of the café. The aroma of crab, shrimp, and the spices and vegetables that made up her famous gumbo, followed her.

"*Bonjour, cherie, mes enfants*," she said, wiping her hands on the white apron she wore. "The gumbo, she is not quite ready, but can I get you servings of Queen conch to whet your appetites for a few moments?"

The local delicacy, a giant sea snail whose flesh was almost as chewy as gum rubber, wasn't Colin's favorite. "I'll just have a mug of rum while the gumbo cooks," he said.

M'nondo licked his lips. "The conch sounds fine with me."

"Me, too," said Elizabeth.

Colin rolled his eyes. He would have to live in the islands at least as long as these two before he developed a taste for conch.

"*Tres bon*, I bring three rum and two conch," Lillie said. "Please, sit yourself. Not many customer today, so you have the choice of tables." She paused and looked at Colin. "Unless you prefer the private room?"

"I think the private room would be nice," he said.

"Very well, you know the way. I bring the drink and food *rapidment*."

As they made their way to Mama Lillie's private room for special customers, M'nondo punched Colin's shoulder. "I thought you were the adventurous sort, Colin."

"I love adventure. What makes you think I don't?"

"You do not eat the conch. That is a specialty of the islands. Everyone eats them."

"Actually," Elizabeth said. "It is quite tasty."

Colin snorted. "Yes, if you put enough pepper and other spices on it. I tried it once, and even with the spices, it was like trying to chew my boots."

The three or four customers watched their banter with interest as they went through the curtains. Colin noticed one man who seemed to be paying special interest and resolved to find out who he was.

They sat at the room's only table, and shortly afterwards, Mama Lillie arrived with a bottle of rum, four glasses, and two plates of conch.

"You should try, Colin," she said. "Conch is good for you. Is like your American buffalo."

"I've tasted buffalo, and believe me, it tastes nothing like conch."

"No, *cher*. I mean because it has many uses, just like the buffalo. You know, the local natives use the shell of the conch to make music."

"Oh, yes. I've seen and heard the conch shell horns. They were originally developed as a way of signaling in the jungle, and when the Caribs were out fishing."

"Ha, you know your island history. Why do you not like the island cuisine?"

"I like it well enough," he said. "Just not the conch."

"Ah well, you like Mama Lillie's gumbo, so that is good enough for me." She poured generous portions of rum in each glass. "So, one toast, and then I go see to the gumbo, no?"

They raised their glasses.

"Here's the life of a buccaneer," Elizabeth said. "Short, but full of excitement."

"I like the excitement, but I'm not too thrilled about the short part," Colin said.

"We all die, my friend," M'nondo said. "We cannot determine the time or place, only whether we die with dignity and honor."

"Aye, I'll drink to that."

"You men," Mamie Lillie said. "Are really very strange creatures."

She drained her glass, heaved her bulk from the chair and disappeared in the direction of the kitchen.

The three passed the time in her absence, drinking and making small talk. Only when she returned and assured them that it was safe to talk would they get down to business.

Colin was beginning to get impatient, and rose to find Lillie, just as she came in carrying a large pot of steaming gumbo in one hand, and a tray laden with bowls, spoons, and a bottle of the flaming hot sauce that everyone liked in the other.

"The gumbo she is ready," she said. "As soon as I have filled our bowls we can get to the business, no."

"Yes," they said in unison, looking avidly at the mixture of seafood, sausage, okra, sweet and hot peppers, and chopped tomatoes. The spicy sweet aroma of thyme and the special gumbo powder that Lillie ground herself filled the air.

Once everyone's bowl was filled, and they began digging in, Lillie leaned forward, her elbows, and a large portion of her generous breasts on the table.

"Now, while you eat, I will tell you what has been taking place since you were here last time.

They all stopped eating and looked at her. She frowned and waggled her finger.

"Do not stop eating *mes enfants*. Can you not eat and listen at the same time?

"Sorry, Mama Lillie," Colin said. "I was just trying to give you my full attention."

"You give me attention with the ears, *cher*. With the hand you put the food in your mouth, and you chew."

"Okay." He resumed eating, as did the others, but all eyes were on Lillie.

"Very well, here is what happen. I am told the English sent a man to the islands with a special mission."

"Yes," Colin said. "We've heard the same thing. He's some kind of spy. We think his presence here is somehow connected to the English plans to attack New Orleans."

"I have heard that they might attack Mobile," Lillie said.

Colin nodded. "That is also a good place, but if they take New Orleans, with their ships blockading the coast, our merchants will suffer greatly. The Mississippi River is our major supply route in the west."

"It will be bad either way. The thing that is *tres important*, however, is that my people tell me that this strange man is coming here."

"Here, as in Cat Island?"

"*Oui*, here to Cat Island. I am wondering if this is perhaps because he has some idea who has been attacking the English ships, or maybe he has the suspicion about me."

"Oh, no, Mama Lillie," Elizabeth said. "No one would ever think you are anything but a jolly bistro owner."

"Maybe, *ma petite*, but I cannot take the chance. I am instructing my people to try and find this man and kill him."

"I wish you would reconsider that, Mama Lillie," Colin said.

"And, why should I do that?"

"Because, it's important that we find out what he's up to. If you kill him, he'll just be replaced, and we'll still be in the dark."

She put a pudgy finger on the side of her nose. "Ah, I guess I see your point, *cher*. Very well, then. I will tell my people to make a special effort to capture this *cochon*. If he resists, though, he will be, how you say, damaged."

Colin laughed. "I can accept a certain amount of damage, as long as he can talk."

"Then, I promise you, I tell them not to hit him in the mouth."

Everyone laughed at that. Colin knew, though, that she wasn't trying to be funny. She would instruct her people, if they found and captured the English agent, he was not to be killed or hit in the mouth, but any other part of his body was a legitimate target. Colin didn't know the man, but he felt a bit of sympathy for him.

"Okay, I can live with that." He turned to Elizabeth and M'nondo. "I won't be going back to base with you two." They looked surprised. "I'll be back in a couple of weeks, but I need to get to Cap Haitien to check on my ship and crew, and to check in with George Hoskins. We need to know the most recent news from Washington."

Elizabeth dropped her gaze, a gesture that didn't go unnoticed by everyone except Colin.

"You have a safe trip, and hurry back," she said quietly. "We'll save the richest ships for when you get back."

"I appreciate that. M'nondo, you're in command of *Avenger* until I get back."

"Aye, captain," the big man said.

Chapter 14

April 1813, Cap Haitien

It took Colin a week to get to Cap Haitien, begging rides on fishing vessels and smuggling boats from Cat Island, hopping from island to island until he finally managed to get aboard a French merchantman headed for Haiti.

The captain of the merchant ship, though bound for Port-au-Prince, was kind enough to make an unscheduled stop at the port of Cap Haitien in the country's northeast to drop him off.

From the pier, he made his way through the shamble of warehouses, where the goods coming in and going out were temporarily stored, the shanties occupied by the Haitians who worked, played, and occasionally, stole on the docks, and the astonishing assemblage of shops and markets that seem to always grow up around docks.

George Hoskins, the rumpled American consul in Cap Haitien, was in office, a run down, two-story wooden building on the first main street after the dock area, giving him access to the occasional American vessel or itinerant seaman, as well as to the merchants and businessmen of the city. Mainly, though, it allowed him to do his most important job; act as the eyes and ears of the American government in the volatile Caribbean region.

The front office of the building was manned by a middle-aged, balding American, who examined seamen's papers and shipping documents before they were passed to Hoskins for signature and seal, and who dealt with the people, local and American, who sought assistance from the consul. Hoskins kept himself cosseted in a back office, when he wasn't prowling the city's streets meeting with his extensive network of agents and informants, seated behind a scarred wooden desk piled high with shipping charts, maps, and other documents.

Colin rapped lightly on the door, and then entered without waiting to be told. Hoskins looked up from a map he'd been studying and smiled broadly when he saw who his unannounced visitor was.

"Aye, Colin, lad, it's been a while," he said. He waved at the chair at the left side of his desk, the only horizontal surface that didn't have a pile of papers on it. "The beard makes you look like a swashing buccaneer, or a dastardly pirate, depending on which side you're on. Have a seat. What can I do for you?"

"Well, George, I'd really like some information on how the war's going at home."

Hoskins frowned and rubbed his unshaven, sun-darkened jaw. "My, you get right down to business, don't you, and unpleasant business at that. Okay, make yourself comfortable, lad, for what I'm about to tell you will not please you."

He pulled a map of the United States from beneath an untidy pile of papers and spread it over everything else, tamping it down as best he could.

"Why don't we start with what you know," he said.

Colin shook his head. "About what's happening back home? Nothing. I've been in the islands since I last saw you. By the way, I didn't see *Intrepid* when I arrived."

"Ah yes, your ship. She was ordered to patrol the gulf to try and interdict any English vessels that try sneaking up that way. That young Comstock, by the way, is turning out to be a competent captain. You might not have a job when this war's over, at least, not on *Intrepid*."

"Albert deserves the chance to show what he can do," Colin said. "I saw his potential early in our acquaintance. Now, the war?"

"Oh, the war. It's more like a Shakespearean tragedy. Foolishly, in hindsight, our first move was to invade Canada."

"That's not such a bad strategy. If we control Canada, it makes it harder for the English to supply their forces to our west, and eventually, when they run out of supplies, they'll have to surrender."

"Yup, it's a good idea, and would've worked, if they'd had a proper commander."

"Who led the forces in the invasion?"

"That, lad, is a good question. There are some who say they had no leader. If, on the other hand, you want to know who was commanding the forces that went to Canada, well, I can answer that. General William Hull was the top dog for that debacle."

"William Hull? I know that name. He's the governor of Wisconsin Territory, isn't he?"

"Yeah, that's him, but he fought in the independence war before goin' into politics, and when the president got congress to declare war this time, they made him a brigadier general. He got himself 2,000 unseasoned militia and headed for Canada."

"I take it that little expedition didn't work out too well." Colin chuckled.

"Ain't funny, boy," Hoskins said. "That fool didn't do a good job of planning, and he don't know beans about moving troops. Got up there, and first time the English shot at him, he beat a hasty retreat back to Fort Detroit."

"I suppose I can understand that. After all, the English troops have been fighting old Emperor

Napoleon, and the French Republican forces before that, while our militia boys haven't done much except harass the Indians."

"I reckon you could be right, but they made a bunch of stupid assumptions from the outset. First, they just assumed that the Canadians would welcome our troops, but instead, they fought alongside the English. Same with the Indians. Most of the tribes on our western frontier are afraid we got eyes on their tribal lands."

"They're not too far wrong about that. Our people in the west are land and power hungry, and they see the tribes as standing in the way of our rightful expansion to the west. That's the bunch that talked the president into this war in the first place. I sympathize with Hull. He was given a hard job, and not very much to work with."

"Well, you're right about that, at least. The damn Ohio militia boys refused to cross the border into Canada. Said they were only fighting in their own state. Now, why in blazes would we start a war without an army that'll go where its ordered to go?"

Colin shook his head. "I have to confess, that puzzles me as well. The navy is undermanned, and we don't have enough ships, but thankfully, the ocean has no borders. We go where we're told."

"The navy is our only hope in this war, son, mark my words. We have some savvy navy commanders, and soon as they build enough ships of the line, we'll give old John Bull what for."

"John who?"

"Oh, that's just a little nickname some English author created back in 1711 or 1712 to represent the English, you know, the portly country gentleman. I've never been sure if it was meant to be mean satire or sympathetic, but that little pot-bellied gallimuffin just seems to be what the dang English are like, you know.

Anyway, as I was saying, if the navy don't come through, our beans are cooked."

"How is the war at sea going?"

"It's touch and go right now. We've won a few and lost a few. I don't have all the details. They got this ship building operation going up in New York, on one of the rivers with access to the lake region. The president is also pushing congress to appropriate more money for the army and approve a national standing army. As you might well imagine, the New Englanders are pushing back, and not all of the Democratic-Republicans are on Madison's side in the matter."

"In other words," Colin said. "The war goes badly."

"No, not in other words, son; in just those words. If things don't start turning around soon, we're gonna be in a peck of trouble. How are things going on your end?"

"We've bagged several merchant ships, and got quite a haul of weapons, ammunition, and other supplies. It's been driving the English in Nassau crazy. Their scouring the islands, but they don't have enough ships or men, and with over 700 islands on the charts, and a few that are not, they could search a hundred years and not find us."

"So, the tales brought by fishermen haven't been exaggerations." Hoskins laughed. "The damned English don't know it, but they're not all that popular with the natives here in the Caribbean. Of course, neither or we."

"Of course. They just want to be left alone. But, of course, neither we nor the English are going to do that."

"Hey, it's the way of the world. The strong exploit the weak. So, things are going well for you?"

"Not completely. We received word of an English agent arriving in Nassau but haven't been able to identify him or his mission. I believe it's related to their plans to attack from the south."

"Anything definite on that?"

Colin pulled the mysterious letters from his jacket. "We found these documents in the captain's cabin of one of the ships we raided. I believe they are either intended for, or related to this mystery man, but I've not been able to decipher them."

Hoskins took the letters and spread them on his desk. After looking at them for a few minutes, his brow furrowed in concentration, he looked up at Colin. "I see what you mean. This makes no sense."

"I was hoping you would know someone who might be able to decipher them."

Hoskins picked one of the letters up and held it up, peering at the words. "Not here in Haiti, lad. But, I might know a fella in the State Department who can do it. He's a real crackerjack with puzzles and codes. Problem is, with the bloody English blockade, getting dispatches back and forth with Washington is a real problem. Might be a few months before I can get you an answer."

"If that's the best you can do, I'll have to accept it." Colin made a huffing noise. "Well, my vacation is over. Unless you have something else for me, I'm back to the war."

His head cocked to the side, and one eye half closed, Hoskins regarded Colin thoughtfully. "You know, boy, it's almost like you're a different man than the one I spoke to a few months back."

"What do you mean?"

"I don't know. It's like you've got a rougher edge to you, but at the same time, you're looser. Dang if you aren't becoming a pirate."

Colin laughed. "I have to play the part well if I'm to be successful," he said. "It's just a coat I put on and take off at will." He wasn't at all sure, though, that the coat could be taken off that easily.

He shrugged and stood. "I'll be taking my leave of you, now," he said.

He and Hoskins shook hands, him with a look of grim determination on his face, the older man, a suspicious look in his eyes.

Charles Ray

Chapter 15

**May 1813, On board *Avenger* in the Atlantic Ocean,
north of Skull Island**

The Vixen and *Avenger* crews had developed a well-choreographed routine during their joint patrols in search of prey.

They alternated the lead ship, with the following vessel about an eighth of a mile astern and to port. When the lead ship, which on this voyage was *Avenger,* spotted a likely target, it went to full sails and mimed a direct frontal attack. The target vessel, assuming a pirate ship was coming alongside to board, would tack an angle away from it, while still heading generally toward its intended destination, the islands of the Caribbean. The trailing ship, in the meantime, would move to position itself so that the fleeing vessel would be sailing right into the maws of its starboard cannons. At this point, the victim had little choice but to either heave to and allow itself to be boarded, or if armed, to prepare to fight.

Preoccupied with the new threat, the captain of the vessel wouldn't notice the first ship until it was lying off starboard, its cannons primed and ready to fire.

It would then be do or die. Broadsides from six cannons starboard and six cannons port, if not sending the target immediately to the bottom of the ocean, would at a minimum damage it so severely it would be unable to do more than limp along at the speed of a rowboat.

For this voyage Colin had added an adaption of his Leyden jar powered lantern which he'd used against *Intrepid* when its then captain, Beauregard Dangerfield, pursued Elizabeth. His adaptation consisted of a slightly smaller lantern, with a hinged metal cover over the lens. The lantern would be lit, and the cover would be flipped in a prearranged pattern. Each ship had one such device, and they used it to signal back and forth over a distance of as much as three miles, a bit farther at night when the bright flashing light was more easily seen. The devices were mounted on a pedestal installed on the quarter deck so that the signaler could more easily send the captain's messages and relay any messages to him.

He had also installed four of the original flash lamps on both sides of both vessels, between the cannons, and slightly forward of the priming holes, so that when lit, they would blind the sailors on the target vessel, and serve as illumination for the gunners on their ships. They had yet to test them, but he was confident they would work as he envisioned. The signal lamps, on the other hand, had been tested on trial voyages around Skull Island, and had worked very well, saving manpower, as now there was no need for a runner between the captain on the quarterdeck and the signaler high up in the rigging.

They had been under sail for six hours without spotting anything, and Colin was just about to give it up and signal *The Vixen* to turn and sail for home when the lookout in the rigging shouted, "Small vessel, looks to be a sloop, off port bow, bearin' southwest."

At the lookout's shout, the deck of *Avenger* came alive. The cannon crews ran to their stations and began preparing them to fire, boarding parties armed themselves and stood near the rails, and four sharpshooters scampered up into the riggings where they would have clear shots onto the target ship's decks. Colin turned to the signalman standing behind him.

"Signal *Vixen*," he said. "We're giving chase."

"Aye, sir," the man, a youngster barely out of his teens, said.

Colin turned his attention back to the helmsman.

"Steady she goes, lad," he said. "Just like we practiced. Aim for her port bow, so she turns to run. Deck crews, prepare for a fast run."

The helmsman acknowledged the order and began making adjustments. Deck crews set the sails for top speed in the direction of the vessel, which Colin could now see was a sloop. He smiled. It would be lightly armed, no match for either of their vessels, and was probably carrying either official dispatches or officials, either of which would make for a good day's haul.

As the gap between the two ships lessened, the sloop began to turn further west, indicating that *Avenger* had been seen, and probably identified as hostile. The sloop was much faster, but that speed would be her undoing because it would take her directly into the sights of *The Vixen's* cannons, and if it was making top speed, there would not be enough time to slow or make an abrupt enough change of course to avoid them.

Colin stood, feet apart and his hands behind his back. Until they closed, or unless something unexpected happened, there was nothing for him to do but observe. He had trained the *Avenger's* crew hard, just as he had trained the men of *Intrepid*, and though they were pirates, he rated them as highly as he did the navy men under his command.

M'nondo, his first mate, having seen to the cannon crews and checked the deck crews, moved silently up beside him.

"It is just as you predicted, Colin," he said. "He is running directly into Elizabeth's cannons, thinking that because he is faster, he is getting away from us."

Colin nodded. "Yes. I almost feel sorry for him."

"Hmph, I do not. He is the enemy, and while it is proper to respect your enemy, it is not helpful to feel sorry for him."

"What's the difference?"

"If you respect him, you will not underestimate him, and you will treat him properly when you have defeated him. If you feel sorry for him, you might let your guard down, and then he can take advantage of you."

"Dang, I never thought of it that way. Okay, I respect the hell out of him. And, besides, I said I *almost* feel sorry for him. That, my friend, was sarcasm."

"Forgive me for not understanding. When I was a young slave in America, I had no contact with people like you, and since I escaped here to the islands, my only contact has been with them at the point of my cutlass, so there has been no time for conversation."

The two men laughed.

"Well, I guess I'll just have to teach you some of the finer points of the English language as spoken by us rustic colonialists," Colin said.

"Perhaps some other time." M'nondo pointed at the horizon to their front. "Yonder lies *The Vixen,* and she is cutting across that sloop's path. I wonder . . . ah, yes, he has seen her, and he is turning. The fool, he has just made his ship a perfect target. I will go and ready the port cannons."

As he trotted off, Colin said, "Helm, adjust course to bring us abeam of her starboard."

He crossed his fingers that things would continue to go as he had planned and anticipated, knowing that any military operation can go awry at any point for the slightest of reasons.

In addition to all the things that could go wrong on his own ship, there was the added complication of his lack of control of events on *The Vixen*. Fortunately, Elizabeth was one of the most competent captains he'd ever seen, better even than he was, so he just sighed, kept his fingers crossed, and waited.

Charles Ray

Chapter 16

On board *The Vixen*

Elizabeth was bored. She had been standing on the quarterdeck for three hours with nothing to do but listen to the flapping sound the sails made or the crash of the bow as it plowed through the waves, and watch the fluffy clouds floating toward the north. They hadn't seen a ship since leaving Skull Island, and the sun was getting low in the western sky.

She was, however, accustomed to being bored. The ocean is vast, and even with the thousands of merchant vessels plying the trade routes between Europe and the Americas, finding one of them in that expanse of heaving water was often a matter of luck. So, bored though she was, she stood impassive behind the helmsman, one eye on him, the other on the sea ahead, where Colin and *Avenger*, at an eighth of a mile were clearly visible.

Then, she saw the flicker of light from *Avenger's* stern. A signal. *Has he sighted a ship, or, like the impatient American he is, is he suggesting we quit and go home?* She peered closely blinking light. **Small ship off port bow. Heading west. Prepare to engage.** Like Colin, she had taken the time to learn the signal code. But, as a good captain, she still waited patiently for her signalman to relay the message to her, which he quickly did.

"Very well. Helm, begin the maneuver to bring us on a parallel course. Starboard cannons make ready." She didn't strain her voice, or shout, but had learned over the years, first standing near Captain Teague, and later standing on the quarterdeck as master in her own right, to make herself heard across the expanse of the ship's deck.

She braced herself as *The Vixen* heeled to port, making the necessary turn to put her on a course that would allow her to bring her cannons to bear on the target. She squinted and recognized the single mast with fore-and-aft rig of an English sloop some distance beyond *Avenger*. It would not be heavily armed but could slip across the water like a stone skipped across a pond. A single ship would be hard pressed to catch it, unless it was caught by surprise near an island, but Colin's plan to use one ship as the hound to chase it into the hunter's trap was masterful. She doubted, though, that the technique would catch on with her fellow pirates, who in the main were not noted for their ability to cooperate with each other.

The distance between the two vessels closed rapidly, and it was only when it was too late to make an evasive maneuver that the English captain realized that he'd been forced into a trap. The flutter of the sloop's top sails indicated an attempt to slow or stop the vessel, which, Elizabeth thought, was a prudent idea, as, in addition to her six cannons that were just now coming into effective range on one side of the sloop, she could see *Avenger* gliding in on the other, already well within the range that would allow her cannons to inflict maximum damage on the smaller ship.

She felt a raging mental conflict; on the one hand, glad to see the captain taking the judicious step of standing to rather than entering into a fight he was sure to lose, but on the other, she had been looking forward to a little dust up to knock loose the cobwebs from the relative inactivity of the past several months. They had only encountered one ship that chose to fight, and that conflict had lasted for only two volleys from *The Vixen*'s cannons. A heated ball from the second volley had found the ship's powder store and the vessel went up in a ball of orange flame and black smoke, with pieces of ship and crew thrust high into the air and as much as a hundred yards from the hole in the ocean into which the ship sank. She was not bloodthirsty and did not gloat over the death of those poor sailors, but she did like the occasional bit of pulse-pounding action that came with sea battles. She could tell that Colin was much the same. He was extremely reluctant to take a life, but when the cannons began firing, he became a different person. In another life, he would have been a pirate, and based on how he was out-foxing the English fleet in Nassau, a successful one.

"Are we gonna board 'er, captain?" The voice of a sailor standing on the main deck at the steps up to the quarterdeck yanked her from her reverie.

"No, we are not," she said. "We are here to provide cover for *Avenger*. Her crew will board."

The man looked disappointed.

"Never fear," she said. "Tomorrow will be our turn to lead. You'll get to board then."

He smiled and touched a forefinger to his forehead in what, among the pirates, passed as a salute.

"Aye, captain, and we'll do a better job of it than them bog hogs on *Avenger* I wager."

"That we will, that we will." She laughed. The men on the other ship had, just a few months earlier, been shipmates of her current crew, but now that they were on another ship, they were competitors, friendly competitors, but that didn't mean they would give an inch to each other. She and Colin both encouraged their rivalry within certain limits. There was no fighting allowed for example, but the arguments during after dinner drinking over which crew was better were so loud at times it was hard to know that they weren't about to

Chapter 17

On board *Avenger*

Colin was delighted to see *The Vixen* respond immediately to his signal and change to an intercept course. He laughed when he saw the frantic attempts aboard the sloop to change course to avoid her, and then, the realization that they were blocked in causing the captain to begin slowing in preparation for stopping and being boarded. He wondered if they knew who was raiding them and that they would, if they offered no resistance, be allowed to row away in the ship's boats. They were, he estimated, about three to four hard days of rowing from the nearest landfall, and with enough food and water, should make it without problem.

"Helm," he said. "Bring her up alongside for boarding."

"Aye, sir."

The big ship responded to the helm like a dream, probably better with Colin's helmsman than she had with the English sailor they'd evicted from his position when they appropriated the vessel.

In a matter of a few minutes they were abeam of the sloop, *H.M.S. Duke of Edington*, cannons loaded and aimed at her waterline and marksmen in the riggings with key people on her deck in their sights. One of those targets was the captain, a tall, imposing figure in his Royal Navy captain's uniform standing on the quarterdeck with a haughty expression on his narrow face, and he knew it, but refused to cower. It always amazed Colin how the English officer class, actually, all of the English upper classes, put on their airs of indifference when he knew that deep down the man's guts were quivering and his legs probably felt like gum rubber. Only a fool or a mad man could stare down the barrel of a loaded cannon or rifle and not feel afraid. It was one thing, he thought, to keep calm so that the men under your command stayed calm and did their jobs, but this went beyond calm, and it grated on him every time he witnessed it. Even though he'd not met that many Englishmen, his feelings toward them were strong, and decidedly negative. And, now that he was engaged in a war against them, all he wanted to do was hit them, and hit them hard.

He would not, of course, act on his feelings. He saw how a captain who had no control over his rages had demoralized a U.S. navy vessel, when *Intrepid* had to endure Beauregard as captain, and he could imagine that it would only be worse on a pirate ship.

So, as *Avenger* slid up near enough to the sloop that grappling hooks could be tossed across and secured to her rails, he stood at the rail, his hands behind his back, with a noncommittal look on his face.

"What do you want from us," a florid faced young officer yelled from the sloop's quarterdeck.

"I want you to heave to so we can board you safely," he yelled back. "Or, would you like a couple of volleys from our cannons. And, by our cannons, I mean the ship on t'other side of you."

Colin pointed across the space. The young officer turned, twitched, and turned back. Some of the red had gone from his complexion, and he looked very uncomfortable—or, Colin thought, very un-English. This was the first time he'd seen an English officer show any kind of emotion other than disdain or anger.

"We're stopping, sir," the man said. "At the speed we were sailing, it takes a bit to bring her to full stop."

Colin knew that but was not about to give them any sympathy. What was it M'nondo had said? Oh yes, give them respect, but do not feel sorry for them. Good advice.

"Very well," he said. "Be quick about it. I am not a patient man."

It took nearly five minutes for the sloop to bleed off its speed and come to a standstill. *Avenger's* crew matched speed and stopped at almost the same instant. Beyond the sloop, Colin saw that Elizabeth's crew had turned in a similar performance. From the open-mouthed looks among the sloop's crew, it was clear that they had noticed as well.

When the ships were still in the water except for the up and down motion from the swells, he ordered the boarding party to begin. Using ropes strung from the yard arms, some with their cutlasses clenched in their teeth, his men swung across, landing lightly on the sloop's deck and surrounding the cowed crew.

Colin swung across in the second wave, but he left his sword in its scabbard, not wanting to trip and fall as he hit the deck and cut his jaw away. That would not look good to his men, or to the crew of the vessel they were about to loot.

Once solidly on deck, he moved toward the man he presumed to be the captain, a thin, ascetic looking man with a high forehead and a hawk nose, which he stared down at Colin as he approached.

Colin touched the blade of his sword to his forehead and bowed slightly. "You are the captain of this vessel, I presume."

The captain copied Colin's bow. "You presume correctly," he said. "Captain Archibald Wadsworth of His Majesty's Navy at your service. To whom do I have the honor of addressing."

Colin looked at the man, the most ferocious expression he could muster on his face, and said, "Teague, Captain Teague to you, you pompous twit."

Wadsworth took a step back as if he'd been struck. His face darkened, almost like an overripe eggplant. "How dare you speak to an officer in His Majesty's Navy in that manner," he said. Spittle flew from his thick red lips.

Colin approached him, the point of his sword leading the way.

"I dare what I please *Captain* Wadsworth, and if you wish to keep that head of yours, it's *you* who'd best be polite to me. Now, here is what you're going to do. You'll assemble your crew, gather enough food and water to last you for a few days, and get in your boats and row away."

"You can't—"

"Oh, I can, captain, and I will. After we've taken everything of value, this ship is going to the bottom of the ocean. Your decision is whether you're in your boats when that happens, or you go with it."

To reinforce his threat, the boarding party brandished their cutlasses and made growling and snarling noises.

"As you can see, my men are thirsting for a little adventure. It's been quiet in these waters the past few weeks."

Wadsworth bowed; not a bow signifying respect, or even the acceptance of Colin's clear dominance of the situation, but an aloof, stiff-backed mockery of a motion that attempted to show that he, a member of the British ruling class, was not under the thrall of this common ruffian. Colin recognized the gesture for what it was and laughed.

"And, why do you laugh, Captain Teague?"

All serious, Colin locked eyes with the man. "For no reason, captain," he said. "You'll find that I am a most serious man, all business as it were. And, speaking of business, where do you keep the official dispatch bag?"

Red circles blossomed on Wadsworth's cheeks, and his eyes became as round as demitasse cups. "Who told you that we had a dispatch bag aboard this vessel?"

"Why, you just did, captain. Now, where is it? In your cabin perhaps?"

Wadsworth sniffed and looked away, but that told Colin all he needed to know. He grabbed the shoulder of an empty-handed pirate who had just returned from tossing a crate of valuable over the rail to his waiting comrades on *Avenger*. "Go to the captain's cabin," he said. "Look for a bag or satchel that will be locked and probably have an official looking seal on it. Bring it to me."

"Aye, cap'n," the man said, and trotted off.

Colin turned back to Captain Wadsworth and his crew who stood looking at him with their mouths agape. Wadsworth looked like he'd bitten into an unripe persimmon.

"You, sir," Wadsworth said. "Will hang for this."

"You could be right, captain." Colin tipped the blade of his sword to his forehead again. "But, it won't be you doing the hanging. Now, I suggest you and your men get to work preparing your boats. You have a long row ahead of you to reach land."

Wadsworth looked as if wanted to say something else, but finally, snorted and spun on his heels.

"All right, men, prepare the boats for launch."

Colin watched for a moment as two of his men guarded the crew as they moved a barrel of water and several crates of provisions to each of the boats. Then, he turned his attention to those who were searching the ship above and below decks, seeking anything of value that could be moved to *Avenger* before they scuttled *Duke of Edington*. He regretted having to do that. She was smaller than *Avenger*, a frigate, and lighter armed, with only four cannons. At about 80 tons, with a headsail and mainsail affixed to the single mast, she was a sleek beauty. Capable of amazing speed, they were the best choice for dispatch boats, which, from appearances, was what this one was. He was tempted to take her as a prize, but his better judgment convinced him not to. They were already stretched to the limit having to man two ships; it would be impossible to operate another without recruiting more men, and with an English agent in the islands looking for them, that would be a risky, even foolhardy undertaking. He sighed as he thought of such a beautiful ship covered in silt at the bottom of the Atlantic.

"Cap'n," a voice behind him said. "Found this here bag in the cap'n's quarters."

Colin took the calfskin bag, noticed the Royal Navy seal on the lock, and slung it over his shoulder. It was heavy, and as he patted it he could tell that it was crammed full. Another batch of coded documents, no doubt, but probably some unencoded missives for the government authorities in Nassau that might be of use to the war planners in Washington. He sighed. It would be a long night for him. He would have to check every document in the bag before packaging them for forwarding to Cap Haitien.

The pace of activity was slowing as almost everything of any use had been transferred to *Avenger*. The sloop's crew were in boats and were over a hundred yards off the starboard bow, heading generally west by southwest. Colin hoped they would make it without incident. He'd seen no American navy vessels in this particular area, and the other pirates had by unspoken agreement moved their operations elsewhere to avoid getting in Elizabeth's way or in her bad graces, but one never knew.

He sighed and shrugged. "Okay, men, let's prepare this ship to be scuttled and get back aboard *Avenger*."

Chapter 18

On Skull Island

Upon returning to Skull Island, they moored the ships in the lagoon, and Colin and Elizabeth left their first mates the job of securing them and offloading the loot and storing it appropriately. They went directly to the big building where Colin dumped the contents of the dispatch bag onto the center of the table.

"Oh my," Elizabeth said. "What a lot of important looking documents. That little ship was a good choice of targets, I presume?"

"You presume right, milady," he said. "This is the biggest haul of documents to date."

"So, you'll be sending them to Hosking?"

"Yes, but I want to examine them first, just in case t here's anything in them that might affect us here. You feel like helping me?"

She pouted. "It's not as exciting as chasing down a merchant ship. Honestly, if not for the raids on shipping, I would regret agreeing to help you in this quest of yours."

He gently grasped chin and looked deeply into her eyes. "Admit it, woman, you like spending time with me."

She swatted his hand away. "Yes, but not doing this." She made a sweeping motion, taking in the jumbled pile of letters and folders.

"Ah, well, I think that after a few hours of reading these documents, a good supper, I could take care of spending time together in the other way . . . that is, if that's what you meant."

Her eyes blazed, and she poked a finger in his chest. "You know very well--, oh, never mind, let's just get this over with."

He sorted the documents into two stacks and pushed one in front of her. "Okay, you work on this one, and I'll do these," he said. "That way we'll be finished sooner."

Without responding to him, she picked a document from the pile, spread it out on the table and began reading. After a few minutes she snorted. "This is just like that other letter. Just a lot of nonsense."

He leaned over to look. "Hm, I see what you mean. It must be a coded message for someone, probably the agent they sent. Let's see if we can figure it out together."

She moved to the side to allow him to see the paper more clearly. He studied it closely. Like the previous letter, it was from Cousin Stanley to his unnamed cousin in Nassau. At a casual glance it seemed to be just gossip between two relatives, but the more he read, the stranger it seemed. He was sure it was some kind of code. He wondered if Hoskins had found someone to decipher it.

Elizabeth stabbed a shapely finger at the paper. "What does this all mean? Here, for instance, where he writes, 'our cousin says that there are rats in the manor and we need to use the ferret to eliminate them,' I have no idea what he's talking about."

Colin stared down at the words on the paper. Elizabeth was right, in a way. The words made no sense if you were reading them in the context of a letter between cousins separated by an ocean. But, if you tried to think like a spymaster sending instructions to one of your agents . . . maybe, he thought, that was the key. He had to think of the words in relation to the situation in the Caribbean.

"I think that I just might, though," he said.

She looked at him, her brow creased. "Really? You know what this totally nonsensical sentence really means?"

"Perhaps. Let's think about it, not as a message from one cousin to another, but from some official in London to an agent out here. Now, the manor, that would probably either be Nassau or the whole region. The rats in the manor would, I think, be us. Rats are annoying vermin, and you must admit, we are very annoying to our English friends right now."

Nodding, she said. "That makes sense, but who or what is this ferret?"

"Ah, that one sort of has me stumped."

"I know that the ferret is a domesticated polecat, could—"

"That's it." Colin almost shouted. "A tame animal used for hunting rabbits, it sleeps a lot, and is most active at night. He must be referring to this agent we've been looking for."

"What a horrible thing to call a person."

"I'm sure there was a good reason for the use of that title," he said. "And, I suspect it means trouble for us. If this person was sent here specifically to hunt us down, we need to take action to stop him."

"But, how do we do that when we don't even know where in the islands he is."

"From the description given by Mama Lillie's people, we have a good idea of what he looks like. I think we can use that, with her help, to track him down."

"We're going to Cat Island, aren't we?"

"I can go alone if you don't wish to go," he said.

"Oh no, I would not miss an opportunity to eat Mama Lillie's gumbo."

Charles Ray

Chapter 19

June 1813, Cat Island

The group that descended upon Mama Lillie's café was larger than usual. In addition to Colin, Elizabeth, and M'nondo. Garcia, the helmsman O'Reilly, and four other men pushed through the door on Tuesday at midday. The ten customers already inside, crewmen from merchant vessels callin at the island's main port, looked up warily at them, but after a look at the confident swaggers and cold expressions, even on Elizabeth, turned their attention back to their food and drink.

Lillie came out of the kitchen and hustled them into the private room.

"What you want now, *cher*? We still have not found this mystery English man," she said to Colin.

"Didn't think you had. But, it's important that we find him quickly, and we need your help to do it."

"Well, of course, *cher*, I will do anything to help you, within reason, of course. But, before we get down to business, *ma petite enfant* looks like she is starving." She pinched Elizabeth's cheeks.

"Not starving, *maman*, but I would really love to have a bowl of your gumbo."

"Well, sit yourselves down and I will bring nine bowls." On her way out of the room, she pinched

O'Reilly's cheek, causing his face to turn redder than his hair.

She was back quickly with a large kettle of gumbo in one hand and a tray of bowls, spoons, mugs, and several bottles of rum in the other. After she'd settled everyone over a bowl of gumbo, with a mug of rum at his or her elbow, she sat at a corner of the table and rested her ample breasts on its surface.

"Now, Colin, what is it you wish for me to do?"

Colin first finished the mouth full of gumbo, and after licking his lips and sighing, turned his attention to her and her question.

"This man, whoever he is, must be found," he said. "I think he knows a lot about British plans for this area, but, more importantly, I think his main mission is to find us. I cannot allow him to continue to roam the islands free. He is too much of a danger."

"Ah, *oui*, I see what you mean. My people in Nassau have been keeping me informed. This man visited the governor's house on several occasions, but then he disappeared for a week."

"Do they know where he went?"

"Oh, yes," she said. "He came here, to Cat Island. He is somewhere in one of the areas frequented by the poor whites who work at the docks. I have no sources among them, and it is difficult for my people to go into the area, *non*. A dark-skinned person stands out, and it is dangerous. Oh, and one other thing, we learned why he speaks English so strange, *non*; he is the Scotsman."

"Hm, perhaps I could go in and look for him," Colin said.

"I don't think that's such a good idea, cap'n," O'Reilly said. "I think I know the area Mama Lillie's talkin' about, 'n ain't nothin' down there but bog Irish, a few Scots, and bloody Englishmen who come to the islands to stay out of jail back home. Bein' a Yank, you'd stand out about as much as a . . . well, as M'nondo."

"He is correct," M'nondo said. "These poor white Europeans dislike whites who are better off even more than they hate blacks, and they think less of you Americans than their fellow Europeans."

Colin blew out a puff of air. "Damn, that really complicates things. We know where this man is, but we can't go after him. There has to be a way."

O'Reilly cleared his throat. "Uh, well now, there just might be."

Charles Ray

Chapter 20

The plan was both simple *and* complicated, and extremely dangerous. O'Reilly, with his pronounced Irish brogue, had a good chance of entering the area where poor whites lived without attracting undue notice, which was the simple part, but then, he had to locate the Scotsman, whose name they still did not know, without arousing suspicion, which was complicated. The danger came from the fact that Colin and the others had to wait outside the area, concealed from public view, without a reliable means to communicate with O'Reilly, and no way of knowing if he ran into trouble.

The always nattily-dressed helmsman stood in front of Colin, his face smeared with coal dust, and his clothing looking like he'd slept in it.

"Well now, I reckon you do look like someone who is down on his luck," he said. "But, you must be careful. If they think you're not who you say you are, they're likely to slit your throat."

O'Reilly chuckled. "It ain't the bog rats what live there that bother me, cap'n. It's this bloody Scotsman what they say is hidin' among 'em. The Irish drink a lot and do love a fight, but we're pikers when it comes to the Scots. They love to fight and drink, and often do 'em both at the same time."

"Good Lord, you make the man sound like some kind of blood thirsty monster."

"Well now, cap'n, that ain't too far off what I know 'bout the Scots."

"I guess the only thing I can say, then is, be careful. I'm worried about not being able to communicate with you while you're in there."

The smiling O'Reilly reached into his pocket and pulled out a white cylinder. "I think M'nondo's solved that problem," he said. "He done give me this here whistle made from ivory. Says it b'longed to his grandda, 'n iffen I lose it, I better hope the Scot kills me, 'cause iffen he don't M'nondo will."

Colin matched his smile. Leave it to M'nondo to come up with a solution to their problem. He patted O'Reilly's shoulder. "Okay, then, mate, be safe."

The helmsman nodded, turned and trotted off in the direction of the shanty town near the docks. Colin watched him until he turned a corner and was out of sight. He heaved a sigh and went back inside the building they'd rented, not so close to the shanty town that their comings and goings would be noticed, but, hopefully, close enough to respond in time if O'Reilly blew his whistle to signal that he needed help.

Elizabeth, M'nondo, Garcia and the others sat around the lantern-lit room.

"O'Reilly get off okay?" Elizabeth asked.

They'd all wanted to see him off, but Colin had argued that it was dangerous for O'Reilly to be seen with such a crowd, because it would attract attention and possibly blow his cover. Colin, dressed in the cast-off clothing of an itinerant seaman, like one of the hundreds who roamed the streets of most of the port cities in the Caribbean, didn't earn a second glance, whereas Elizabeth, regardless of how she dressed would be looked at by every man on the street, and the tall, imposing figure of M'nondo was almost impossible to disguise.

"Yes," he replied. To M'nondo he said, "That was a good idea giving him that whistle to signal, but are you sure we'll hear it?"

"I have no doubt," M'nondo said. "My grandfather used it when out hunting. The sound carries a long distance on the savannah. Here in the city, with so many buildings for the sound to bounce off, we should hear it even farther away."

"What if someone else out there has a whistle, and we mistake it for O'Reilly's?"

Colin knew he was being a devil's advocate, but it was the only way to discover as many weaknesses in their plan as possible.

"It does not matter if there are a hundred other whistles," M'nondo said with a note of testiness in his voice. "I know my grandfather's whistle. I could pick it out from any number of others. Do not worry, Colin. He will be okay."

Outside the building, just as he entered the narrow, crooked street, littered with trash and lined with rundown dwellings, O'Reilly felt anything but okay. As he walked, he felt as if someone had pinned a large red circle to his back with a note that read, 'stab me.' He imagined eyes looking at him through every window, and assassins lurking in every doorway.

"Upon me sainted mother," he muttered. "Why'd I ever volunteer for such a dangerous job? I don't belong in this place no more'n M'nondo." Then, realizing that his muttering might be overheard, he clamped his lips tight and continued walking.

His progress was, indeed, being watched, and he was seen as someone not native to the neighborhood, but from someone he would never have thought of. As he turned down another equally narrow, equally crooked lane, a short, stocky man wearing a priest's cassock stepped out of a doorway, blocking his way.

"Ah, me son, and where are ye off to this fine day, and whyd'ya have sich a morose expression upon yer face?"

O'Reilly stopped just before plowing into the man, and stared down at him for a few moments, at a temporary loss for words. Then, he gathered his wits. "Father, what are you doin' in a place like this?"

"I notice ye di'nt answer me question, lad," the priest said. "But, I'll forgive ye, and answer yours first. I be here because here is where I be needed. This place is filled to the gunwales with sinners, so what better place for a priest to be, eh? Now, ye tell me, who are ye, and where come ye from?"

This would be, O'Reilly realized, a first opportunity to check the story he and Colin had cooked up to explain his presence in shanty town, and had the advantage that if it didn't work, at least the priest wouldn't cut his throat—he hoped. They had decided to stick fairly close to the facts that might be known by many, and hope that O'Reilly didn't run into anyone who had firsthand knowledge of events.

"I was part of the nonmilitary crew on a frigate out of Southampton, bringin' supplies for the army at Nassau," he said. "We was hit by pirates. The cap'n and crew was put in boats and the ship was looted and burned."

"Ah, and I've heard of that," the priest said. "T'was a pity what happened. How'd ye end up here on Cat Island? I heard that bunch went to Nassau."

"The bloody cap'n only cared about the gobs on board. The few of us who weren't navy were given a handshake and a bugger off. I been bummin' 'round these bloody islands since, lookin' for work."

"Heh! Our English friends. They call it Great Britain, but it's really just bloody England that counts. The rest of us are nothin' but serfs."

O'Reilly smiled. "So, you be Irish to, eh?"

"Aye, lad, born and bred in Galway. Come over here to minister to the heathen some ten years ago. Now, the heathens are me own people cast adrift in a foreign land. So, lookin' for work, are ye? What kind might I ask?"

"I'd rather get work on a ship sailin' somewhere," O'Reilly said. "But, right now, I ain't too fussy, long's it pays me enough for something to fill my belly and pay for a place to lay my head at night. I heard talk over to the other side of town that there was a Scotsman down here lookin' to hire some lads. You wouldn't know anything about that, would you?"

The priest's expression clouded. "Aye, I've heard about this Scot, a new arrival he is. I hear he was on a ship that was attacked by pirates, too. Lot of that goin' around it seems. You'll be takin' my advice, lad, you'll steer a wide path around that one."

"Why? If he's hirin', he's just the man I need to see."

"But, what he's lookin' for men to do . . . well, it ain't exactly on the right side of the law."

"Beggin' yer forgiveness, father, but right now, I can't be too fussy. 'Sides, the law ain't done much for me lately."

"I pray you'll change your mind, lad." The priest made the sign of the cross. "But, if you've yer mind set, I believe you'll find the Scotsman down t'end of this lane. It's the shop with the black skull and crossbones drawn on the door—a most appropriate sign for what I hear goes on inside the place."

O'Reilly smiled. How appropriate that he, a pirate, would enter a place marked with the universal symbol of pirates, seeking a man who, in his opinion, was worse than any pirate.

"Thank you, father," he said. "I promise I'll try and keep most of the commandments."

"Yeah, and which ones will that be, not coveting thy neighbor's ox or ass?"

O'Reilly chuckled as he walked toward the building indicated by the frowning priest. He put his hand in his pocket and felt the comforting presence of M'nondo's whistle.

When he arrived at the building, a one-story, wood slat structure with a thatched roof, the skull and crossbones roughly painted on the door made it look forbidding. It was not a place he would approach in darkness. The door was closed, but he could hear the hum of conversation from inside, so he pushed it open and stepped in. The conversation stopped abruptly, and the sudden silence sent a shiver of fear up his spine. But, he kept his expression calm as he walked across the dirty wood floor in the direction of the haphazardly constructed wooden bar at the back.

A toothless, hairless, hard-to-determine gender individual stood behind the bar, wiping at the greasy glasses with a dirty rag.

"What ken I git ye, stranger?" The voice was too deep to be a woman, so O'Reilly assumed he was talking to a man.

"I'd fancy a bit of rum," he said.

The man pulled a bottle and pewter mug from beneath the bar, blew the dust off the mug, and filled it to within a finger-width of the rim. He pushed it across the bar toward O'Reilly. "Thet'll be one bit, stranger."

O'Reilly grimaced at the inflated price for what he was sure was second- or third-rate rum but reached into his pocket and withdrew a silver coin which he slapped on the bar. "There be a peso, friend," he said. "Leave the bottle."

The man picked the coin up and pressed his bluish gums into it. Satisfied it was real, he dropped it into the cash drawer, and began polishing the bar in front of O'Reilly with the same rag he'd been using to wipe the glasses. "You be new here," he said. "Whereat you from?"

O'Reilly repeated the story he'd told the priest. "I be lookin' for a Scotsman. I hear he be hiring men for some kind of job."

He looked at O'Reilly, his eyes narrowed to tiny slits. "And, where'd ye be hearin' such?"

"Around." O'Reilly shrugged. "I was told he could be found here."

O'Reilly heard the scrape of a chair behind him, but no sound of boots on the wooden floor, so he forced himself not to turn.

"Well now, I ain't sayin' whether or not any Scotsman's here, or that he's hirin', not until I know why you be. What ship was you on?"

"I was on *Whitechapel*. It was made up to look like a reg'lar merchant vessel, so they had some of us reg'lar seamen among the crew, but mostly they was royal navy."

"Aye, heard of it. Pirates hit her. They put the crew in boats and shoved 'em off, I hear."

"That they did, the bloody bastards. Then that bleedin' English cap'n, when we got to land, he cut us non-navy types loose to find our own way."

"Now, ain't that just like the feckin' English, ain't got no use for Irish or Scot, and just barely get along with the Welsh."

"That'll be the last time I do anything for the bloody English military, I can tell you that."

"In it for yourself, eh? Makes sense. Ain't nobody else gonna look out for you. You finish your rum, and I'll go see if the Scotsman will see you."

O'Reilly was on his second mug of rum when he felt a presence behind him. He turned slowly.

The man standing there wasn't at all impressive looking, but the cold glint in his gaze and the tight way he held his body caused O'Reilly to shiver. His were the eyes of a cold-blooded killer, a man without compassion.

"You be lookin' for the Scotsman, mate?" the man asked in a commanding tone, the burr of the highlands strong in his voice.

"Depends," O'Reilly said. "Be ye the Scotsman? I hear you be hirin' men for some kind of special job."

"Yeah, laddie, it depends, but it depends on who you be, and why you be wantin' to hook up with the Scotsman."

"Now, I'm figurin' the barkeep had already told you my story. I'm in need of a job, and I'm willin' to do just about anything 'cept hurt women and children."

The cold eyes narrowed even more, but not a muscle in the man's face moved. His eyes were like pebbles, and his gaze bored into O'Reilly's very soul. In his twenty-six years of living, though, O'Reilly had faced death more than times than he could count, and had, on occasion dealt it out. While he felt the fear that is normal in the face of danger, it was a controlled fear, deep down inside his gut where only he knew of it. The two faced off, two alpha animals vying for dominance of the pack.

"So," the man said. "The innkeeper say's that you were on *Whitechapel.*"

"Aye, that I was."

"Well now, that's passin' strange, 'cause I was on the ship that was sailin' along with *Whitechapel,* and I don't recollect seein' you at any time before or durin' the voyage."

That cold stab of fear again. This confirmed that this was the man they were looking for, but it put O'Reilly deeper into mortal danger. He could feel the tension on the other man.

"There was a whole passel of men in the crew of that ship," he said. "I'd hardly likely to be noticed among 'em."

The man chuckled. "Oh, I think I'd of noticed a tall redhead bog Irishman like yourself." His right hand wandered to his left forearm, which he began to caress softly. "Now, why don't you be tellin' me your true story, laddie."

O'Reilly held his hands up in mock surrender.

"Okay," he said. "You got me. I was not on *Whitechapel*. I made that up 'cause I was forced to beg on the streets to get coin to buy a meal, and people was more generous when I told 'em I was a sailor in distress. Guess it's impossible to fool an old hand like yourself. Truth is, I *was* on a ship, merchantman out of Dover, *Gallant* was her name. Got tossed off last time she come here for fightin'." He'd stayed close to truth again. The merchant ship *Gallant* had been in the vicinity of the islands, and he *had* fought on her decks—when they had boarded her after waylaying her just east of Nassau.

"So, you're a scrapper, are ye?"

"When I've a reason to be."

With gazes locked the two stood there. Out of the corner of his eye O'Reilly could see that the man's right hand was resting just above his wrist and he had pulled the cuff of his shirt up revealing the wiry muscles of his lower arm. Accustomed to wearing a weapon in plain sight, at first, he didn't think, weapon, but his agile pirate's mind quickly came to the conclusion that the nerveless man standing before him wouldn't engage in a gesture indicating nervousness. That meant he had a weapon, most likely a knife, under his sleeve. The muscles in O'Reilly's body tenses reflexively.

"So, are you the Scotsman, and do you have a job that I can do?" he asked. He slowly slid his hand toward the pocket containing the whistle.

"Well now, laddie, here's the problem. Well, two problems, really. One; I don't believe a bleedin' word of what you're sayin'. I been dealin' with people for a long time, and I know when a bloke's lyin' to me, and you, my lad, are lyin' like a fancy carpet."

"I'm not lying," O'Reilly said. "But, just out of curiosity, you said there was two problems. What's the other?"

"Oh, the other is that, now I've got to kill you, and Henry the innkeeper's goin' to be put out havin' to clean your blood off the floor."

With that, both moved. The Scotsman slipped the dirk from beneath his sleeve, and O' Reilly pulled the whistle from his pocket.

As he put the whistle to his mouth, the Scotsman took a jerky step backwards. When O'Reilly blew it, he cringed and put his hands over his ears. O'Reilly took that opportunity to dash for the door.

The Scotsman was quick to recover.

"Ain't no use in runnin', laddie," he said. "The folks down here are mine. They'll stop you before you can leave the area. But, thanks for not makin' me mess up my friend Henry's place."

He ran to the door and exited. By this time, O'Reilly was twenty feet from the door, in a full-out run back the way he'd come. The Scotsman smiled. Several seedy looking individuals stood across the street looking at the scene with smiles on their grimy faces.

"Ten pesos to the one what catches that bloke for me," the Scotsman yelled.

Like a closet full of cockroaches when the door is opened and light is let in, they stirred, momentarily confused, but as the meaning of his words sank in, they recovered, and began running full tilt after O'Reilly. The Scotsman loped easily behind them, a vulpine smile on his narrow face.

O'Reilly, his heart pounding and his breath coming in ragged gasps, glanced over his shoulder, and when he saw the crowd of ragged looked men chasing him, turned back and redoubled his efforts to reach the safety of the streets outside the shanty town. But, in that last moment before he turned away, he saw that he would not make it. The yelling, slavering crowd seemed to be motivated by a devil-force as it ate up the distance between him and them. He could hear the slap of their feet on the dirt, and in some places, poorly-placed cobblestones, and hear the hunger in their voices. He thought he could almost feel their moist breaths on the back of his neck.

Running straight for the exit to the shanty town was clearly not a wise option, because the crowd would catch him many yards from safety. In an effort to confuse them and hopefully thwart their efforts to catch him, he turned right down an alleyway that was dark in shadow.

It didn't take him long to realize that, in turning, he'd made a fatal mistake. The alley, turned lazily to the left—in the direction of safety—but ended suddenly in a stone wall, the side of a building that must be close to the outside, or even part of the outside of shanty town. He turned, his back against that stone wall, took out the whistle, and blew as loud as he could.

The mob came around the corner, and upon seeing him, let out a howl of glee. He could see the greed and hunger in their eyes.

"We got 'im, boys," someone in the mob shouted. "Should we take 'im back to the stranger alive, or in pieces?"

"He di'nt say nuffin 'bout catchin' 'im alive, guvnor," someone else said. "I says we kill 'im 'n take the body back."

"No, you'll not kill him," a voice with a pronounced Scottish burr said. "I'll give each of you two bits for cornerin' him." O'Reilly heard the clink of coins hitting the hard ground behind the mob, which was no longer interested in him. "I'll take care of him," the voice said.

The mob turned away from O'Reilly and began scrambling on the ground, snatching up the coins. The Scotsman stepped past them, his gaze fixed on O'Reilly.

"You put up a good run, laddie," he said. "Now, are you goin' to put up a good fight for your life, or will you keep blowin' on that child's toy?"

O'Reilly blew the whistle one last time, and then put it back into his pocket. "Reckon I've no choice but to fight, mate," he said. "But, before you gut me, would you do me the honor of at least lettin' me know my killer's name?"

The Scotsman laughed. "I like your style, boyo," he said. "If I didn't have an important job to do, I'd be thinkin' on forgivin' you for lying to me. But, alas, it's not to be. The name, laddie, is Liam Macintosh, here on His Majesty's service." He bowed slightly, never taking his eyes off O'Reilly. His right hand came up, showing the wicked blade he carried. "I hope knowin' my name gives you some comfort in the hereafter."

O'Reilly smiled. "Probably not, but it's always good to know the name of the man who is aimin' to kill you. Too bad you'll be disappointed."

Macintosh's face contorted in confusion. "I dinna think so, laddie. Many's the man I've gone up against, and as you can see, I'm still here. Now, shall we get this over with?"

"I think not," Colin's voice said from behind Macintosh. "If you wish to live, drop the knife. Or, don't drop it and die, it's up to you."

Macintosh turned slowly, the knife still held low, point of the blade forward. When he saw Colin and M'nondo, their expressions grim, his smile faded.

"I've never gone up against three at the same time before," he said. "And, I have *never* had the pleasure of guttin' a blackamoor. This should be interesting."

M'nondo stepped forward, a deep frown on his dark face, and his curved saber pointed at Macintosh's heart.

"I do not think that small pig sticker you have is a match for my blade, friend," he said. "But, I am happy to give you the opportunity to try."

Colin brandished his saber. "And, just to make it interesting, I'd be happy to see how deep into your carcass I can stick this fine blade."

Macintosh looked from the menacing hulk of M'nondo to the smooth delivery from Colin, his eyes narrowed in concentration. He sighed and dropped his blade. "A smart man knows when he's outclassed, and me mam didn't raise me to be stupid." He bowed. "To whom am I surrendering, sir?"

Colin walked over and kicked the blade away. "I'll be the one asking the questions, Mr. Macintosh, just as soon as we get you to a more comfortable place . . . for us." He nodded at O'Reilly. "Good to see you're okay, lad. Now, bind this man and put on a blindfold. We're going for a sail."

"Aye, cap'n," O'Reilly said. "I take it you heard my whistle for help, you 'n M'nondo getting here so fast and all."

"We heard it loud and clear."

"When Co-, the captain heard it the first time, he ignored the stares from the derelicts on the streets and raced here so fast, even I had trouble keeping up with him," M'nondo said. "But, as you see, I was right. It was easy to hear, and there was no doubt when we heard it, that it was you."

"Well, just glad you got here when you did. I'm not sure I could've taken this one."

Just as O'Reilly began wrapping his bandana over Macintosh's eyes, the Scot said, "You can be sure you would *not* have taken anything but my blade in your gut, laddie."

"You're a tough one, all right," O'Reilly said. "But, we'll see how tough you be when the cap'n gets through with you."

Charles Ray

Chapter 21

On Skull Island

They made their way out of the shanty town under the wary eyes of many of its denizens who were shocked to see the feared Scot, Macintosh, led away with a blindfold over his eyes and his arms bound behind his back. More than one shrank back under M'nondo's steely glare.

After rejoining the others, they went directly to the ship and set sail for Skull Island.

Contrary to O'Reilly's threat, Colin had no intentions of using harsh methods on Macintosh. He let the threat linger, though, deciding that when he didn't use force, it would throw the man off balance.

They secured him, under constant guard, in the same hut they used to confine ship's officers when they captured them. Canvas was lashed over the windows to keep out light, and everyone was cautioned to maintain absolute silence near the building. Colin wanted the period of deprivation of light and sound to soften his prisoner up before he began questioning him. To add to his discomfort, his arms and legs were tied to the hard cot in the room, securely so that he couldn't turn, and forcing him to call for the guards when he needed the toilet, which was more often than he desired, because Colin only allowed him water, and instructed the guards to give him plenty.

After ensuring that Macintosh was all secure, he went to the big house where Elizabeth and M'nondo waited, sitting at the big table with mugs of rum at their hand. Across from Elizabeth was an empty mug. As Colin entered, M'nondo filled it to the brim with the fiery golden liquid.

"Is our prisoner comfortable?" Elizabeth asked.

Colin laughed. "It depends upon how you define comfortable," he said. "He hasn't been beaten or tortured, but I doubt he would write a glowing recommendation of his accommodations."

"I don't understand why you subject the man to such misery if you want him to talk to you," she said.

M'nondo snorted.

"If he was an ordinary man, my dear, you would be right. In such a case, the soft touch would be the way I choose. Macintosh, however, is a hard man, and hard men must first be softened. Simple discomfort, not being to take a piss without asking permission, or not being able to scratch an itch can drive a man mad if he's subjected to it long enough. I plan to let Macintosh wait until the brink of madness, then when I relieve him of his discomfort, you watch, he will be cooperative."

"I do not know," M'nondo said. "This one strikes me as much harder than a normal human. In fact, he is most inhuman. I think perhaps the hard way might be required with him."

"You mean, you *hope* the hard way will be required, don't you?" Colin laughed.

He'd seen the look on M'nondo's face when the man called him a blackamoor, a term of derision that many Europeans used for Africans and the darker people from India, often without considering how the recipient of such treatment might feel about it. He thought that he might, after getting all the information he could from Macintosh, place him in the not so tender hands of M'nondo, just to teach him a lesson in manners.

"I am just saying," M'nondo said in an insistent tone. "That this Macintosh seems to be a very tough man. He has the eyes of a killer. I imagine he has tortured more than a few people, so he will know how to resist most methods of questioning."

Colin shrugged. "We'll see. For now, though, let's enjoy this fine rum."

Two mugs of rum later, and a bit unsteady on his feet, Colin headed for the prison hut.

At the entrance he handed his saber to the guard. "If I call for help, come in, and bring this."

"You think he'll be dangerous, captain? He ain't had nothin' but water for the past three hours, and most of that he done pissed out. Last time I took him to the privy, he was so weak he could barely walk."

"Some people know how to fake weakness. I am taking no chances with this one. And, keep the door open, so you can hear better."

The guard nodded and unlocked the door.

The hut wasn't large, and the smell of sweat was heavy in the air. In the dim light from the open door, Colin could see Macintosh curled up on the cot with his knees up to his chest, shivering like a man with influenza. As he neared, he noticed that in addition to the smell of sweat, the acrid ammonia-like smell of urine indicated that he'd pissed himself. Perhaps, he thought, the guard had been right. Lack of food had made the man weak. All the better for his interrogation.

Holding his breath, he reached over and shook Macintosh's shoulder.

"Wake up, Macintosh," he said. "It's time for our talk."

Macintosh slowly straightened out and rolled over. Colin was shocked at his appearance. His face was gaunt and grayish, with large dark bags under his bloodshot eyes, and when he sat up, he moved like an old, arthritic man. He blinked at Colin, as he swung his legs off the cot.

"So," he said in a cracked voice. "You've come to see how the condemned man fares, have you?"

"I'm sorry you were treated this way," Colin said, trying to sound sincere. "When was the last time you ate?"

Macintosh blinked again. He closed his eyes and cocked his head to the side. When he opened them, he regarded Colin suspiciously. "I don't recall," he said. "M-must've been a couple of hours before your man walked into the Skull and Crossbones."

"My God, man, you must be starved. Guard, send a runner to the kitchen and have some goat meat stew and bread sent here immediately."

"Aye, sir," the guard shouted. "Will you be okay while I'm gone?"

"I'll be fine, now just hurry with that food."

Macintosh sat on the edge of the cot, his hands on his knees, looking at Colin like a man who has just awakened in a strange place.

"You're not foolin' me, captain," he said. "I know you ordered them to give me only water. What was it supposed to do, make me grateful when you came in and corrected that little . . . mistake?"

"I assure you I did not order such treatment," Colin said. "That is *not* the way I was taught to treat a prisoner."

"Say, you're a colonial, ain't you? One of them Americans? And, a gentleman by the sound of you. What are you doing out here?"

The guard came running in carrying a clay bowl and a woven basket. "Here's the stew and bread like you ordered, captain," he said. "I'll go get some water so he can wash it down."

"Thank you, guard." Colin turned back to Macintosh. "What I'm doing now is waiting for you to get some food in your belly. After that, we'll have a little talk."

If Macintosh noticed that Colin didn't answer his question, he didn't let it show. His attention was fixed on the heady smell of goat meat coming from the bowl that the guard sat on the end of his bed. He looked at it as if it was the last life boat on a sinking ship.

"Go ahead," Colin said. "The food's not poison. Eat. But, since you haven't eaten in a while, it'd be better to take small bites, and eat slow."

Ignoring the warning, Macintosh picked up the bowl and wooden spoon and began shoveling food in his mouth like a starving man. He alternated, a spoon of stew and a bite of bread, and didn't stop until there were only a few tiny crumbs of bread left, and the bowl had been licked clean. He then sat back, balancing with his left hand and rubbing his belly with his right.

"That was pretty good stew, captain," he said. "Please give my compliments to the cook."

"I will. Now, let's get started. Your name, you said in that alley, is Liam Macintosh, and you work for the British government. What is it that you do for that government?"

"Ah, now, captain. I canna be tellin' you that, for that would be betraying a sacred oath."

Colin smiled. "A man of principle. Interesting, considering what I've heard about you, Mr. Macintosh."

"Eh, and what is that you've been hearing?"

"I heard that you like killing men with that little knife of yours, for one thing. For another, I know you're here in connection with English plans to invade America from the south."

Macintosh blinked, but said nothing. He didn't have to. His reaction told Colin that he'd hit on the truth.

"Well," Colin said. "What have you to say?"

"Laddie, if you already know so much, there's nothin' I could tell you, now is there?"

Colin frowned. "So, you're going to be difficult. You know, we can do this the easy way, or we can do it the hard way. Personally, I would prefer the easy way, but that is entirely up to you."

"Are you sayin' that you'll torture me, laddie?"

"I'm saying that I'll do whatever it takes to find out what the damn English plans are for the south."

"So," Macintosh said. "You *are* a bloody American. I thought the rumors that the colonials had sent an agent here to the islands were just that. Looks like I was wrong."

Colin almost missed the import of the man's words. Then, some of the cryptic phrases from the letters he'd failed to completely decipher resurfaced in his mind.

"You mean the rumors you heard from your American cousin?"

Macintosh looked as if he'd been slapped, and for Colin, it all began to fall into place. He could hardly believe what he was thinking, it was, in fact, unthinkable.

"The English have an agent in America," he said.

He could see the resolve fade in Macintosh's expression.

"Well, you *are* the well informed one, aren't you," the Scotsman said. "Looks like my masters in London were misinformed about the ability of you bloody colonials to make war like big boys."

"So, you do have a spy. Who is it?"

"I don't know, laddie, and that's the God's truth. I think only one man in all of London does know, and like all good spymasters, he keeps things close to his chest. All I can tell you is that he is, or was, pretty high placed, and knows a lot about your navy."

Colin's body tensed. Could it be that a senior naval officer was a traitor? It wasn't without precedent. During the fight for independence, Benedict Arnold, a native of Connecticut and owner of a fleet of merchant vessels, had been promoted to major general because of his bravery at the outset of fighting. He'd been given command of the fortifications at West Point, New York, and because of the refusal of the continental congress to promote him higher, and his disagreement of the new nation's alliance with France, had plotted to surrender the fortifications to the British. When his duplicity was discovered, he defected to the British side. Colin knew that there was still a strong English sentiment in America, especially in the northeastern states, where trade with the former colonial master was the lifeblood of local economies. He also knew that congressional reluctance to expand the navy or to authorize a standing army had frustrated or cut short the careers of many officers.

"Do you have any idea where this spy is located?"

"Nay, laddie, I don't, but one of the messages that got through to me—by the way, intercepting the dispatch bags like you been doin' is more of a nuisance than disruptin' the supply shipments—where was I, oh yes, one of the messages indicated that 'cousin' was in London, and might be headin' this way."

"Why would an American spy for England come here?"

"You really don't know the effect you're having on the royal navy, do you, lad?"

"Are you saying this American is coming here to try and flush me out, or to identify me for the damn English?"

"Just so, lad," Macintosh said. "Matter of fact, getting rid of you was my main mission, until this traitor in your midst let on that the pirates who were givin' the navy fits out here were bein' led by an American. I'll tell you, that got their attention. You, laddie, are the fly in the milk of their plans to take New Orleans."

Colin felt a flicker of excitement but tried to keep his expression placid. So, of the choice between Mobile and New Orleans, the English invasion target was the city on the Mississippi. It made sense, he thought. Controlling the mighty river, which was the main transportation route in the country's west, would cripple an already limping war effort.

There was no doubt about it. Macintosh had to be transported immediately to some place where professional interrogators could ferret out whatever other information he possessed. \

Macintosh looked up at him and smiled. "So, laddie, you didn't know which city we'd attack, did you? Looks like I let the cat out of the sack." He held his hand up and blew on his nails. "Oh well, if the bloody snobs can't handle your little colonial militia, they deserve to lose. Now, tell me, laddie, what are you planning to do with me."

Colin decided not to tell him until they were boarding the boat bound for Cap Haitien and a meeting with George Hoskins.

Chapter 22

July 1813, Cap Haitien

The voyage to Cap Haitien and George Hoskins' consulate office was less circuitous or long as previous trips. Colin simply went to the docks at Cat Island and chartered a fishing vessel to take him and his 'cargo', which consisted of a large trunk into which the bound and gagged Macintosh had been stuffed to the Haitian port city.

Once the ship was at sea, there was no longer a need to keep Macintosh out of sight, so Colin had him taken out of the trunk, but either he, M'nondo, or O'Reilly, with a saber readily at hand, kept a close watch over him for the entire voyage. Once in the port at Cap Haitien, his hands were again bound behind his back, and he was led off the ship and walked the short distance to Hoskins' office. The sight of a bound prisoner, even a white man, was not unusual in the island republic, and one being guarded by a tall, muscular black man delighted the people they passed along the way.

Hoskins welcomed them himself and had one of his staff take Macintosh away to secure him until he could be transported to Charleston, South Carolina, where naval officers would question him in detail about the British invasion plans. Hoskins then suggested that M'nondo and O'Reilly avail themselves of the refreshments in the tavern across the street and invited Colin to join him in his private office.

When they were seated, he put his hands on his stomach and eyed Colin with a paternal gaze.

"You seem out of sorts, boy," he said. "What is it?"

"I don't think it was necessary to dismiss my friends like you did," Colin replied. "They know just about everything I know about what's going on."

"Sorry, Colin, but they're not government employees, and are not authorized to know what I'm about to tell you, at least not until this damn war's over."

Colin's frown deepened. "That must mean it's bad news."

"Pretty much the worse I'm afraid. Remember last time I told you that that fool Hull went and invaded Canada, then turned tail and ran when the first shots were fired?"

"Yes, I recall, but I still think he might have had a good reason to withdraw his forces."

"He didn't *withdraw*, boy, he retreated, he ran back south with his damn tail between his legs like a yellow dog. Anyway, that's neither here nor there. The damn fools in Washington let him take another go at it."

"I take it he didn't . . . retreat this time?"

"No, well, not right away. Say, would you like a cup of coffee, or maybe a drink they like here made from cocoa beans, it's pretty good with milk and sugar in it."

Colin nodded his acceptance. Hoskins called for his secretary and bade him bring two cups of that 'cocoa stuff.'

"Now," Colin said. "Tell me about the second invasion of Canada."

"I think you'd better wait until you have some of that cocoa drink in you. It's a gruesome story."

As if he'd been waiting at the door for Hoskins to utter those words, the secretary rapped lightly and entered without waiting to be admitted. He carried two large white ceramic cups that had steam coming from them. He handed one to Hoskins and the other to Colin. Inside the cup was a milky brown liquid that had a strange, but pleasant aroma. Colin watched as Hoskins first blew on the surface of the liquid and then took a sip. He copied the man's actions. At first, the hot liquid burned his tongue, but as his mouth became accustomed to the heat, the taste penetrated his consciousness. Hoskins was right, he thought, this is quite the drink. Like coffee, yet not like coffee. He took another sip, swallowed, and sighed.

"You're right, sir," he said. "This is a nice drink."

"The Indians on the South American mainland, and on some of the islands, chew the nuts, and on occasion boil them in water and drink it. Chewing it is an acquired taste, one that I have yet to acquire, but prepared like this, with milk and sugar, well, as you can see, it's pure ambrosia."

"Now, sir, the war," Colin said.

"Ah, yes, the war. If you'll recall, the last time we spoke, I told you about William Hull's disastrous invasion of Canada, well that only got worse."

Colin winced. "Don't tell me, he tried and failed a second time."

"Oh no, worse, lad, much worse. His job after failing in Canada was to defend Detroit. Well, a month after his withdrawal from Canada, the English, under the command of General Sir Isaac Brock, moved on Detroit, and Hull surrendered without firing a shot."

Colin sputtered, sending the milky brown liquid across Hoskin's desk, where it spattered some papers. The gruff consul didn't seem to notice. "You're tell me," Colin said, when he got his breath back. "That he didn't even put up token resistance?"

"Nope, not according to what I heard. Brock had a bunch of Indians make a lot of racket around the perimeter, and poor old Hull thought he was surrounded, I suppose, so he put up the white flag.

Brock let him and his garrison withdraw, which was really bad for Hull, because one of his subordinate captains also happened to be a political rival. He accused Hull of cowardice in the face of the enemy. The old man was court-martialed, convicted, and sentenced to be shot."

"That seems a bit harsh," Colin said.

"Apparently the president thought so to because he commuted the sentence. Can't say I disagree. Hull did do some heroic things during the war for independence, and the man was over sixty, way too old to be out in the field leading troops."

Colin shook his head. "So, we lost Detroit, and failed to take territory in Canada; that puts our lake fleet in dire straits."

"Yeah, the failure to take anything of strategic value during the second invasion of Canada adds to the misery," Hoskins said.

"What happened? Who led the second invasion attempt?"

"General Pike."

"Zebulon Pike? He is, er, was the man who explored the western frontier. I can't imagine him being involved in a failed expedition," Colin said.

"Oh, it was doomed from the beginning. The original objective was Kingston at the northeastern end of Lake Ontario, which is where the English have most of their ships based, but someone got the bright idea that York, the capital of Upper Canada, would be an easier target, even though it's of no strategic significance, which is why it was so lightly guarded."

Colin shook his head. He had little understanding of how the army made strategic decisions. "So, if it wasn't heavily fortified, why was the mission a failure?"

"Pike's troops had the English regulars and their Canadian militia and Indian supporters outnumbered. When they attacked the town, the regulars withdrew to

Kingston, leaving the poorly defended town to the Americans. The English general had the fort's magazine blown up, Pike, along with some of his senior officers were killed. We held the damn town for three or four days, during which time out troops burned and looted. The surviving officers swear that no order was given to do this, and that the men just did it in the heat of battle, and because they believed that the Indians had scalped some of the dead and injured Americans. Whatever the reason, it was a disgusting display of lack of control and professionalism."

"They looted and burned the provincial capital? I thought we were trying to get the Canadians on our side. That's a funny way to go about it."

"Hell, son, it's the way to get the exact opposite. Even the Canadians who *were* supportive are mad as hell about that. And, you can bet your brass buttons the English are not gonna allow an act like that to go unanswered."

He could only imagine what the English response might be, probably an attack on a poorly defended town or settlement near Detroit now that they'd taken control of that strategic port at the southern end of Lake Erie. The western settlements had always been vulnerable to Indian raids instigated by English officers stationed in the lake area and farther west on the country's western borders. Now that it appeared they controlled both Lake Erie and Lake Ontario, unless the navy pulled a magic trick out of its hat, the war could very well be lost, especially if British forces were also able to take New Orleans.

"Damn, it sounds like things are really bad."

Hoskins slammed his hand on the desk. "Now, don't you go talking like that, boy. Remember, it's always darkest just before dawn. We beat the bloody English once, and we'll do it again. The damn politicians in Washington just have to get their heads out of their asses and start thinking straight, and they have got to stop giving military rank to politicians. If we don't get ourselves a professional army, we're gonna be ripe for picking by some country that does have one."

"I guess we're lucky they don't play the same political games with the navy," Colin said. He sighed. "Not that we don't have some deadwood but handling a ship and crew at sea will expose the unfit pretty quickly."

"Yeah, but even the navy gets short shrift from the politicians who seem to be more interested in getting elected and lining their pockets than really doing what's good for the country."

"I don't have much use for the English, the upper classes at least, but I have to say, old Samuel Johnson had it right in his critique on patriotism, politics *is* the last refuge of scoundrels. Lord knows, we have more than our fair share."

Hoskins waved negligently. "Don't let it get you down, boy. We're gonna come out of this just fine, you mark my words. Now, I've given you my bad news, what do you have to tell me about what's going on in your neck of the woods."

Colin couldn't help smiling at the man's quaint turns of phrase. Neck of the woods indeed. "Well, we've been making it difficult for the English to stockpile supplies for their planned invasion of New Orleans. That, by the way, is their target, not Mobile, according to our friend, Macintosh."

"I'm surprised you got anything out of him. He looks to me to be a real hard case."

"Oh, he is, but he's a Scot, and frankly, he doesn't like the English much more than we do. I think he's willing to work for whoever pays him best. Once I got him to start talking, I think he told me everything he knows."

"Well, when we get him to Charleston, we'll see. I'll bet you he has more to tell, it just takes someone who knows how to make him want to talk."

Shaking his head, Colin said, "I know what you mean, but that's not my way. I might threaten violence, and I'm not above depriving a prisoner of food or water, or making him uncomfortable, but outright violence, well, I just don't think the information you get that way is really trustworthy."

"You might be right, but you got to remember, it's wartime, and the normal rules of behavior don't apply."

"That, sir, is where you're wrong. If we don't apply civilized rules of behavior to wartime, it's . . . well, it leads to situations like York."

"Maybe you're right, Colin, I don't know. All I know is what I've seen, and that's the fact that so-called gentlemen become animals when the muskets and cannons start firing."

Colin was at a loss for words. How could he explain to this man that even though he'd killed in war, he took no pleasure in it, and the few times he'd looked into the faces of the men he'd killed, he had never been able to erase that look in their eyes when they know they're dying. How anyone could lower himself to engage in gratuitous violence was something he could not understand.

"That may well be, sir," he said. "But, I'll still fight my war by the rules of conduct taught to me by my mother and father. Now, if there's nothing else, I think I'd better round my men up and head back north."

"Good luck, young man, and stay safe," Hoskins said. "We need more officers like you." He stood and took Colin's arm, guiding him to the door. "Give my regards to that lady pirate of yours."

As Hoskins opened the door for him, the secretary appeared. He looked at Colin with a quizzical expression. "Sir, the prisoner wishes to speak with you before you leave."

Colin turned to Hoskins.

"Sure," the consul said. "Go ahead. Jackson, show Captain Worth to the cells."

Colin followed the man down the long, narrow hallway to a door at the end. The man opened the door and turned to Colin. "Careful on the stairs, Captain Worth," he said. "There's no light until we reach the bottom."

That, Colin thought as he squeezed past the man and stepped down onto a stone step that looked like it had been carved from the earth upon which the building stood. When the man closed the door, it was pitch dark. Colin gingerly felt for the wall to his right. As the man eased past him, he said, "This old basement was in the building when Mr. Hoskins bought it. I think the original owner used it as a wine cellar. Oh, and the steps aren't carved from the bedrock, but they were set into the earth to make it look that way. The old man who owned it was a rich eccentric."

To Colin the secretary sounded like a man who had delivered this speech many times before. It was interesting, but the only thing he really wanted to do was get the visit with Macintosh over with and get back to the surface. He did not like dark places, and especially hated being underground. Once when he was twelve, a cousin who lived in a village west of Philadelphia, while Colin was visiting for the summer, had taken him exploring a cave on the family's farm. They'd gotten lost in the convoluted cavern system for nearly a day before his uncle found them. From that day, the only dark places he'd ever entered were below decks on ships, or his bedroom.

"How far down does it go?" he asked.

"Not far, maybe twenty feet," was the reply.

Colin shuddered. *Deeper than a grave.*

He breathed a sigh of relief as they neared the bottom of the stone steps. A lantern hanging from a hook on the wall at the base of the stairs gave off a faint glow, just enough light for Colin to see that the walls were rough timbers with some kind of plaster caulking, supporting his guide's story about the stairs being installed instead of carved out of the surroundings. The floor, when he stepped off the last stair, was hard-packed clay, shiny in the lantern light from the many feet that had trod upon it.

The space at the bottom of the stairs was a little vestibule, about five feet on each side, with a door to the right. The secretary opened the door and motioned Colin through.

He entered a long, rectangular room, with a row of lanterns hanging on the wall to his left, and a row four of iron-barred cells on the right. He could see Macintosh in the last cell, standing at the door, his hands gripping the iron bars.

When Colin stood before the bars, he could see that Macintosh was no worse for wear, apparently, Hoskins was not doing any 'interviewing' himself. Through the bars, he could see empty eating utensils on the simple wooden cot against the back wall of the cell. A large earthenware jug sat on the floor. In the right corner was a porcelain pot, and from the smell, Colin could guess its purpose.

"I'll be outside in the vestibule, sir," the secretary said. "Just call when you're ready to leave."

He bowed slightly and departed.

Macintosh waited until the door had closed behind him before speaking.

"Thanks for coming, laddie," he said.

Even though he knew that Macintosh was probably a cold-blooded killer, Colin couldn't help but feel a degree of grudging respect for him.

"No thanks necessary," he said. "I see they're treating you well."

"Aye, fattening the lamb for the slaughter, they are. I don't think my accommodations will be this grand when I get to America."

"You know that you can make it easy on yourself just by telling them what they want to know."

"I could, but where's the fun in that, eh? Besides, I have to make these boyos earn their pay."

Colin shook his head. "Liam Macintosh, you are one tough man."

"Have to be to be in this business." Macintosh shrugged and smiled. "Look, laddie, I just wanted to see you before you left. Before I met you, I had a jaundiced view of your people, you . . . Americans. I thought you got lucky when you defeated the English and won your independence, but seeing the way you operate, I think more than luck was involved. You people are more like the bloody English than I think you care to admit."

"Well, many of us have English forebears, but except for the bloodline, I don't think we're anything alike."

"Oh no, laddie. The English with their bloody empire so vast the sun never sets on it, and you Americans stretching your wings here in the new world, pushing the aborigines aside and taking their land, using slaves to build your mansions and grand estates—oh, yes, you're a lot like the English. But, that's not what I wanted to say. If the people I'm meeting when they get me to America are like you, I'll make them work, but I imagine I'll tell them what they want to know. You might not know it, laddie, but you make a damn good spy."

Colin's cheeks flushed. He was a man of many talents, and wasn't shy about admitting it, but being a spy was the last thing on his list of talents he wished to possess.

"Thank you, I think," he said. "But, I'm no spy. I'm just a . . . man doing his job."

"As am I, laddie. Now, Mr. non-spy, you go on back to that non-spying you're doing. I'm goin' to take a wee nap before they take me away."

Without a further word, Macintosh went to the bunk, removed the used eating utensils, lay down, and put his left forearm over his eyes.

Colin was fascinated at how calm the man was about his situation. If he was in Macintosh's shoes he doubted that he'd be able to relax the way the man was doing.

He shrugged and headed for the door.

Charles Ray

Chapter 23

August 1813, Skull Island

Colin found M'nondo and O'Reilly in the tavern across from Hoskins' office, and after prying them loose from their beer and sausages, had to fend off their questions about what went on between him and the consul after they were dismissed, and hustled them to the dock to find an outbound ship to get them back to Cat Island, or some other place from which they could get a message to Elizabeth to pick them up. They were unhappy at being left out on the gossip, but he promised that he would share what he could when they were back at Skull Island—he had no desire to tell the same story twice.

They sulked at his answer and remained quiet during the entire voyage to Cat Island, spoke hardly a word while they waited in Mama Lillie's for one of the ships to arrive and pick them up, and didn't break their silence on the sail to Skull Island.

Once their feet touched the sandy beach of the cove in which the ships were anchored, both rounded on Colin, faces scowling.

"Now, will you tell us what you learned from that man Hoskins?" O'Reilly asked.

"I told you," Colin said. "You'll hear it when everyone else hears it. Now, go and assemble the crews in front of the big house, and I'll share what I can."

M'nondo looked at him skeptically. "Which, if I read Hoskins right, is not very much."

"You are a good reader, my friend." Colin laughed. "But, *I* will decide what the people here need to know. After all, you're the ones putting your lives on the line, so you have a right to know what's at stake."

M'nondo chuckled. "I have read you correctly as well, Colin. You are, what is the word, a renegade. You live by your own set of rules. I wonder how it is that you have survived as long as you have in your government."

"Hm, sometimes I wonder that myself. Oh well, no sense in wasting thinking on imponderables. I need to say hello to Elizabeth, and then I'll talk to everyone."

M'nondo nodded and trotted off after O'Reilly. Colin continued his walk across the sandy beach toward the big house where Elizabeth awaited him on the veranda.

"Welcome back, stranger," she said. "For a while there I feared that you might have decided to go back home."

He stopped at the foot of the steps and looked up at her. Home? An interesting concept. All the time he spent in and around the islands, he realized that he had never once thought of his home back on the mainland, but a few weeks at sea and in Haiti, and all he could think of was getting back to Skull Island.

"I am home," he said.

Her eyes misted. "Do you have time for a proper welcome?"

"How long do you think it will take for M'nondo and O'Reilly to gather everyone to hear what I have to say?"

"At least twenty minutes."

"Well, that's not enough time for a *proper* welcome, but it will be adequate time for a pleasant welcome."

She smiled as he mounted the steps and took her hands. They were both smiling when they entered the house, her head rested against his shoulder.

They were still smiling fifteen minutes later when they came back out, to find M'nondo standing on the veranda with his back to them, watching as the pirates and those of their families not involved in important housekeeping duties, assembled on the broad, sandy area in front of the house.

A cheer went up from those who were there when Colin and Elizabeth emerged from the house. M'nondo turned, and when he saw them a broad smile lit up his brown face.

"You two look happy," he said.

"Big brother, you're just jealous because you don't have a woman," Elizabeth said.

"Hmph, I have many women, just not here on the island. But, we will be going to Cat Island soon, and I will get *my* welcome home there."

"M'nondo, my friend, you have a dirty mind," Colin said.

M'nondo thumped his chest with a meaty fist. "But, my body is clean, and quite presentable."

Elizabeth punched Colin lightly in the chest. "Do not get him started, Colin. He might seem like this stoic, unfeeling person, but when you get him started talking about his romantic conquests, he will talk your ears off."

Colin looked out at the crowd. There were still a few stragglers arriving, but it looked to him like most were there. "Okay, but I think I'd like hear some of his stories." He ducked as Elizabeth poked at him again.

He stepped up to the edge of the verandah and raised his hands to quiet the murmuring of the crowd. When there was silence, he began by telling them of the capture of the English spy, Macintosh, and O'Reilly's bravery in that endeavor. Then, he gave them an abbreviated version of what Hoskins had told him about the progress, or lack of progress, in the war.

"As you can see, the loss of Fort Detroit and the failure to take Canada leaves us vulnerable in the

165

north. Now, this might lead you to think the English will shelve their plans for a southern invasion, but I think otherwise. This would be an excellent opportunity to catch our unprepared forces in a pincer movement and crush them. There's still a chance that the navy will be able to hold them off in the lake area, but if they have to worry about English forces at their back, they will be lost."

"Is it true that the Americans burned the town of York?" O'Reilly asked.

"Yes," Colin replied. "How did you know about that. I didn't mention it."

"Oh, one of the serving girls in the tavern was talking about it. Says she heard it from one of the guards who works in the building across the street."

Colin sighed. Hoskins had pulled the bureaucratic ploy of keeping Colin's men in the dark but was unable to control the flapping lips of his own staff. It was the typical way things worked in bureaucratic organizations; rules foisted on outsiders, and those on the inside playing fast and loose with those same rules. Well, he thought, to hell with him and his rules.

"I don't know what you heard, but the fact is that the troops who invaded Canada in April looted and burned York, and there were a lot of civilian casualties."

"The English will not like that," M'nondo said.

"Bloody well right they won't," Colin said. "They will want revenge, and I shiver at the thought of what they might do to get it."

"Do you think they'll burn an American city in retaliation?" Elizabeth asked.

"Yes, I'm pretty sure they will, and during the trip back here, I gave some thought to which cities they might select, and what came to mind gave me a bad case of the shivers."

All eyes were on him now. Colin wasn't sure he should share this particular thought. He hoped that he was just being paranoid, and perhaps over thinking the situation.

"Well, don't keep us in suspense, Colin," Elizabeth said. "What city do you think the English will attack?"

As usual, Elizabeth had cut through the fog of indecision. He had no choice but to share his thoughts now.

"I tried to think like the English," he said. "Our troops burned a provincial capital, a symbol of the might of the British crown in Canada, so they'll have to attack a similar symbol on our side. Now, there's only one city really that stands for the whole country, and that's the new capital city on the Potomac. I think they'll attack Washington."

There was a long moment of silence as his words sank in. M'nondo was the first to break the silence. "Isn't that taking a big chance? Your capital should be heavily guarded and fortified. Their losses in attacking it would be great."

"I wish I could say that Washington is a fortress, but I really don't know. I know there are forts around the city, but how they're manned, and how capable the forces manning them are, well, that's anyone's guess. We don't have a large national army, and the state militias, though well meaning, are not very capable. Hell, most of them won't fight outside their home states. I can't imagine the states will send militia to protect a capital that belongs to no state."

"If the English take your capital, the war is over," M'nondo said.

"Well, not really. It's not like ancient warfare, when the chief is killed or captured, the warriors stop fighting. We're such a fractious bunch anyway, with each state insisting on its own rights, it's not necessarily true that losing the capital would end the war. The northeastern states already don't support the war, but the southern and western states might just fight harder if Washington is attacked. I hope I'm wrong, and nothing will happen."

M'nondo shook his head. "I do not think you are wrong, Colin."

"You, my friend, are so reassuring."

Chapter 24

December 1813, Cat Island

For the following four months, they continued to conduct hit and run raids on English shipping in the Caribbean, taking ten merchant vessels and another Royal Navy dispatch boat. Colin kept expecting the hammer to fall, and that their two ships would run into a British armada, but there was no noticeable increase of British naval vessels in the area. Word from their informants in Nassau indicated that the authorities were still stockpiling arms and supplies, but there had been no appreciable increase in troops.

The hunt for them seemed to have been abandoned after they captured Macintosh. But, Colin didn't believe in leaving things to chance. For him, the lack of action indicated that something was going on that he didn't know about, and that worried him. So, in mid-December, he convinced Elizabeth that they should cease operations for the rest of the month to allow the men to spend time with their families during the holiday season—a conversation that was overheard by one of the men who was passing by, and was quickly spread throughout the island, making Colin everyone's hero—and, along with M'nondo, they go to Cat Island and find out what Mama Lillie's spies were hearing around Nassau.

The day before they were due to sail, Elizabeth tripped over a bucket someone had left carelessly in the kitchen and sprained her ankle, so only Colin and M'nondo arrived at Mama Lillie's in the early afternoon just after the midday rush. There were only two people in the place, Lillie, sitting behind the counter looking glum, and an elderly, brown skin man with a fringe of wooly white hair around the sides of his shiny head, sitting at a table in the corner loudly eating a bowl of gumbo.

Lillie smiled when they came through the door, but then her frown returned.

"Where is my *Lizbet*?" she asked, regarding the two men through narrow slits.

"She sprained her ankle and is resting in bed for a few days," Colin said.

"Oh, *j'sui desolais*, you must take her a big pot of my special gumbo when you return. It will make her ankle better *toute suite*."

Colin thought the curative powers of Mama Lillie's gumbo were about as valid as chicken soup, but if feeling better helped a person to heal, it would do the trick because it was without doubt the best stew he'd ever eaten."

"Great." He looked around the nearly empty room. The old man was only paying attention to his food. "Could we go to the private dining room?" No sense taking unnecessary chances, he thought.

Lillie hopped off the stool upon which she was sitting, came around the counter, and beckoned them to follow her. Just before she parted the beaded curtain, she looked at the old man. "Pierre, I must go out. If you wish more gumbo, it is in the kitchen, so help yourself. If you finish before I return, put your money under the towel on the counter."

The old man mumbled something that sounded to Colin like 'okay, thank you,' but with his mouth full of food it was hard to tell.

Inside the room, they sat at the table in the center, Colin with his back to the wall and watching the entrance, M'nondo to his left, where he always stood, saying that he didn't want to block Colin's sword arm, and Lillie facing him.

"So," Lillie said. "What is so important that you come without Elizabeth, and that you are afraid that a half-deaf old man might hear?"

Colin began by explaining the lack of British naval patrols in the area where they'd recently seized four merchant ships. "I'm concerned at this apparent lack of activity, or interest, in what we're doing," he said. "It's important that we divert their attention away from an invasion."

"*Oui*, it is strange that the English authorities no longer seem interested in what you are doing, but my people in Nassau tell me that part of the problem is they do not know what happened to their agent. You must be careful, by the way, because they know he disappeared after coming here. There are men from the constabulary all over the island."

"I have never come to their attention before," Colin said. "So, they are not likely to look at me suspiciously." He glanced at M'nondo.

"I am just another black man to them," M'nondo said. "Unless they see me commit a crime, they do not notice when they pass me on the street."

"He is right, *cher*," Lillie said. "They are certain that their man was captured by secret American agents." She looked at Colin. "So, it is better if you do not speak in public. You do not sound at all *anglais*. If they hear you speak, they *will* be suspicious of you."

"That's fine. I'll let M'nondo do all the talking if needed and pretend to be a mute."

"If only that was true," M'nondo said. "My ears would thank you."

Colin tapped him playfully on the shoulder. "I do not talk a lot."

"Not about women, like me, but you talk about everything else."

Colin raised a finger as if to disagree, and then lowered it when he realized that he did have a tendency to go on at length on some subjects. He smiled and turned to Lillie. "What news do you hear from America, Mama Lillie?"

"A Dutch ship captain was in here a week ago. He'd just sailed from the port of Boston, and he says the city was all excited by some ship battle that your Americans won," she said. "Said a few American ships forced a whole English fleet to surrender."

Colin felt his heart pound. "Are you sure he wasn't just making up a story?"

"I thought to myself, at first, that he was just, how you say, spinning the yarn. But, he had so many details, it just sounded true, you know."

"Well, for heaven's sake, woman, tell me. What happened, and don't leave anything out."

"Oh, *cher*, you are so impatient. I will tell the story my way, *non*, so sit there and keep quiet. Now, this Dutchman said that an American fleet commanded by . . . Perry, I think—"

"He must mean Oliver Perry," Colin said. "I know him. Served with him during the war against the Barbary pirates. I always thought he'd make something of his naval career. He's young, though, only twenty-eight or twenty-nine. He was barely out of his teens when we were in Tripoli. He's from a navy family, you know. His father—"

Lillie held a hand up in front of Colin's face.

"Quiet, *cher*! First you want me to hurry and tell you the story, and then you keep interrupting me. Now, decide; I tell the story or you talk. It cannot be both."

M'nondo chuckled. "Did I not tell you? You talk too much."

Colin's cheeks turned red. "Sorry, Mama Lillie. I'll keep my mouth shut. You tell your story."

"Ah, that is better. Now, this Oliver Perry, in September, he take a fleet of six or nine ships on Lake Erie, and he fight with six English ships. Even though he have more ships, they are smaller, and the English they damage his ship so he has to move to another ship, but he still force them to surrender. The Dutchman say he like bulldog, he get teeth in and not let go. It is first time an English fleet ever defeated, and by former colony. There must be many red faces in London."

Colin nodded. "I would imagine, oh, may I speak?"

"Of course, you may, *cher*, as long as you ask nicely like this."

"This is truly a stain on the reputation of the English navy, the fleet that ruled the world," he said. "And, it will just fuel their desire to strike back at us in some really significant way."

"Well, it will not be from Detroit, or even from Canada. Your General William Harrison attack the English in Detroit in October. With the English ships gone from Lake Erie, General Proctor, the commander of the English in Detroit decide is better to withdraw. Harrison chase him all the way to Upper Canada. They have a big fight at place called Moraviantown. Many English killed, but even more of the *Indien* who fight with the English. They killed the chief, and the rest of his people just faded away."

"Killed the chief," Colin said. "That must be Tecumseh the Shawnee warrior. He is, was, a real firebrand. Pulled the western tribes together to fight against westward expansion into their lands. He talked several of the tribes to forget their differences and join the English against us. If he's dead, I imagine that confederation is dead as well. That, the loss of ships at Lake Erie, and the loss of Detroit spells big trouble."

"For the English, you mean," M'nondo said.

"Yes, but for us as well. Now that they've lost in the north, they will be even more set on a southern invasion. We might have dealt them a significant blow, but they're just down, not out."

"Do not be so negative, Colin. Do you not always say, it is darkest just before the dawn?"

"Yes, my friend, but it is now midnight, the time when the night is darkest."

Chapter 25

January 1814, Cap Haitien

Liam Macintosh sat on the edge of his cot listening to the sound of water dropping from a height. The condensation that formed on the ceiling of the basement in which he'd been kept for nearly six months dropping to the hard-packed dirt floor. He sat perfectly still, his hands resting on the tops of his thighs, as immobile as a statue, the only movement, the occasional blinking of his eyes.

His guards only came now twice a day, once in the morning with his breakfast, a bowl of oatmeal and a cup of water, and in the evening with his supper, various local dishes that were greasy and cold by the time they reached him. A Haitian in Hoskins employ came every other day to remove and empty his chamber pot. Other than that, he was left totally alone. There were no other prisoners, and in the cold, dankness of his underground cell, not even rats for company.

This would have driven a lesser man crazy. But, Macintosh was not a lesser man. In his career working for the British government he had endured far worse.

He had, in fact, appreciated the solitude, for it gave him time to work out a plan. He was always planning ahead, like a master chess player, figuring out what his opponent's moves might be, and preparing countermoves. He was, therefore, upset when he heard the door from the vestibule slam against the timber walls, followed by the thump of a pair of boots on the hard floor.

It was Nelson, the fat guard with the bad breath and the constantly sweating forehead, staring at him through the bars.

"Okay, princess, up and at 'em, it's time for your trip," Nelson said.

Macintosh took his time opening his eyes, and when he did, he looked at the man like a snake would look at a plump mouse wandering by unaware of a reptilian presence. Of the many plans he'd mentally mapped out during his months in this underground cell, the one involving Nelson was by far the easiest, and the one that pleased him most, because, while the other guards did their jobs and mostly ignored him otherwise, Nelson seemed to take pleasure in taunting him, and on occasion when no one was looking to jostle him a bit too roughly against the rough timber walls. Oh yes, he thought, this will be a pleasure.

He stood, his posture loose but ready.

"So, I am finally to be moved to America," he said. "It is about time."

"It's not for your convenience, friend. We had to wait for an American vessel that had a good reputation with the government, ours and the Haitians. I suppose, though, I oughta thank you. Escortin' you gives me a chance to get outta this shit hole. I ain't seen my ma, pa, and younger brother for nearly two years."

Macintosh smiled. If things worked out the way he'd imagined them so many times sitting in his cell in the dark, the fool wouldn't be seeing his kin ever again. Maybe, he thought, I won't mess him up too much, and leave him where he can be easily found. That way, at least his kin might get a last look at him. He stood and stretched like a cat after a long nap. The look of the jungle cat about to go on the hunt was in his eyes.

"Well, Mr. Nelson, let us be off," he said. "We Wouldna want to be keepin' you from your kinfolk, no would we?"

Nelson looked at him with a funny expression on his bloated face, not sure if he was serious or not, but seeing the completely blank expression on Macintosh's face decided he was being serious in that English way of his.

"Well grab your socks and let's be off," he said.

Nelson unlocked the cell, put a pair of iron cuffs on Macintosh's wrist, and held his elbow tightly as they made their way up the stairs and out the back exit of the building. Outside in the alley he pushed Macintosh toward the docks.

They were less than two hundred yards from the docks when Macintosh struck.

As he suspected Nelson would do, rather than call for a carriage, he'd decided they would walk. He placed a jacket over Macintosh's manacled wrists, not that anyone on the street would have been particularly surprised or upset at seeing such a sight, and walked him at a brisk pace for a man of his girth. Macintosh had for many weeks been feigning weakness, occasionally refusing to eat all of the slop they called food, and he did the same now, reeling like a drunk, and gasping as if he was out of breath. As a result, by the time they entered the last street before the docks, a narrow lane lined on both sides by one and two-story wood frame buildings whose occupants were either all at work, or otherwise occupied, for the narrow, trash-littered sidewalks were empty, Nelson was paying less attention to him, and his hand no longer rested on the handle of his pistol.

Near the middle of the long block of houses, two-story buildings stood on either side of the street, casting long shadows over everything, and between the building on their side and its neighbor was a dark, narrow alley, even more littered with trash and debris than the sidewalks.

Without warning, Macintosh spun, and grabbed Nelson's pistol from the belt at his waist, and with his shoulder shoved him into the alley. The fat man, caught off guard, back pedaled until his heels hit a large plank on the ground, and he fell backwards, landing on his fat rump.

"What the—" He looked up, confused, at the large, dark circle that was the end of his own pistol's barrel pointing at his face.

"Shut up and you just might come out of this okay," Macintosh said. "Now, take the keys to these manacles out of your pocket and slide it over here to me. And, do not be tryin' any funny business. I've seen what the ball from one of these things can do to a man's face up close. Believe me, you do not want me to have to pull the trigger."

Nelson's face went white. He fumbled in his pocket and pulled out the brass key. His hand trembling, he put it on the ground and flicked it toward Macintosh.

"W-what are you gonna do?" Nelson asked, his eyes never straying from the pistol barrel.

"Just shut your trap until I get out of these cuffs," Macintosh said. He knelt, and keeping the pistol pointed at the guard, slowly retrieved the key with his left hand.

A right-hander, he fumbled getting the key into the lock of the manacle on his right wrist, but finally got it free. Hands free now, he pocketed the key and waved the pistol at Nelson. "Get up to your knees and turn around," he said.

"You're not gonna shoot me, are you?"

"No, you fool. A gunshot would have half the town descending upon us. Now, do as I say, or I might just take a chance on being able to outrun 'em."

Nelson pushed himself up, got to his knees and shuffled around until his back was to Macintosh. His flabby body trembled like a willow tree in a strong breeze.

Macintosh approached him and raised the pistol. He then brought it down with all the force he could muster, making contact with the back of Nelson's head. The force broke the skin, and the big guard pitched forward. He twitched once, and then lay still.

Macintosh put the pistol into his pocket and knelt over the still body. "I wish I could say I'm sorry for what I'm about to do, laddie, but I need time to get away. Can't have you waking up and sounding the alarm. Besides, you been giving me grief ever since you locked me in that cellar."

He wrapped his hands around the man's neck and squeezed. The unconscious Nelson never felt a thing. Macintosh continued squeezing until he felt the pulse in the neck stop, and then maintained his grip for a minute longer, until he was sure he could feel the man's life leave his body.

He rose and dusted off his trousers.

"Now, to find a way out of this bloody place."

He retrieved the key and removed the manacle from his wrist, dropping it and the key beside the body. Then, casually, he walked away.

Charles Ray

Chapter 26

February 1814, Governor's Residence, Nassau

"So, you allowed yourself to be captured by the very pirates you were hunting. Not very professional of you, Mr. Macintosh." Alwyn Brice's voice had, if anything, Macintosh thought, gotten even more condescending since they'd last met.

Biting his lip to hold back an angry outburst, Macintosh considered explaining that he was outnumbered, but decided against it. He explained himself only to people he considered his equal, and Brice wasn't even equal to the stuff he scraped off the bottom of his boots.

"Yes, a bit of bad luck," he said. "But, I think I know where they hang out. With a large enough force, we can go in and wipe them out."

"Are you seriously trying to tell me that these pirates told you where their base is?"

"They didna actually tell me. I was blindfolded when they captured me on Cat Island, but we got on a boat, and I know how long we sailed. I could also tell that we sailed east mostly, until we arrived at this isolated looking little island. They keep their ships in a cove, out of sight from the sea, and I doubt you can

181

see the entrance to the cove if you don't know what you're looking for. But, given a few days, I think I can find it."

Brice scratched at his chin. "I've no doubt you probably could do just that, Mr. Macintosh. There is just one problem with your plan, though."

"And, that is?"

"We have neither the ships nor the men to spare for you to go on some wild goose chase."

"It's not a wild goose chase. These pirates are a thorn in our sides, and if we don't wipe them out, we'll be hard pressed to mount a southern invasion to support our forces in the north."

"Ah, our forces in the north. I see that you have been out of circulation and are not aware of what has happened in that area. The American navy completely defeated our lake fleet and took Fort Detroit back. They now control Lake Erie and our access to the Ohio Valley. We're planning an assault on their east coast, but it's primarily designed to do as much damage as possible in retaliation for the Americans looting and burning York. No, the attack on New Orleans is now our main card to play. There will be more ships and forces coming here, but they won't be here to look for pirates, they will be here to plan an invasion."

"So, you won't help me find these bloody pirates?"

"I am sorry, Macintosh, but there are priorities, and what you want to do is very low on that list."

Macintosh growled deep in his throat.

"Well, feck the bloody lot of ye," he said. "I'll hunt the beggars down myself, and when I bring you their leader's head in a bag, I'll dump it in your lap, blood and all."

Before a shocked Brice could respond, he spun and strode out of the office, a look of rage contorting his face.

Chapter 27

March 1814, Cat Island

When word arrived at Skull Island that Macintosh had killed his guard and escaped from Haiti, Colin knew that the man would resume his hunt for their base. He would have to find him first to keep their secret. With Elizabeth, M'nondo, Garcia and O'Reilly, he set out for Cat Island, reckoning that Macintosh would start his search at the place where he was first captured.

They found Mama Lillie in a tizzy when they arrived at her café.

"What's put a bee in your bonnet, Mama Lillie?" Colin asked.

"You have heard, *non*? The Scotsman you captured escaped from Haiti."

"Yes, as a matter of fact, we did hear. That's why we're here."

"He is not here, *cher*, at least, not now. He was here for a few days looking for men and a ship."

"Did he find either?"

"*mais non, cher*. Everyone on the docks knows Mama Lillie. They would not dare work for some stranger without first asking me. When they came to me and told me, I knew it was this *cochon*, Macintosh, so I told them to say no."

"You think he went back to Nassau?"

"No, he went to Little Abaca Island. There are many boat captains there who will work for anyone, do anything for the right amount of money, and I think this Macintosh has much money."

Colin nodded. "He has the entire British government behind him. I'd say he can get whatever funds he needs."

"Do you think he is looking for ships and men to come after us?" Elizabeth asked.

"It has to be," Colin said.

"Why does he not just get the English navy?" M'nondo asked.

"I have no idea. Why don't we go to Abaca, find Macintosh and ask him?"

M'nondo made a fist. "I will be happy to ask him."

Chapter 28

Little Abaca Island

They anchored off a deserted beach of Little Abaca Island and took boats to shore. After hiding the boats in the palm trees lining the beach, Colin, M'nondo, Garcia, and Elizabeth made their way into the nearby town that also served as the island's main port.

It didn't take them long to discover that Macintosh had indeed been recruiting on the docks and had been successful in acquiring a modest sloop and a crew of thirty men willing to do just about anything for the money he offered. With M'nondo cajoling them, the dockworkers, some of them former slaves, parted with information freely, and in short order they obtained directions to Macintosh's base of operations on the island.

A twenty-minute walk from the docks, it was a modest looking wood frame house with a rusted metal sheet roof. The only thing that distinguished it from its neighbors were the two men holding wicked looking sabers who stood to either side of the front door warily eying all who passed by.

"Hm," Elizabeth said. "If what we heard on the docks was right, he has twenty-eight more men inside that building, and I'll bet they are all armed. I guess we'll have to let Mr. Macintosh go."

"I hate to do that," Colin said. "That's like walking past a poisonous snake and leaving your back unprotected."

She looked as frustrated as he did. "What other choice do we have?"

Garcia stepped up. "This Macintosh *hombre* knows you, Colin, and he also knows O'Reilly and M'nondo, but I have never had any contact with him."

Colin nodded, but frowned. He thought he knew where Garcia was headed, and he worried that, as O'Reilly almost did, the man might get in over his head.

"True, but what does that have to do with anything?"

"I am thinking, he is hiring men. What if I present myself to him as a sailor who has been kicked off his ship, and I am desperate for money? I could tell him that I have heard of this pirate who is raiding the English, but when I tried to get work from them, they turned me down. *Esta muy Bueno, si?* He will think that I am seeking revenge, and when I tell him I know where these *putas* are based, and will take him there for . . . how much gold should I ask for?"

"Diego, that is a stupid idea," Elizabeth said. "The man is merciless. He'll cut your throat and feed you to the fishes."

Colin held his hand up. "I agree that it's dangerous, but Diego is right. Macintosh doesn't know him, and it might just work. He could lead Macintosh and his crew to some place where we could ambush him."

She looked skeptical. "And, where would that place be?"

Colin smiled. "Why, Skull Island, of course."

"What? Are you crazy? You would invite this dastardly man to our base?"

"I know it's taking a risk," Colin said. "But, I imagine he has a fairly good idea where to look for us. Taking him to a different place might make him suspicious. Besides, on Skull Island, we would have the advantage. We know the ground, and he doesn't. Nor to any of the slackers he's hired off the docks here."

"That is a crazy plan," M'nondo said. "But it is just crazy enough to work."

"I do not like it," Elizabeth said.

"Do you remember how we defeated Colin's old captain, little sister?" She nodded reluctantly. "They were more than thirty. I think we can do it again. If we defeat Macintosh, we need not worry about anyone knowing where our base is, because if he lives, we will not allow him to leave until the war is over."

"And, we can get Chief Kojomo and his warriors to help us as we did the last time," M'nondo said.

"I'm not sure I want to put the islanders in danger."

"We put them in danger just by being there." M'nondo looked grim. "We should at least allow them the honor of defending their home. The chief will be insulted if we have a battle on his island and do not invite him to take part."

Colin shook his head, but he smiled. "You warriors and your warrior codes never cease to amaze me. Very well, here's what we'll do. Diego, get yourself dirtied up and make your approach to Macintosh. Give us until tomorrow at noon to prepare and then bring him to the island. The rest of us will return right away and set up our ambush."

"The chief will be happy," M'nondo said.

"It should be interesting," Colin agreed.

Elizabeth looked from one to the other, a wry smile on her face. "I suppose it will," she said.

Charles Ray

Chapter 29

Garcia walked in a shambling gait, like a sailor who is trying to get his land legs back after a long sea voyage, directly toward the two guards at the door to the building.

When he was six feet away, the guard on the right, a hulking six-footer with a shaved head and a scar from over his left eyebrow down to the corner of his mouth, raised his sword and stepped forward.

"What you want?" he asked.

Garcia stopped, swaying like a man who had drunk too much. "I hear there is *hombre* here hiring men to go after the pirate who is attacking the *Ingles* navy. I have come to offer my services."

The man, who towered over the diminutive Garcia, glared down at him. "Why do you think he'd want a runt like you, stranger?"

"Now, I think I should tell him that."

"You tell me, little man, or you begone."

"Okay, but when he finds out that you let a chance to catch that pirate slip away, no, *amigo*, you sent it away, I do not think he will be very happy."

The big man looked uncertain. His companion said, "Mayhap you should let him go in. If Mr. MacIntosh won't want to hire him, that's his business. But, if he got the information he wants, he's right, you could be in big trouble."

"Okay, runt," the big man said. "You wait here. I'll see if Mr. Macintosh wants to talk to you."

Garcia stood there, his thumbs hooked in his pants pockets, for five minutes. Then, the big man came back, a sour look on his face.

"You can go in," he said. "He'll talk to you. But, you gotta leave your saber here."

Reluctantly, he handed over his saber to the grinning man. He then took a deep breath and brushed past him and pushed through the door. As he closed the door, he heard them laughing.

The room he entered was dimly lit by six lanterns; one each on the two tables flanking the door, and four spaced along the waist-high wooden bar that ran across the back wall. Men sat at table around the room, their heads bowed over large mugs. Garcia smelled the mixed scents of rum and whiskey. He wanted a drink, badly. His mouth was dry. Except for a slender white man standing with his back to the bar and his left forearm resting on its surface, the only other person at the bar was the bartender, a tall, cadaverous looking man with dark brown hair in a widow's peak. He stood near the man with a whiskey bottle near at hand.

Garcia assumed the man at the bar was Macintosh. Even from the distance he could see the air of command the man possessed. He stopped at the door to control his breath and calm the tremor in his legs. His first thought was to turn around and go back to the docks and join the others before they sailed away, but he took a deep breath and began to walk forward. His comrades were depending upon him to get this right, and he was determined not to get himself killed.

He stopped in front of the man, holding his hands in front of his crotch.

"I'm told you have something I might want," Macintosh said.

Garcia heard the menace in his voice, and the implied threat of the consequences if he didn't have something that Macintosh wanted.

"I understand you are looking for the pirate who has been troubling English shipping," Garcia said. There was a nervous tremor in his voice.

"Where did you hear this?"

Garcia and Colin had briefly discussed how he should go about his approach and had decided that sticking close to the truth would probably be the safest route.

"I was on Cat Island, and there was talk all around the docks about a Scotsman who was hiring men and looking for a ship. I am in need of work, so I asked where I might find him. Someone there told me I would find you here on Little Abaca."

"You are an experienced sailor?"

"I have been going to sea since I was a boy. I once sailed with a pirate, maybe you have heard of him, Jack Cleague? He was killed by the Americans many years ago, and since then I have been sailing on any ship whose captain would hire me."

"That, laddie, is not too different to any of the thirty other men here. What do you have that is so important that I should hire you?"

"I know where you can find this pirate you are looking for."

The bait was in the water, now he had to wait for Macintosh to bite.

"How do you know who I am looking for, laddie?"

"Like I have said, people on the docks they talk. And, I sailed before with pirates, and I know many of them still. I have heard that the leader of the pirates is an American, and I know where they sail from, because when I sailed with Captain Cleague, it was where we hid out between raids."

He saw a flicker of interest in Macintosh's eyes.

"You say the leader is an American? How do you know this?"

"People talk. A man on the dock described him." He described Colin and Macintosh's eyes widen further. "This American was here before the war, and he sailed with pirates then."

"Where can I find him, this American pirate?"

"It's a small island to the southeast. It has no name, and no one lives there. The pirates hide their ships in a cove that is almost impossible to spot unless you know what to look for. I can guide you there . . . for a price."

Macintosh smiled. "I see you still have the guile and greed of a pirate. Okay, laddie, you're hired. But, steer me wrong, and you'd better be able to breathe under water."

Chapter 30

April 1814, Skull Island

While Garcia wormed his way into Macintosh's confidence, Colin and the others sailed for Skull Island, arriving on the first day of April. M'nondo went off immediately through the jungle to the village of the escaped slaves who lived on the other side of the island, to recruit warriors for their ambush. Colin and Elizabeth sat on the verandah where he outlined for her his plan for the ambush.

"We need to somehow get their ship to enter the cove," he said. "Even better, get his men to come ashore."

"It is unlikely that he will bring the ship into the cove where he would not have room to maneuver," Elizabeth said. "It is more likely that he'll lay off the inlet to the cove and bring a force ashore in boats. But, I have a plan for dealing with that."

"Oh, you do, do you?" Colin smiled. "For someone who was opposed to this idea, you seem excited about it."

"I just wish to ensure it does not fail, Colin. Now, will you listen to my idea, or not?"

"I'm sorry. Go ahead."

"As I said, I think he'll leave the ship off the island with a skeleton crew, and land in boats. I think I should take *The Vixen* and a boarding crew and lie in wait on the ocean side of the island. While you and M'nondo take care of their landing party, we can attack and take the ship."

He looked at her, pride swelling in his chest. "That, my dear, is an amazing idea, and it's just the piece that was missing from my plan. You know, you and I make a great team."

She leaned over and kissed his cheek. "In more ways than just making war on the English, too. Oh, look, here comes M'nondo and he's brought his friend, Chief Kojomo and some warriors."

M'nondo strode out of the trees. Beside him, his chest out, and attempting to walk with a strut, a maneuver that was hampered by his legs, gnarled and swollen from age, was the aging, grey-haired chief of the village. Behind them came a band of twenty young men, their dark chests bare and glistening with sweat. They carried spears, bows and arrows, and clubs, and were prancing and singing in a tongue neither Colin nor Elizabeth understood.

The entourage stopped at the edge of the verandah. Kojomo bowed slightly at them. The young men fell silent.

"Elizabeth, Colin, I have brought Chief Kojomo and some volunteers," M'nondo said. "I explained to him what we plan to do, and he is more than happy to join us."

The old man stepped forward and slapped a fist into his chest. "It has been too long since the young men had a worthy challenge. When the bad white men come, they will get to test their warrior skills."

Colin stood and stepped off the verandah. He placed his right hand on Kojomo's shoulder.

"We are glad to have you, chief. Your warriors look like they could use some refreshment. M'nondo, why don't you take them to the cookhouse and get them something to eat and drink. Have the cook send over some for us, and you come back and join us. I'll explain what my plan is."

After one of the women had brought them a platter of fruit and nuts, a jug of water for the chief who was a non-drinker, and a bottle of rum and mugs for the others, Colin put a piece of paper and a stick of charcoal on the table and began to speak.

"If Diego does his job well, they'll come after dark, and it'll probably be by small boat into the cove. I think they'll beach the boats here." He used the charcoal to sketch in a rough map of the cove and put an 'X' at a spot near the entrance. He then drew a series of circles to the left of the 'X.' "We'll be waiting for them in the trees here. When they're getting out of the boats is when we attack."

The chief's head bobbed up and down. "That is the time they will not be paying attention. Is a good plan. We will kill them, of course?"

"If they fight, they die. We will, however, give them a chance to surrender. I would like to take their leader alive if possible."

M'nondo nodded at him. "I do not think he will surrender this time."

"You might be right, my friend, but it would be nice to know what he has told his English masters."

"I don't think he has told them anything," Elizabeth said.

Colin's brows raised in surprise. "Why do you say that?"

"If he had briefed his superiors in Nassau, he would be coming with English warships, not with a rented ship and a band of hired men."

He rubbed at his chin. "You know, I think you're right. He's doing this on his own. But that raises another question; why are they not helping him?"

"Hm, maybe we should try asking him," she said.

"He will not answer." M'nondo's voice had a note of finality in it. "I believe he only surrendered the first time so that he could discover our base. He will not do that again."

"We won't know for sure until the battle starts," Colin said. "In the meantime, we should get some rest. This will be a long night."

Elizabeth stood and smoothed the legs of her trousers. "I must go and get *The Vixen* ready to sail. We need to be east of the island before the sun sets if I am to surprise their ship."

"Do you wish me to go with you, captain?" M'nondo asked.

"No, I think Colin will need your skills here. I'll take O'Reilly as my first mate this time. It's time he started assuming more responsibility."

"As you wish, captain." The big man nodded in agreement.

Colin took her hand. He wanted nothing more than to pull her into an embrace and kiss her, but, in front of the others it would diminish her authority as a captain, so he just squeezed her hand gently, a gesture that was returned.

"Good hunting, captain," he said.

"Stay safe, Colin," she said.

She pulled her hand away, turned, and walked off the verandah.

When M'nondo had taken the chief away to be with his men and tell them what they were to do, Colin went inside the house and sat on the sofa in the main room. He was soon fast asleep, and slept soundly until just before midnight, when he awoke with a snap.

Still dressed, he rubbed his eyes, stood, and mentally prepared himself for what he knew was to come.

M'nondo was waiting for him on the verandah, along with the chief and his warriors, and all of the able-bodied men who hadn't gone with Elizabeth on *The Vixen*.

"I was afraid I would have to come inside and wake you up," M'nondo said. "But, you are awake and ready just at the time you said to be ready."

"A habit I picked up aboard ship when we fought the Barbary pirates. Get sleep when you can, but always wake up when you're supposed to."

Kojomo grunted. "The habit of true warrior."

Colin acknowledged the compliment with a slight bow of his head. "Let's get everyone in position. I have a feeling we'll be having guests soon."

Pirates and village warriors moved together, and while not quite as orderly as a military unit—although, Colin noted, as well as most of the state militia units—moved into the palm trees and bushes that lined the beach where the inlet spilled into the cove. Within minutes they'd concealed themselves in the bushes where they had a clear view of the beach.

And, not a moment too soon, for just as Colin knelt beside M'nondo and patted his shoulder, two ship's boats came through the foliage that hung from branches that spanned the inlet. In the moonlight, Colin saw eight men in each boat, with Macintosh clearly visible standing in the bow of the lead boat, his finger stabbing toward a point on the beach twenty yards in front of where they waited.

"It is as if he is following your plan," M'nondo whispered. "He will come ashore at exactly the point you predicted."

"It wasn't hard to guess," Colin said. "He couldn't risk coming too close for fear the noise would alert us, and if he landed too far away, we might also hear them moving through the jungle. This point seemed to be the happy middle point. Now, quietly pass the word for everyone to hold their fire until I fire."

Colin pulled his pistol and checked the charge.

"We'll first hit them with a volley of musket and pistol fire," he said. "And, then we'll close with bladed weapons."

M'nondo smiled. "Chief Kojomo's warriors will like that."

He scuttled quietly down the line, stopping and whispering quickly. In two minutes he was back at Colin's side just as the bow of the lead boat scraped the sand, and Macintosh jumped onto the beach.

The other men followed him, pulling the boat up on the sand to keep it from drifting away. A few seconds later, the second boat pulled in beside them, and within a minute, sixteen men, armed with muskets and cutlasses stood around Macintosh awaiting orders.

"I don't see any sign of activity up ahead," Macintosh said. "So, it looks like the new man, Garcia was right; they don't even post sentries. Mayhap I should have let him come with us instead of leaving him on the boat. Oh well, if they have anything of value here, I'll see that he gets his share. We'll move into the jungle and hit them from this side." His voice carried clearly to the edge of the jungle.

"We takin' any prisoners, sir?" a voice asked.

"No, and we're not leaving anyone to talk about tonight's events," Macintosh replied.

He turned and started walking directly toward Colin. From the sound of it, Garcia had done his job well, but Macintosh's last words had infuriated him. He knew that the man was ruthless, but to plan to slaughter everyone on the island, even the women and older people, was not just ruthless, it was inhuman. He raised his pistol and aimed it at Macintosh's chest.

"Mr. Macintosh, there be a path yonder just like—"

Just as he pulled the trigger, a burly man with a braided beard stepped in front of Macintosh, pointing to the left. The pop of the pistol was unnaturally loud in the stillness of the moonlit night, and it cut the man off mid-sentence. It was followed by a succession of pops and bangs as pistols and muskets fired as Colin had ordered.

All of this took place in a matter of seconds, but to Colin everything seemed to move in slow motion, a sensation he'd often experienced during sea battles.

First, the bearded man, his eyes widening as the ball slammed into his chest, then the rictus of pain and the dark stain growing on the front of his shirt, as he crumpled slowly to the sand. Second, the smoke from the many weapons firing, and the noise of firing and the screams of men as they were hit, sounding muffled as if through cotton in his ears. Then, he stood and drew his sword. He raised it high.

"Get 'em, boys," he yelled, and time resumed its normal pace.

Four of the sixteen invaders had been felled in the volley of fire. Those remaining were momentarily confused by the noise, of the shooting and the war cries of Kojomo's young warriors as they charged at them.

M'nondo sprinted past Colin, making a beeline for Macintosh who was waving his arms and shouting, trying to restore some semblance of order. He stopped when he saw M'nondo charging toward him. He turned and thrust the blade of his knife forward, crouched in a fighter's stance.

M'nondo stopped six feet away and smiled.

"Your small knife is no match for my blade," he said, brandishing the curved-blade saber that was his weapon of choice.

"We'll see about that, blackamoor," Macintosh said. "I dinna think a jungle ape like you has the skills to take me."

If his words were intended to inflame M'nondo, they had the exact opposite effect. The tall man went perfectly still except for the slow blinking of his eyes. When he spoke, his voice was just loud enough to be heard over the din of the battle that raged around him.

"Why do we not test that belief?" he said.

He took a step forward, waving his blade in a circle, the tip pointed upwards.

Macintosh dropped into a lower stance, his blade forward, his left hand guarding his midsection.

The fight swirled around Colin, one of Macintosh's men took a swing at him with a saber, which he blocked and then knocked the saber-wielder out by smacking him in the temple with the hilt of his saber, but half of his attention was on the drama playing out between M'nondo and Macintosh. The latter was obviously skilled in the use of the blade. He kept it low and kept his eyes on his opponent as he circled, looking for an opening for his thrust. But, M'nondo was no slacker when it came to using bladed weapons. He kept his saber pointed up, with his arm in close to his body, robbing his opponent of the knowledge of when and from where his thrust would come. He turned slowly, keeping Mcintosh in front and slightly to his left, which would allow him to stab in from the right, going for the left side of his opponent's chest, not to stab his heart, but to puncture a lung, or, if he missed the torso, perhaps sever a major artery in the arm. Colin had watched him practice, sometimes for hours, a stab-slash maneuver, where he would stab the target lightly on its left side, or nick it with a right-to-left motion, and then flip it back and up at a point where a man's throat would be, slashing deep. He wondered if Macintosh had ever encountered a move like that before, but even if he had, Colin doubted that there was an effective way to counter it.

Seeming to be losing interest, M'nondo let the tip of his blade dip. Macintosh jumped forward, his arm out, the knife an extension of that arm, aimed at the center of M'nondo's chest.

So fast, if Colin had blinked he would have missed, M'nondo's saber came up, and started its swing to the left. The tip of the blade nicked Macintosh's arm, a shallow cut that bled freely, causing him to hesitate and wince in pain. Before he could look down at the cut in his left arm, though, M'nondo's blade had completed its left swing and was coming back on an upward diagonal path, and his throat was in the path of that swing. He realized what was happening a fraction of a second too late and tried leaning back, so, instead of lopping off his head, M'nondo's saber cut a half-inch deep slash across the front of his throat.

Blood spurted from the gash. Macintosh opened his mouth to scream, but only a gurgling sound came out. He reached for his ruined throat with his left hand, but his life was ebbing out along with his blood.

The fingers of his right hand loosened their grip and his knife dropped to the sand. His eyes crossed.

The last thing he saw was M'nondo's smiling face, and the last thing he heard was the big man saying, "A man is foolish to bring a knife to a sword fight."

Charles Ray

Chapter 31

Aboard *The Vixen*

Elizabeth and a crew of fifty had made *The Vixen* ready and were on the east side of the island thirty minutes before Macintosh's ship appeared. They were positioned so a man in the bow could see the likely point on the western horizon from which the ship would said, and an hour before midnight, he spotted its lights.

Instead of calling out the sighting as he normally would; because sound carries exceptionally well at night; he had a companion with him who he sent back to the quarterdeck with the information.

In a conversational tone, Elizabeth told the messenger to tell the deck crew to set the sails for movement and told the helmsman to bring the ship around on a west by northwest course.

The Vixen sailed without lights, but on board, they had one of Colin's lanterns. The device was mounted in the bow and manned by one of the younger members of the crew. Elizabeth charted an arced course that brought them around the stern of the vessel and then to a position about twenty yards off the port side. The men aboard, their focus on the island and the boats that had just disappeared into a dark area, had their backs to *The Vixen* and unaware of her presence until they were bathed in a bright light and a booming female voice called from behind them, "Ahoy, unknown vessel, you have entered forbidden waters. Surrender your ship or you die."

Elizabeth, standing on the quarter deck, had a clear view of the deck of her prey, bathed as it was in the light of Colin's Leyden Lantern. She smiled as that deck erupted into a scene of chaos. It was hard to believe that six men, which was the number she counted on the deck, could generate such activity—well, five actually, for one figure, standing near the vessel's quarterdeck, stood calmly, watching the chaos around him.

Elizabeth brought her spyglass to her eyes and focused on the serene-looking figure, and her smile broadened. It was Diego Garcia, hands on hips, awaiting their arrival.

"Your time is running out," Elizabeth said in a more commanding tone. "In a few seconds I'll give my cannons the command to fire. What will it be?"

She looked directly at Garcia as she spoke. He turned to a man next to him and began talking, pointing at *The Vixen* as he did.

The other men gathered around them. There was some arm waving, but most of the heads were nodding. Then, Garcia turned to face her. "All right, captain, we surrender if you promise our safety," he yelled.

"We won't harm a hair on the head of any man who offers no resistance," she replied.

There was some more animated discussion, and then the man who had first been talking to Garcia came to the rail. "All right, we surrender," he said. "But remember, you said you'd harm no one."

Elizabeth stiffened. How dare this common wharf rat question her word. Then, she smiled. Of course, in his place, I suppose I would be skeptical too.

"Very well," she said. "We're coming alongside, and I'm sending a crew aboard to take over your ship. You will come aboard this ship where I promise you that you will be well treated."

And, just like that, the battle was over before it started.

Charles Ray

Chapter 32

June 1814, Skull Island

The battle of Skull Island was talked about for days afterwards. Four of the marauders, including Macintosh, had been killed in the encounter, and several were severely wounded, but by June were completely recovered. Colin and Elizabeth had talked with each man after getting Garcia's opinion of him and offered each a place on the crew of one of the, now, three vessels. The captured ship, a gaff-rigged, two-masted schooner, only had two cannons, but they gave it six more from ones they'd taken from captured vessels and rechristened it *Hellhound*. Every one of the surviving men accepted the offer, especially when they were told that they would get full shares of any booty taken. Macintosh and the other dead were buried at the edge of the jungle without much ceremony, but in carefully marked graves.

"When the war's over," Colin said. "The decent thing to do would be to offer his remains back to his government."

Elizabeth doubted that the English would want him back, after all he'd failed his mission, but she said nothing.

With three ships now, *Hellhound* under Garcia's command, Elizabeth on *The Vixen* with O' Reilly as her new first mate, and Colin, with M'nondo assisting him, commanding *Avenger*, their pincer tactic was even more effective. During the two months after they started the three-ship raids, they captured ten merchant vessels, and even surprised and defeated a Royal Navy frigate when, preoccupied with *Hellhound* on its starboard side, and *Avenger* threatening to 'cross the T' at port, fell prey to *The Vixen's* cannons into its aft section, destroying the quarterdeck and killing the entire quarterdeck crew, including the captain.

They even managed to harass a convoy of five merchant ships guarded by two frigates, not capturing any, but damaging two, and causing them to scatter in all directions.

Colin suggested that they take the last week in June off to allow the men to rest and spend time with their families, many of whom had made their way to Skull Island, leaving Lost Island sparsely populated mostly by the elderly who didn't take well to sea voyages, pregnant women, and the children, so time off on Skull Island became a time for festivities similar to the ones they held on Lost Island after successful voyages.

It was at one such festival, held in the open area in front of the big house, that Colin, Elizabeth, Garcia, and M'nondo sat at a roughly-carved wooden table in front of the house, mugs of rum at hand, and discussed their operation.

"I must say, we've done rather well the past few weeks," Colin said, opening the discussion.

"And Macintosh's men seem to be getting along well also," Garcia said.

"I still do not trust them," said M'nondo.

Elizabeth punched his muscular bicep. "Is there anyone you trust?"

He looked around the table. "Yes, and most of them are sitting at this table."

Colin laughed. "My friend, M'nondo, you are ever the pessimist, but in this case, I am with you. They have done a good job so far, but only time will tell if they can truly be trusted. I remember an old Russian man who had a shop not far from my father's place when I was about ten who always said 'trust, but get proof,' or something like that. We need to keep an eye on them to make sure they are truly with us."

"I agree with Colin," Garcia said. "I only mention it, because they have not caused any trouble, and the ones you assigned to my ship follow my orders without complaint."

"Watch the ones who are too compliant," Colin said. "A warrior who never complains is usually hiding something."

"I see your point." Garcia nodded. "I suppose I was just happy that they cause no trouble."

"Just keep an eye on them." Colin cleared his throat. "Now, let's get to some serious business. I've heard nothing about how the war is going, but I've noticed in the past week there have been fewer ships coming this way."

"I have noticed that, too," Elizabeth said. "There seem to be more ships heading north than south. I wonder why that is?"

Colin could think of a number of reasons. The British could be preparing an attack on a coastal city to avenge the American burning of York, or, smarting from their defeat on Lake Erie, the first time an English fleet had been beaten, they could be planning a major offensive in the north. Either would spell trouble for the young nation. Without a standing army, loosely organized and poorly motivated militia, and a deficit in military leadership for the land forces, it would be hard pressed to withstand a major English offensive.

"They're up to something in the north," he said. "So, we have to step up our operations down here to distract them."

"What more can we do? We have sunk dozens of their ships, and yet they seem to be ignoring us." M'nondo looked as frustrated as Colin felt.

"I've been thinking about that," Colin said. "Perhaps we need to send them a louder message."

"What can be louder than sinking so many ships?" Elizabeth asked.

He looked around the table, knowing that what he was about to say would shock them. "Let's attack them on land," he said.

He hadn't been wrong about shocking them.

Chapter 33

July 1814, Government House, Nassau

Alwyn Brice was not a happy man. Morose by nature, he found little in life or his job to smile about. But, on this day, his facial muscles were so taut with anger they ached, and he felt that he was grinding his teeth down to the gums.

Ships were being attacked and destroyed by pirates at an alarming rate, and according to reports of survivors of their raids, they attacked in packs of two and three ships, and even had the audacity to take on a small British warship; and had come out the victor in that encounter, killing the captain and several officers and crew, and damaging the ship so badly that it would be months before it was again seaworthy.

They *had* to be stopped, and not just because they were disrupting plans for the invasion of New Orleans, for, in truth, he cared not a whit about that, but because they disturbed the peace of what should be for him a tranquil assignment, with nothing more bothersome than listening to the complaint of a native laborer who felt mistreated by his master, or some colonist from home who couldn't understand why things were not like they were back home. Instead, his desk was piled high with reports of lost shipments, armaments and supplies that the army needed to support its landing and subsequent operations.

He needed a fleet of well-armed ships to hunt the pirates down and destroy them, but did the authorities who controlled the allocation of vessels listen? No, they did not.

Accustomed as he was to being on the receiving end of supplications, standing before a bevy of senior military and navy officers, resplendent in their uniforms with arrogant expressions on their faces, he seethed with repressed anger. How dare they treat him like some junior functionary, he thought, he, the man who had manipulated events for the past six years, reporting to the colonial governor only those things he needed to know, and given free rein to act on his own volition on matters great and small. Of all the officers sitting smugly behind the ornate mahogany table, though, the one who rankled him most was Rear Admiral George Cockburn. Cockburn was commander of a squadron of ships in the area, and the man who had the authority to grant him the ships and men he needed. But, instead of listening to his request and evaluating it on its merits, he insisted on delivering a lecture.

"Mr. Brice," he said. "You do not seem to understand the gravity of the situation we currently face, or you would not come to us with such an outrageous request."

"Quite the contrary, admiral. I am aware that we have lost dozens of ships, and millions of pesos worth of supplies and equipment to these marauders, and that something has to be done about it."

He realized as he spoke that his tone was insulting, but it wasn't his tone that the admiral chose to address.

"That may be so, sir," Cockburn said. "But, you do not seem to be aware that this barbarian Spanish currency is not the currency of the British realm."

Brice shrugged. *Oh well, in for a pence, in for the whole quid.* "No, admiral, I am quite aware of the specie of the home island, but out here in the colonies we tend to use the currency most familiar to the natives. You are quite right, though, as an officer in His Majesty's government, I should use the official currency, even when speaking to those who do not know what I am talking about."

The stiffening of Cockburn's facial muscles told him he'd hit home with that last barb.

The admiral made a harumph noise and drummed his fingers on the table. "No matter," he said. "The fact is, your request cannot be honored. All military and naval assets must be diverted to our new mission."

Brice's eyes widened. "Does this mean the invasion of the south is cancelled?"

The two army officers, generals Edward Pakenham and John Lambert, stiffened and glared at him.

"No," Pakenham said. "It is definitely *not* cancelled."

"Nor is my plan to take the port of Mobile," Lambert added.

"Of course not," Cockburn said, making a placating hand gesture at the two army men. "But, for the nonce, those operations are to be delayed until the new one is concluded."

"And, what is the new operation, admiral?" Pakenham asked.

Cockburn pointed at another army general, who had been sitting quietly at the end of the table to Brice's right. "Gentlemen, you all know General Robert Ross," he said. Brice didn't, but then, he didn't think Cockburn was including him in the conversation in retaliation for him forgetting his proper place. "General Ross and his 2,500 men have a very important mission. My squadron will take them up the Chesapeake from where they will launch an assault on Baltimore." Now he looked at Brice. "That city is a den of privateers, and instead of dozens of ships, they have taken over a thousand. We intend to put a stop to it."

Ross smiled and nodded.

"But," Cockburn went on. "Before attacking Baltimore, we plan a s surprise visit to the Americans' quaint little capital city on the Potomac River, and teach them the consequences of burning one of His Majesty's capitals."

"Won't Washington City be heavily guarded?" Brice asked.

"In a civilized nation that would be the case, but according to Admiral Sir Stanley Kensington of the admiralty, the city is only lightly guarded, and by militia at that."

"How does Sir Stanley come by this information?" Pakenham asked.

"Apparently, he has a high-placed American officer on his payroll, or, a formerly high-placed officer at least. He swears by the man."

As much as Brice hated to admit it, the plan was sheer audacity, and it would serve the bloody colonials right to have their capital sacked and burned.

"Well, if that is the case," he said. "You and General Ross should be back here in a few weeks. At that time, could my request be reconsidered?"

Cockburn rubbed the end of his nose. He looked at Brice like he would look at a stubborn horse.

"Oh, very well," he said. "We will take a look at it after our Chesapeake operation. In the meantime, Admiral Sir Alexander Cochrane will be arriving this afternoon. He will be preparing the way for you gentlemen to pay a visit to New Orleans and Mobile by arming and equipping the Creek Indians who live in those areas and encouraging them to harass the Americans. You, sir, are to extend him every courtesy, and help him in any way you can."

Brice knew when he was being dismissed. But, there was nothing he could do about it but smile and incline his head.

"Rest assured, admiral, Sir Alexander will get my undivided attention."

He rose and turned to leave. A murmuring conversation began immediately and was going full blast as he exited and closed the door.

Charles Ray

Chapter 34

August 1814, Cat Island

In early August, Colin received word from Mama Lillie, conveyed by a local fisherman who just 'happened' to know where to find him, that she needed to talk to him. She had news, the fisherman said, that she didn't want to put into writing lest it fall into the wrong hands. They sailed *Avenger* to one of the secluded spots on Cat Island they used infrequently, and Colin, leaving M'nondo in command of the ship, made his way by mule cart to Mama Lillie's place.

She was all aflutter when he entered, and without even greeting him properly, took his arm and pulled him into the private room.

"What is it, Mama Lillie?" Colin asked. "What has you so flustered?"

"I received news from *Cap Haitien* that Mr. Hoskins asked be delivered to you immediately," she said. "I think it is *tres important.*"

"Well, what is it?"

"Let me think so I get it correct. He said to tell you that *Monsieur* John Adams and four other gentlemen have traveled from Washington City to Ghent in the Netherlands where they will be meeting with agents from the English government. They will be trying to end the war."

For a moment, Colin was speechless. This was the news he'd been hoping to hear from the day he left Charleston. But, his elation lasted only a few seconds. He knew how long diplomatic negotiations could take, and that both sides would be maneuvering for more favorable bargaining positions while they were underway.

"Did he say who is representing the English in these meetings?"

"He was not sure, but he heard that the *Anglais* sent only low-level officials."

"Typical of the snobs," Colin said. "John Quincy Adams is the son of our second president, and a very educated man, so of course, the English would insult him by sending mere clerks to talk to him. Heaven forbid that a senior official from the foreign minister would lower himself to talk directly to a mere colonial."

"They are also insulting your president," she said. "One of the men in Adams' delegation is Mr. Albert Gallatin, the secretary of the treasury. For them to insult a private citizen, regardless that he is head of the delegation, is one thing, but to treat a cabinet minister in that manner, *merde*, such pigs they are."

"I don't disagree with you on that. This, however, is both good and bad."

"How is it bad? The war will soon be over, *non?*"

"Maybe, maybe not. Who knows how long they'll be haggling over terms and such? In the meantime, I expect the war will only heat up as each side tries to get into a better bargaining position. While the diplomats talk, soldiers and sailors on both sides will continue to die."

"Oh, Colin, *cher, j'sui tres desolais*, to be the bearer of such bad news."

"Don't worry, Mama Lillie. I don't believe in killing the messenger. I'd best be getting back. I have a feeling that things have just gotten more interesting."

Chapter 35

October 1814, Cape Haitien

After reading the top message in the dispatches sent from the chief of consular services in Washington, George Hoskins slammed it down on the desk.

"Dammit, dammit all to hell," he said. "This is just ridiculous."

His secretary rushed into the office.

"Is there anything wrong, sir?"

Hoskins held the single sheet of foolscap up. "Here, read this."

The man, shortsighted, held the paper close to his face, and moved his lips as he read. A few words into the document and his face went pale.

"They b-burned the p-president's residence and sacked the Capitol Building. That's outrageous. How could they do such a thing?"

As angry as he felt, Hoskins couldn't keep from smiling at the young man's reaction. He looked as if he was about to burst into tears.

"Well, in ancient times, it was common practice to sack your enemy's capital," he said. "We don't do it so much these days."

"Why would they d-do such a terrible thing?"

"You forget, son, our boys burned York up in Canada. I reckon the British feel it's only fair they burn us back. Besides, that's now what I was fuming about."

"No? What then?"

"Look at the date, boy, look at the date."

When he held the paper close again, his eyes got as round as small tea saucers.

"Oh, my goodness, this happened in August, and we're just hearing it in October."

"Hell, boy, for all we know, the war could be over already. How are we supposed to represent our country's interests when it takes so long for us to get information about what's going on back home is beyond me."

The secretary shrugged. "But, what are we to do, sir? The only way to send and receive messages is by ship. We're better off than our missions in Europe. Think how long it takes for a message to get to them."

"I suppose you're right. Here, give that back to me. I need to read it closely and see if there's anything there that impacts on us down here—other than the possibility that we might lose this damn war, that is."

After handing the paper back, the secretary scurried out. Hoskins chuckled, and began reading.

The report from the chief of the State Department's chief of consular services was short and written in a painstakingly precise hand:

From: Chief of Consular Services
Department of State
Washington City
To: All Consul General and Consuls
Subject: British Attack on Washington

On August 24 of the year of our Lord, 1814, British Forces landed near Bladensburg, Maryland, and after defeating our forces stationed there, marched on Washington City.

After occupying the city, this invading force embarked upon a campaign of burning and looting and terrorizing the good citizens of the capital city. Buildings damaged or destroyed include, the Presidential Mansion, the Capital, the Treasury, and the War Departments. The Washington Navy Yard was completely destroyed, and the offices of the Washington Intelligencer were dismantled.

The city was set ablaze, and but for the timely and Divine intervention of heavy thunderstorm on August 25 prevented the total destruction of the city, and a tornado sent by the Almighty, though it also killed several citizens, killed many British soldiers, as did an explosion of powder at Fort McNair.

The British occupied Washington City for a day, but, their losses and the storm damage to their ships forced them to withdraw. They are reported to be moving toward the port city of Baltimore.

More to follow.
Yours Respectfully

The dispatch was brief, and told him little, but raised many questions in his mind. For example, how many casualties, what happened in Baltimore, and the like. He knew, though, that each letter to the 60 American consular posts worldwide had to be laboriously drafted by hand, which could take several hours per letter, and with only nine senior officials—including the secretary of state—and a small number of clerks, in the aftermath of the attack he was lucky that anything had been sent.

He noticed, though, that included with the dispatch were a number of newspaper clippings reporting on the British attacks, although, whoever had done the clipping had neglected to identify from which paper they'd been taken.

WASHINGTON CITY SACKED

British armed forces under the command of the brutish General Robert Ross, after savaging American troops at Bladensburg, Maryland on August 24, in the late afternoon, entered the capital, Washington City.

The undisciplined hordes sacked and burned the Capitol, the President's Mansion, Treasury, and several other government buildings in an outrageous act of barbarity.

The offices of our sister paper, *The*

Short on details and long on emotional rhetoric, that article, Hoskins thought, was sure to arouse the ire of the fence-sitting northeasterners. The next article, though, raised his hopes.

Baltimore's defenses hold against English onslaught. Fort McHenry still stands

After looting and burning the capital, English forces moved north to attack the city of Baltimore.

At dawn on September 13, English warships began a bombardment of Fort McHenry, at the mouth of Baltimore Harbor. Despite the intense rain of rockets and cannon fire for more than 25 hours, the fort's flag remained aloft, and finally, unable to penetrate the city's defenses, the cowardly English put their tails between their legs and ran away. Without naval support, General Ross's army was forced to abandon plans for an invasion of the city.

Hoskins could imagine the fuming and gnashing of teeth in London when these articles were read, while in many parts of his homeland, there would be jubilant celebration.

"Dang, maybe we can win this war yet," he muttered. "Of course, that'll depend on whether or not we can repulse an invasion from the south, which I know is coming. Colin Worth, wherever you are, and whatever you're doing, may the fates look kindly upon you."

Carefully, he folded and stacked the papers and called his secretary in to take and file them.

Charles Ray

Chapter 36

November 1814, Cat Island

It seemed that Colin was making the trip from Skull Island to Cat Island at Mama Lillie's request more and more during the months of October and November. He mumbled to himself as the mule cart carried him over the bumpy streets to her café, wondering what was so urgent that she would summon him back for the third time in the same month.

When he entered her café, the first thing he noticed was that she looked worried. The ache in his back from being jostled around in the mule cart was forgotten.

"Mama Lillie, you look like someone stole your gumbo recipe. What's so urgent that you needed to see me again so soon this month?"

"Oh, *mon cher*, please, come with me to the private dining room."

That seemed unnecessary as there was no one else in the place except the woman she had helping her with the place, who was in the kitchen standing over a pot of something that smelled delicious. He didn't argue, though. Mama Lillie wasn't usually one to over dramatize things. If she was worried, he too was worried. He followed her waddling form.

Once inside the room, she closed the door and went to the table in the center, beckoning him to come close.

"Okay, I doubt anyone's listening," he said. "Now, what's your news?"

"You know, *cher*, that *les anglais* failed in their attack on Baltimore?"

"Yes, that word filtered even to our little backwater. It appears that our forces are finally getting some spine. I hear that the fort guarding the city withstood a 24-hour naval bombardment, and when the English ran out of ammunition, they simply withdrew."

"*Vraiment, cher*. The ships and the army troops all left, except for a few who are raiding small coastal villages. Do you know where they are coming?"

"I think you mean going, but, no, that was not part of the news that we received."

"Here, *cher*, they are all coming here to the islands."

"That makes sense. They're preparing for a move in the south. It appears that we must step up our raids if we're to distract them."

"*Oui*, my people are hearing that they plan to send an army and some ships to attack New Orleans, but, that is not all they plan to do."

Now, she had his attention. What else besides the southern attack could the British be up to? He had a sinking feeling that he knew but wanted to hear it from her.

"What else do they have on their sly, evil little minds?"

"This man who works for the governor, Brice, is obsessed with finding you and Elizabeth. I am told that they have promised him one hundred soldiers and five ships to find and destroy you."

But for the details, it was as he'd suspected.

"That's what we've been trying to do, and it looks like we've partially succeeded. Now, if I could only think of a way to get them to divert even more ships and men."

Lillie shook her head. "I do not understand you, *cher*. Did you not hear what I have just said? They are coming after you and my precious Elizabeth."

"Oh, don't worry your head. We can handle five ships and a hundred redcoats. You know, we have three capable ships and nearly two hundred able-bodied and armed men. I'll put my men up against the damn British any day of the week. A hundred soldiers . . . we'll have them for supper."

She grabbed his arm. "I think you are, how you say, hard-headed and fool hardy, but you seem very sure of yourself. Just do not let anything bad happen to *ma petite Elisabeth*. If she is harmed, I will hold you responsible."

Colin laughed. The idea of someone having to look after Elizabeth Parker, master of *The Vixen* and scourge of the Caribbean, was funny. If anything, she would be looking after him. But, the steely gaze that Lillie skewered him with left no room for wit.

"I will, Mama Lillie, I promise. As long as there is breath in my body, I will be there to protect her."

She stretched up and kissed his cheek.

"I know you will, and not because of me. I have seen the way you look at her. Go well, *cher*, and how do you *americains* say it. give them the hell."

He kissed her back and took his leave. Hell was exactly what he planned to visit upon his enemies.

Charles Ray

Chapter 37

Skull Island

When he arrived back at Skull Island, Colin called for an emergency meeting with Elizabeth, M'nondo, Garcia, and O'Reilly.

They gathered around the large table in the front room of the big house.

After the serving woman had placed plates of food and mugs of rum in front of them and left, Elizabeth lifted her mug and held it toward Colin.

"Welcome back sojourner," she said, smiling at the uncomfortable look on Colin's face. "What delightful news do you bring back from this trip?"

He took a long drink of rum, wiped his mouth with the back of his hand, and gave them the depressing news that Mama Lillie had given him.

"So," M'nondo said. "The English did not do well in their attempt to take the city of Baltimore, and they have turned their attention to the south . . . and to us. Is that not what we wanted them to do?"

"We wanted them to pay attention to us so it would relieve the pressure on our forces in the north. True, they are doing that, but, and pardon me for saying this, it would be better if they diverted more forces toward us rather than the south."

Garcia shook his head. "I suppose we could take the hundred *soldados*, but I am not so sure that our three ships can do well against five of their war vessels. Five to three is not good odds."

"Not if we go head to head with them," Colin said. "But, if we do the unexpected we have a chance. I think we should treat them like cattle."

"I do not understand," Garcia said, looking puzzled.

"When you raise cattle, and you need to deal with one of the herd, you don't wade into the herd, you cut that animal out of the herd. The English tend to like ship to ship battles, and conventional tactics. If we confuse them it'll take some time for them to adjust. In the meantime, we can even up the odds with the ships by destroying them one at a time."

Garcia still looked puzzled. "I have never worked with the cattle. You will have to explain it to me."

"Well, I've never worked with them either, but I know a few southern cattlemen, and I've heard them talking about it. Let me think on it for a while and I'll come up with a plan. There is one other thing we must do, though, and you're not going to like it."

"What is that?" Elizabeth asked.

"We can't be sure they haven't figured out our general location, and if they attack us here, there are too many innocents who could be hurt. I think we should move."

She looked as puzzled as Garcia had at the cattle issue. "Move where? One island is as vulnerable as another."

"I wasn't thinking of moving to another island. I think we should move aboard our ships. Keep on the move, stopping only for provisions and an occasional chance to regain our land legs. A moving target is not only hard to hit, it's hard to find."

Elizabeth put a finger on the side of her nose. "Well, we have lived aboard ship for weeks at a time when the authorities were putting too much pressure on. I suppose we could do it, but what about the wives?"

"We send them back to Lost Island. If the English find that place, they'll find nothing but women, children and elderly. If they come here, they'll only find Chief Kojomo and his people, and I don't think either group will give us away. But, even if they were pressured into talking, they won't know where we are at any time—only that we sailed away."

Elizabeth laughed. "Colin Worth, you come up with some of the most audacious plans. Are you sure you're not really a pirate disguised as a navy officer?"

Charles Ray

Chapter 38

December 1814, In the Atlantic Ocean, east of the Bahamas

Their three ships, *The Vixen, Avenger,* and *Hellhound,* honed their operations during the waning days of the month of November, and during the first two weeks of December were known throughout the Caribbean. Even other pirates and privateers gave them a wide berth, for it was known that the captains of this wolf pack didn't like sharing their territory—or so the stories around the docks went.

This meant, though, that the British efforts to find them intensified, raising the level of stress on each vessel, sometimes to the breaking point. Each captain had to discipline men for fighting on more than one occasion, especially during the four-day period when they didn't spot a single vessel.

They were sailing northward in what Colin called the spearhead formation, or goose flight, with *The Vixen* at the tip, *Avenger* on the starboard wing, and *Hellhound* at port, keeping a quarter mile between each ship, enough distance to make it difficult for a squadron of naval vessels to engage more than one of them at a time, but close enough for each to come to the others' aid if necessary. They were exchanging signals among the vessels using the Leyden-powered signal lanterns that Colin had fabricated, routine

messages just to keep in touch and, Colin hoped,
divert the crew's attention from the boredom of
nothing to do but keep the ship on course.

Hellhound: Oatmeal supply running low. Willing to
trade rum.
The Vixen: Have two extra hogsheads of oatmeal.
Six casks of rum?
Avenger: We will give eight casks of rum.
The Vixen: Avenger, do not upset the market.
Avenger: It is a free market.
Hellhound: Ships off port bow heading south.
Avenger: How many? English or American?
Hellhound: Six. Too big to be American, must be
English.
The Vixen: Do we engage?
Avenger: No, follow and see where they go.

They changed course, running parallel to the six
British warships far off to the port side of the
formation, changing to a file with *Avenger* leading,
Hellhound in the center, and *The Vixen* at the end, with
spyglasses trained on the enemy vessels which seemed
unaware that they'd been sighted.

They dogged the six ships for the rest of the day,
sailing southward as merchant ships bound for the
Bahamas would, never coming too close, but not
moving away. *The Vixen*, with her black-timber hull,
stayed farther away than the other two, fearing that
someone aboard one of the ships would have heard of
the feared black pirate ship, but the other two were
able to occasionally wander close, having English
ships originally, and Colin had had the foresight to
keep the ensigns they flew at the time of capture,
which were now flapping in the southerly breeze.

He'd given strict orders; other than the normal
gawking at naval vessels that would be expected of
merchant seamen, no special attention was to be paid

to the ships. Now and then, he would sweep each of them with his spyglass when they came within his range, and what he saw confirmed what he'd suspected when they were first sighted. Four of the six were troop ships, with hundreds of English soldiers in their easy-to-spot red uniform coats lounging about on the decks, their muskets stacked nearby. He assumed them to be the troops who had attacked and burned Washington City, and the ships part of the armada that had failed in its attempt to attack the port of Baltimore.

He had a small chart of the area nearby, and as he estimated their course, he marked it on the chart. If his measurements were correct, these ships weren't bound for Nassau. It's possible, he thought, that they would land at one of the other islands, but his gut told him the Bahamas, except for a possible stop to replenish supplies, was not their final destination. These forces were bound for New Orleans.

Whether they were the entire invasion force, he didn't know, but doubted it. Nevertheless, he would do all within his power to see that this group never reached the Gulf.

Charles Ray

Chapter 39

Government House, Nassau

"I am sorry, Mr. Brice," the ruffled-looking navy captain said. "But, my orders were explicit. You are to be given five ships and three platoons of Royal Marines. That should be more than sufficient to deal with a band of bloody pirates."

"Captain," the long-suffering, just about at the end of his patience Brice said. "You don't know these pirates. They have three ships, with a crew of about 300 to 350 bloodthirsty, capable fighters aboard. Unlike our navy, every man on a pirate ship is a fighter."

"You've been out here too long, sir, if you think any five pirates is worth a single marine."

Brice shook his head. "We can agree to disagree, sir," he said. "I still think the force you're giving me is not even half of what's needed to do the job properly."

"Well, if you'll just be patient, we have someone coming in who will give you some information that might be of assistance."

"I do not need information, I need fighters." Brice's face was turning red.

The two men's attention was diverted to the door of the captain's office which opened with a bang.

Brice could only describe the figure that came through the door as a creature, a mad creature at that.

The man wore a long, black great coat and a bowler hat over unkempt hair, and his facial hair looked like it had been applied to his face by an insane swallow. Bits of food and flecks of tobacco clung to the wiry hairs. He glared at the two men with bloodshot eyes. Brice tensed, expecting a confrontation of some kind, but the captain smiled and offered his hand to the newcomer.

"Welcome, sir," he said. "You must be the gentleman Admiral Kensington told us about."

"That I am, sirrah," the man said in a gravelly voice. "Beauregard Dangerfield, formerly *Captain* Beauregard Dangerfield, late of the United States Navy, at your service."

Brice's mouth dropped open. So, this was the admiral's American spy. Like Macintosh, he looked dangerous, but not in a controlled, calculating way, more like a deranged maniac who might go berserk at any moment.

"This is Mr. Alwyn Brice, the governor's private secretary," the captain said. "It is his task to find and rid us of these pirates who have been disrupting operations. I understand from the admiral that you have information that might help in that endeavor."

Dangerfield smiled, showing crooked, tobacco-stained teeth. "That I do, sir, that I do." He looked at Brice with an expression that said he was not impressed; a feeling that was reciprocated on Brice's part. "Well, Mr. Brice, shall we retire to some place private? I have a story to tell you that I think you'll find quite interesting."

"Yes, Mr. Brice, you should take him to your office," the captain said.

"Before I go, captain, I think you lads should know that the defenses at New Orleans are nothing like they were in Baltimore. There's no Fort McHenry to block your passage, and the forces on the ground are ill-trained and poorly equipped. Andy Jackson, though he be a fearsome Indian fighter, is reduced to using Indians, slaves, and even pirates to defend the city."

"Does he not have regular forces under his command?"

"A few, but most are militia from Mississippi and Louisiana. All told, he won't have 5,000 men under arms."

The captain smiled. "Admiral Cochrane and General Pakenham will have over 14,000 of His Majesty's finest. As long as the Americans don't have warships to impede their passage, it will be a slaughter."

"Don't worry about that, captain," Dangerfield said. "Other than the pirate ships, there won't be anything of any size. A few small gunboats, and they'll be operating mostly in the river. I think your ships of the line will have no problems with them."

"Very good, Captain Dangerfield, very good. That is information the admiral will apprcciatc rccciving."

"Now, lad," Dangerfield said to Brice. "Let us retire to your office, and I'll tell you about these pirates you're after."

Charles Ray

Chapter 40

Unnamed island east of Nassau

They ran parallel to the English ships until they were certain of their destination, one of the ports on an island near Nassau, but not the main port. This made sense to Colin. If they were planning an invasion, the fewer people who were aware of their activities the more secure the plan would be. He had no doubt, though, that the main planning was taking place at the colonial government headquarters in Nassau.

A hundred miles north of Nassau, he signaled the other ships a change of course, to the southeast toward a string of jungle-covered islands, some no larger than a half-mile across, but many with inland coves where they could drop anchor and let the men off the ships for a few hours, while the commanders conferred. They found one that was ideal. Unnamed, and uninhabited except for monkeys and jungle birds, and well off the usual trade routes, they could rest undisturbed.

They sat in a circle on the soft earth under the towering trees at the edge of the beach; Colin, Elizabeth, Garcia, M'nondo, and O'Reilly.

Colin let silence linger in the air for a while before speaking, because he knew that when he told them what he had in mind to do, the discussion would get loud and lively.

Finally, when the uncomfortable expressions at the silence reached a peak, he cleared his throat for attention.

"I think it's safe to say that the ships and troops we saw today are intended for an invasion of New Orleans," he said. "And, we have to do something to disrupt their plans."

"What more can we do?" Garcia asked. "We raid every merchant ship we find, and they just keep coming."

"Maybe it's time we hit them where it will really get their attention," Colin said.

"You mean like attacking London or something?" O'Reilly, new to the command group, looked and sounded like a first-time sailor, a little groggy and unsure of himself.

"Something like that." Colin smiled. "Their headquarters out here is Nassau. If we attacked something there, maybe even a military or government target, that would get their attention."

It took a few seconds for the import of his words to sink in, but when they did, the outburst was much as he'd anticipated. Among the phrases launched, 'are you out of your mind?', and 'that would be suicide', were the least profane. He let the furor swirl around him until it looked like everyone, except Elizabeth who remained quiet like a mountain in a storm throughout, had run out of steam. Then, he raised his hand for quiet.

"I know it sounds crazy," he said. "But, think about it. Nassau is the last place they expect us to operate. Like you, they probably think only a crazy man would do such a thing, therefore, they are not prepared for it."

The incredulous looks softened with the commonsense of his words.

Elizabeth finally spoke, "While I can understand how you all feel about this, after all, we are pirates, we operate best at sea, what Colin says has some merit. It is also not without precedent. There have been pirate raids on villages in the past."

"Nassau is hardly a village," Garcia said.

"You know what I mean, Diego."

"Besides," Colin said. "I didn't mean that we would attack in the central part of the city, or the government house, for example. Maybe some military outpost outside the city. Just close enough to make them think they might be next. Maybe even the harbor. Damaging military vessels moored there would really get their attention."

"It is not a *bad* idea," M'nondo said.

"But," Colin said before he could say more. "It needs a carefully thought out plan. I know. That's why I plan to do a thorough reconnaissance of Nassau before we do anything else."

"I should go with you," M'nondo said. "Two sets of eyes are better than one."

"I was going to ask you to come along," Colin said.

Charles Ray

Chapter 41

Nassau

Two days later, Colin and M'nondo were sneaked ashore northeast of Nassau in one of *Avenger's* boats, while the ship lay off the coast two miles. Colin's instructions were for the boat to meet them back at the same spot two days later, which should, he figured, give him and M'nondo sufficient time to get the general layout of the area and select possible targets for attack.

They decided to walk into town instead of hiring a donkey cart to avoid drawing more attention to themselves than necessary. Not that a tall, muscular black man and a white man, almost as tall, but not quite as muscular, but who walked with a distinct military bearing no matter how much he tried to adopt the shuffling gait of the pirates, didn't draw attention. But, fortunately, that attention came mostly from the young women working in the shops or fields.

They entered the city and made their way to the docks, a good starting point to find targets and obtain information about what was going on in the city. On the way to the docks they passed near government house. The presence of Royal Marine guards at the gate and entrance doors confirmed for Colin that high level officials were in residence. He would have liked nothing more than to attack government house when many bigwigs were there, just to rattle the English, but knew that such a mission, even with the fighting prowess of the pirates, would be suicidal.

At the last corner before entering the docks, Colin saw two men walking ahead of them, a tall, familiar looking figure leaning over and talking to the shorter man who walked with him. There was something about the way the tall man walked and waved his hands when he spoke that stirred a memory. Then, the man turned his face to the side to say something, and Colin stopped short, grabbing M'nondo's arm.

"Holy jumping Jehoshaphat, that's captain, or former captain, Dangerfield up there, and I think I recognize the man he's talking to. He's one of the English colonial officials."

M'nondo's eyes narrow to slits as he looked in the direction Colin was pointing. "You are correct," he said. "The short man matches the description of a man named Brice who works for the governor-general. What is your former captain doing here talking to him?"

In a flash of insight, Colin *knew*. "He must be the American cousin referred to in the letters we seized from that courier ship. I'll be double damned if Dangerfield's not a spy for the bloody English."

"They must be paying him a lot to get him to betray his country."

Colin shook his head. "Not all traitors do it for the gold, my friend," he said. "During our war for independence, Brigadier General Benedict Arnold defected to the British side in a fit of pique, mainly because the Continental Congress passed him over for promotion. He planned to give the fortifications at West Point, New York to the English, but thankfully his plan was discovered before he could carry it out." He pointed at Dangerfield. "Beauregard Dangerfield was relieved of his command and cashiered out of the navy for incompetence. He was an angry, demented man before that, and I imagine that since then his anger has only intensified."

"What do we do about him?"

"I'd like nothing more than to run up and drive my sword into his treacherous heart, but we have more important things to do now. Afterwards, well, we shall see."

Charles Ray

Chapter 42

In the Atlantic Ocean, northeast of Nassau

While Colin and M'nondo did their reconnaissance in Nassau, the three ships, under Elizabeth's overall command, sailed to a point near the shipping lanes a hundred miles northeast of Nassau. The plan that she and Colin had agreed to was that they would create havoc in that area to draw British attention away from Nassau, thus enabling them to identify and attack a target, which should create additional panic and confusion.

Four hours into the voyage, in the middle of the afternoon, the lookout on *Avenger* spotted two sets of sails on the horizon, and the news was transmitted to the other two ships.

They went into a spearhead formation, with *Avenger* as the tip of the spear, *Hellhound* at port, and *The Vixen* at starboard, with an eighth of a mile between them. Elizabeth signaled that they would swing east and run parallel to the two vessels until dark, and then swoop in and attack them under cover of darkness.

When Colin first introduced his Leyden lanterns, she had been skeptical, but the devices had worked so well in their first few concentrations, she had become a disciple. The looks on the faces of startled deck crews when the night was suddenly lit up, and they were staring at tiny suns bobbing along beside their ships was priceless. It also enabled them to take control of most vessels without a shot being fired, beyond the obligatory one across the bow which was a universal call to either surrender or fight.

"Signalman, tell the other ships to make sure boarding crews are fed and rested," she said to the man, no more than a boy really, who operated the signal lantern on *The Vixen*. "And then pass the word to the crew on board this ship."

"Aye, cap'n," the boy said, and he trotted to the station near the quarterdeck rail and began flipping the cover on the lantern.

Elizabeth knew that there was a chance that someone on one of the ships they followed might notice the regular flashes of the lantern, but they were far enough back that, if spotted, it might be mistaken for sunlight glinting on the ocean's surface. At night, they used dark shields on the sides to block peripheral light, making it necessary to be in a direct line to see, thus minimizing the danger of being spotted. Even so, she thought, knowing how superstitious most seamen were, anyone seeing flashing lights at night was likely to attribute them to some demon of the sea.

Once his messages had been sent and acknowledged by both vessels, the boy trotted down to the main deck to relay the information on *The Vixen*.

With five hours until sunset, activity on *The Vixen* settled into a relatively quiet routine. Those of the crew not assigned to man the sails, lounged around the deck, playing cards, or just napping. For Elizabeth this was always the hardest part. She liked the action and excitement of the attack and boarding, but the sometimes long wait times for the ideal moment to strike chafed and tested her patience. Unlike Colin and M'nondo, so different in appearance, but almost identical in personality, who could stand in the same position on the quarterdeck for hours with nothing moving but their eyes, she needed to always be on the move.

So now, she left the helmsman and her first mate in charge of the quarterdeck and went down to the main deck where she wandered from group to group, man to man, chatting about their families, joining in the occasional card game, and just letting out her excess energy, and calming herself for the action to come.

The hours went by slowly, much too slowly for Elizabeth's liking, but finally, the sun sank below the western horizon, the sky turned a deep purple, with a few wispy clouds illuminated by the half moon. She went back to the quarterdeck.

"Are those two ships still in sight?" she asked the helmsman.

"Aye, cap'n," he said. "And since it started to get dark, they been kind enough to light lanterns to make it easier for us to see 'em."

"Good. Douse all lights," she commanded in a loud voice. To the signalman, she said, "Tell the other ships to run in closer, and head straight for the nearest ship."

"Aye, ma'am."

And, the chase was on. Like a pack of hounds that have caught fox scent, the three ships came in close together, a few hundred yards apart, and bore straight at their prey.

Running dark, they were invisible to the two merchant ships, wallowing galleons that rode low in the water, until *Avenger* came alongside the slower one and had the Leyden lantern turned on, lighting up the galleon's main deck and turning night suddenly into day.

The sailors aboard the vessel, stunned by the sudden bright light in their eyes, stood transfixed for precious seconds as *Avenger* closed the gap between them enough to allow a boarding party to swing across on ropes affixed to the yard arms. Within minutes, twenty pirates, armed with pistols and cutlasses, were rounding up the officers and crew of the hapless vessel. Elizabeth had a signal sent to *Hellhound*, 'Let *Avenger* take care of this one. We go after the other.'

Sailing in close formation, full sails to take advantage of every breath of wind, *The Vixen* and *Hellhound* took up the chase after the lead galleon, sailing along, unaware of the drama playing out less than an eighth of a mile behind her.

They covered the distance quickly, with Elizabeth taking her ship to port while *Hellhound* moved to starboard, sandwiching the hapless ship between them.

Both ships turned on their lanterns at the same time, hitting the crew of the galleon with bright lights no matter which direction they turned. There was a flurry of activity as several men made a dash for the two cannons on each side of the galleon, but a few well-placed shots from the snipers in *The Vixen* and *Hellhound's* top masts.

"Gentlemen," Elizabeth yelled across to the galleon. "You are surrounded and outgunned. You can yield, or you can die. The choice is yours."

There was a moment's hesitation, and then, in a wise move, the captain of the galleon called back, "We yield. I demand that you not hurt anyone."

"You, sir, or in no position to make demands," Elizabeth said. "But, for your information, we will not hurt anyone who offers no resistance. Gather your crew on the main deck and cooperate with the men who will be coming aboard."

Securing the ship took about thirty minutes. They put the officers and men in ship's boats and put them overboard, telling them to row south for about fifty miles and they would reach land and safety. Then, they took portable items; rations, rum, ammunition, and muskets; aboard their ships, set fire to the galleon, and sailed away.

Chapter 43

January 1815, Nassau

Colin and M'nondo were picked up on schedule after their reconnaissance, and they sailed to a small island chain south of Nassau where he outlined his plans for an operation in Nassau.

Colin squatted in the sand up on the beach, surrounded by as many of the crew of the three ships as could push their way in to see, and, with a twig, began drawing in the sand.

"Just south of town there's a magazine," he said. "It looks like they keep powder for cannons there, but it's not the main munitions storage point. There are four guards, so it won't be a difficult target."

"We gonna steal the powder?" a voice from the crowd asked.

Colin looked up, smiling wolfishly, and shook his head. "No, my friend, we are not. Stealing it would get their attention, but I don't want to just get their attention. I want to strike fear into their hearts and infuriate them. Nothing like a nice powder explosion to achieve both aims."

The cheering that erupted was deafening.

He asked for twenty volunteers, and then had to explain to all those who he didn't select that they would be busy with Elizabeth attacking ships to divert

English so the raid could take place without anyone in Nassau knowing. "As for you men I've selected, I'll explain the operation while we sail for Nassau. Now, get your gear and let's go."

Once aboard *Avenger,* and underway, Colin began briefing the twenty men, sitting in a loose circle on the main deck, on their mission.

"We'll have to infiltrate the area in small groups," he said. "A large group like this can't travel together without drawing unwanted attention. We'll move under cover of darkness, and attack the magazine just before dawn, which is the time when the guards are likely to be less alert."

"How many groups you figurin' on there bein', cap'n?" a muscular, gap-toothed man near Colin asked.

"There will be twenty-one of us, so I'm thinking three groups of five and one of six. Hopefully that size group will just be seen as a bunch of sailors out carousing."

"That will be two groups of five, and two of six," M'nondo said.

"But, you should remain here to command the ship," Colin said.

"Every man here can command this ship." M'nondo folded his arms across his massive chest. "One of the jobs of a first mate is to protect the captain, so where you go, I go."

Colin cocked his head to one side and closed an eye. M'nondo leaned in close. "Besides," he said in a voice just above a whisper. "If I let anything happen to you, my little sister would kill me."

The two men laughed.

"Okay, that's it, then," Colin said. "Two groups of six, two groups of five."

He then drew a detailed sketch, showing the routes around or through the town, the location of the powder magazine, and suggested routes to get back to the cove where he planned to anchor the ship.

"Any questions so far?" he asked.

The same gap-toothed man raised his hand. Colin nodded at him.

"You say there by four guards at the magazine? How we gonna get in to blow the place up without making noise?"

"Good question. I want eight of you to sneak in and disarm the guards at the gate, as quietly as you can. The other two guards are just inside the entrance to the bunker, so we should be able to get them without much problem."

The gap-tooth man drew his index finger across his throat. "Aye, we can take them quietly, can't we lads?"

General laughter greeted his bloodthirsty gesture. Colin winced. He wasn't averse to killing in battle, for that was a warrior's duty, but this seemed so sordid, sneaking up on unsuspecting men and killing them. He pinched the bridge of his nose and sighed. *War*, he thought, *calls upon us to do extraordinary things, and treat them as ordinary.*

"Okay, then," he said. "Get some rest, for we have a busy night ahead of us, and it goes without saying that there will be no drinking of spirits until after this operation is over . . . am I clear on that?"

"Aye, cap'n, clear as a sunny day, but there'll be no limits on the rum afterwards, right?"

"Once we're safely back onboard *Avenger,* you can drink until it's pouring out of your ears."

The men cheered loudly. Colin smiled and shrugged. What an assemblage of humanity. They appeared to be as anxious to undertake a mission without loot as an objective as they would be to board a fat merchant ship. Then, it hit him like a kick to the stomach; they were doing this because of him. They were willing to follow him anywhere, and risk dying on his behalf. *Oh, Lord, please don't let me fail this.*

They ate an early supper, and just as the sun was sinking below the horizon, they anchored in a secluded bay an hour's walk north of Nassau. The men assembled in their designated teams, accepted the good wishes of their shipmates remaining with the vessel, and set out. Colin's group led the way, but at the outskirts of the city, where the small farms thinned out, giving way to merchants, tradesmen, and small vegetable gardens around humble wooden huts, they separated, each group taking a predesignated route to the target.

Their transit through Nassau was without incident, save for a group of three bawdy ladies who saw Colin's group as potential customers, and dogged them for nearly ten minutes, cursing and importuning them.

It was shortly after midnight when the last group of five men arrived at the assembly point on a slight rise just north of the powder magazine, from which they were concealed by scrub brush, but had a clear view of the magazine.

As Colin had expected, the two sentries at the gate, probably on duty since around eight in the evening, were swaying at their posts, fighting to stay awake. In another few hours, they would be asleep on their feet.

He decided to assign the duty of silencing the guards to the last team to arrive. The wicked smiles on their faces when he informed them, though, made it clear that they didn't think of the duty assignment as any kind of punishment for their tardiness.

The five men selected moved forward and soon were swallowed up in the dark shadows of the brush that grew around the installation. Colin kept an eye on the two guards, now engaged in conversation with each other, possibly discussing some mundane subject in an effort to keep each other awake. At first, he missed it; a movement in the shadows to the right of the guards. Then, the shadow resolved itself into the shapes of two men, running swiftly but quietly toward the guards. The guard on the left was the first to notice, but as he started to raise his musket, three shapes sprang out of the shadows behind him.

It was over almost before it had begun. One moment the two guards were in an animated conversation, and the next, they lay bleeding and lifeless with five smiling pirates standing over them. One of the pirates looked in Colin's direction and raised a bloody knife.

Colin looked at M'nondo. "Very efficient, aren't they? Well, let's move out."

M'nondo only grunted. He rose and the entire group, with Colin and M'nondo in the lead, began jogging toward the magazine.

By the time they arrived, the bodies of the two guards had been dragged into the bush, and their assassins were wiping their bloody blades on their leggings.

"That quiet enough for ye, cap'n?" one asked.

Colin winced, but managed a wan smile. "Very well done," he said. "Now, let's take care of the two sentries inside and set the charges."

The two interior guards were even sloppier than their dead comrades. They were inside a small hut with the door swung wide open, kneeling on the floor playing some kind of game with polished pebbles. They were never even aware of the intruders until two knife blades appeared at their throats, and that awareness lasted only long enough for those blades to slice across their Adam's apples, opening an obscene gash in their throats from which bright red blood spurted. Their killers let the bodies slump to the dirt floor of the hut and came out to rejoin the others.

Colin's plan to destroy the magazine was simple. He would use its contents to do the job. The magazine itself was a log-lined cave carved into the low hillside. Inside, kegs of powder were stacked, four high in four long rows, twenty barrels deep, from back to front, just as he'd imagined it would be. Each time was assigned a row. Their job was to insert a length of oily rag in every other bottom barrel and light it. The rags would burn slow, giving them enough time to set and ignite them all, and then get out of the bunker.

The job was completed in under two minutes, and the first rags ignited had burned almost down to the powder by the time the last man scampered through the entrance of the magazine.

They ran as fast as they could but had just passed the front sentry post when the first barrel blew, followed in quick succession by others in a rumbling like thunder. The earth over the top of the bunker erupted in a spout of orange flame, white smoke and dark earth, sending rocks, dirt clods, splinters, and burning embers in all directions. The force of the explosion knocked them off their feet, but they quickly pushed up and kept running, some of them slapping at clothing set aflame by floating embers. The concussion had deafened them, and to Colin, the absence of sound was eerie. He could feel his boots slapping the hard earth but couldn't hear the sound. He knew that everyone around him, himself including, was breathing hard from the exertion of running and the excitement of being so nearly blown to bits, but couldn't hear, like being in a dream where you're falling, but can't hear or see anything.

They didn't stop running until they were a mile north of the magazine. Colin directed them into a grove of trees and called for a few minutes rest. Everyone collapsed where they stood, looking around in wonder that they'd survived. Mouths were moving, and eyes were wide as they realized that they were deaf.

After a few minutes, Colin could hear muffled sounds. He breathed a sigh of relief that he'd not been rendered permanently deaf. He looked at M'nondo, whose lips were moving, and slowly, words began to trickle into his ear, and then his brain.

". . . .go back to the ship now," M'nondo said.

Colin cupped his hands over his ears and blew a hard breath, feeling a popping sensation, and finally sounds came clearly to him.

"No, not quite yet," he said. "You take the men back. I have one more mission before leaving Nassau. I'll join you by the afternoon. If, however, I don't arrive before sunset, sail without me."

'No, Colin, my friend. You forget what I said. Where you go, I go. I know what this mission is, and I would be honored to assist you. I do not think it will be possible for one man to do it alone, but the two of us, just maybe." He turned to the others. "You men go to the ship and wait for us. As the captain said, if we are not back by sunset, leave and find Captain Parker."

"Any message for her if we have to do that?" one of the men asked.

M'nondo shook his head. "No, if we do not return, she will know what happened. Now, go."

Charles Ray

Chapter 44

Government House, Nassau

Brice and Dangerfield were working late in Brice's office, trying to develop a plan to use the few ships and men Brice had been given to hunt the pirates, when the powder magazine blew.

Dangerfield was just explaining that he was sure that the leader of the pirate operation was his former first officer, navy captain, Colin Worth, and that his knowledge of his former subordinate's way of thinking made it possible for them to prevail even with such a paucity of forces, when there was a muffled booming sound like thunder, and the building shook.

"What the— I didn't know you people had earthquakes out here," he said.

"We don't," Brice said. "At least, we've had none in all the years I've been here. That sounded like an explosion."

Brice got up and went outside. Dangerfield followed. On the front steps of Government House, they could see the orange glow to the south. The Royal Marine assigned sentry duty at the entrance stood at the edge of the entrance platform, staring in awe, his weapon held loosely at his side.

"Looks like something's burning," Dangerfield said.

"I can see that, captain. I wonder . . . oh, no, we have a powder storage facility in that general area. It can't be—"

Dangerfield laid a hand on his forearm. "I assure you, my good man, it *can* be. That's just the kind of thing Worth would do. Even when he was under my command, he had little regard for traditions or formality."

"B-but, to attack a government facility right here in the colonial capital. Why, that's mad. It's crazy. He can't think he'll get away with it. The soldiers and constabulary will descend on that place like a pack of hungry dogs."

"And, Worth won't be there. I assure you, he's a long way from that fire at this moment. Probably laughing his head off at sticking a finger in your eye like that."

"We'll see how much he laughs when they slip the rope over his neck." Brice was sputtering in rage, his fists clenched at his side so tightly the knuckles were as white as bleached whale bone.

"We have to catch him first, Mr. Brice, and that will not be easy I can see. The boy was always a bold one, but he seems to have grown quite a large pair since I last encountered him."

"A large pair of what?" Brice's anger was tempered by his confusion.

"Balls, man, the essence of manhood. I swear, we speak the same language, but it's not mutually understandable."

"Ah, I see. Well, let us put our heads together and see how we can cut those big ones off."

"Now, that's language I understand," Dangerfield said. "But, I get the pleasure of doing the snipping."

They turned and went back into Brice's office.

Brice sat behind his desk, while Dangerfield sat on a chair in front of the desk, with his leg draped over the arm. Brice was shuffling the stack of that day's dispatches, which he always read and annotated before sending them in to the governor.

Suddenly, he picked up a single sheet of foolscap and peered at it, his eyes wide. "My, my, this *is* interesting," he said.

"What is it?" Dangerfield feigned interest, but his main objective was to find and kill Colin Worth. Everything else was just a distraction, but he needed the little English popinjay in order to get what he wanted.

Brice held the paper up, his cheeks red, and a smile so broad it caused the muscles under his eyes to bunch up, giving him, in Dangerfield's eyes, the look of a chubby oriental.

"The treaty negotiations at Ghent have ended," Brice said.

"So, they couldn't come to agreement. No surprise there. Both sides were asking the impossible."

"No, you do not understand. The treaty was signed. On Christmas Eve of all days. As of December 24, 1814, the war is officially over, and things go back to where they were when it started."

Dangerfield snorted. "And, we're just now hearing this? Your General Pakenham is enroute to attack New Orleans. Do you think he's received this news?"

"I doubt it, but that means there will be no more ships or troops sent from here, which means more for us to use in our hunt for this pirate friend of yours."

"He's no friend of mine, but I take your point. So, when do we start looking for him?"

Brice opened his mouth to answer but was distracted by a thumping sound outside his office, and then the door crashed open, and two figures strode into the room.

At first, with the beard he'd grown and his hair down to his shoulders, Dangerfield didn't recognize Colin, but the tall, mahogany-colored man with legs like tree trunks and corded muscles in his arms was all too familiar. He'd seen him before, on a ship that was sailing away as he beheaded its former captain. That black devil who sailed with Jack Teague, he thought, but the other . . . "Oh, my Lord," Dangerfield said. "Colin Worth in the flesh." He turned to Brice. "Did I not say he would do the last thing you expect of him? He's come here to Government House to turn himself in to be hanged."

Colin held up the sword he carried, and M'nondo brandished his saber.

"Not really, captain," Colin said. "I expect to walk out of here in just a few minutes."

Brice looked from Colin to Dangerfield, sensing that what was taking place was private between them. He contemplated calling for help, but the black man waved the point of his saber under his nose and shook his head. He clamped his lips shut.

"So, tell me, Worth. How do you plan to get out of this building alive, and what did you come here for?" Dangerfield let his hand rest on the hilt of his sword.

"As to the first," Colin said. "My friend and I plan to leave the same way we came; through the front door. Oh, don't worry, the guard won't stop us. He's a bit tied up at the moment. We put him in the coat closet in the hall outside this office. He's sleeping peacefully, thanks to my friends sleeping medicine." M'nondo held up a fist the size of a small ham. "He'll have a bit of a headache when he wakes up, but at least, he'll wake up. Now, your second question; why am I here? Simple, captain. I came to kill a cowardly traitor."

Dangerfield laughed. "Really? So, you think you can take me with a blade, boy? I was using one of these when you were still shitting your nappies. Unless your friend there is planning to help you, you don't stand a chance."

Colin turned to M'nondo. "He's mine. Don't interfere, no matter what happens."

M'nondo grunted. Colin knew that there was a lot of meaning in that grunt. Mainly, that he wouldn't interfere as long as Colin lived and was winning the fight. But, if he lost . . . well, that would be Dangerfield's problem.

"Now, Captain Beauregard Dangerfield," Colin said. "I am not a fan of dueling, but I call you out as a coward and a traitor, and I challenge you to a duel, right here and right now. My friend, M'nondo, is my second. I assume this gentleman will stand for you?"

Dangerfield looked at Brice. "Well, Mr. Brice, you heard the young pup challenge me to a duel. Will you be my second?"

Brice bowed. "It would be my honor, sir."

Dangerfield drew his sword and moved into a classic sword fighter's stance, his left hand on his hip, right foot forward, with most of his weight on his left or trailing foot. He held his sword forward, tip of the blade angled toward Colin as he shuffled forward.

"Prepare to die, dog," he said.

Colin was not a classic sword fighter, and his time with the pirates had taught him that the only way to win a blade duel was to be forceful, fast, and furious.

He waved his blade tip around in a figure eight, took a half step back, and then lunged forward, swinging it, cutting edge forward to the left, aiming at Dangerfield's sword hand.

Thrown off balance by Colin's unorthodox maneuver, Dangerfield pulled back, but with the weight on his back foot, he was a fraction of a second too slow, and Colin's blade sliced his wrist. Not deep enough to hit a major blood vessel, but it took off a small patch of skin, hurting like the devil, and the capillary bleeding made his hand slippery.

Colin smiled and took a step backwards.

"Looks like I drew first blood, sir," he said.

"That, sir is because you do not fight like a gentleman," Dangerfield said through clenched teeth.

"I am *not* a gentleman, sir. I am a pirate."

"You are, were, an officer in the navy. You should fight like a gentleman."

"You, too, were an officer in the navy. You should not betray your country."

Dangerfield made a growling noise and thrust his sword forward, aiming at Colin's chest. But, when the blade tip arrived, Colin was no longer there. He'd pivoted left, causing the blade to slide past, nicking his shirt, and then, flipped his blade up and thrust upwards, the tip of his sword entering Dangerfield's throat and piercing his tongue. Dangerfield made a gurgling sound, as he jerked back, causing the wound in his throat to be enlarged as the blade was yanked out.

He opened his mouth, but instead of speech, blood bubbled out. His eyes rolled back in their sockets, and his lifeless fingers released his sword, which clattered to the floor.

He sank to the floor, first to his knees, and then pitched forward, face down on the polished wood floors, a dark pool of blood forming under his face.

Colin walked to the window and polished his blade on the curtain, and then turned to Brice, who stood, eyes wide, face ashen, quivering like a willow.

"D-do you plan to kill me, now?" he asked.

"No, I do not, sir," Colin said. "I do not kill unarmed men. I will, however, have to make sure you cannot give the alarm until we are well away."

"H-how will you do that?"

Brice was so focused on Colin wiping his bloody sword on his curtains, he didn't hear M'nondo come up behind him. He probably felt the hilt of M'nondo's saber when it hit the back of his head, for a fraction of a second before blackness descended on his world.

Colin looked at the two bodies on the floor, only one of which would be getting up on his own. As he walked past Brice's desk toward the door, he noticed the document Brice had been reading when he and M'nondo came in. He stopped and glanced at it.

"Well, well, what do we have here?" he said.

"What is it?"

"It's a letter from the Foreign Office in London to the governor, informing him that the treaty to end the war has been signed. The war is officially over since December 24th."

"So, no attack on New Orleans?"

"I hope not, but even if they do, according to this, everything goes back to the way it was the day the war started. If they do attack, it will be a wasted effort."

"So, that means our work is done."

"That's right, my friend," he said. "Our work here is done. Shall we go to the ship?"

Charles Ray

Chapter 45

Aboard *The Vixen,* southeast of Nassau

Once *Avenger* reunited with the other two ships, Colin called for a meeting of the captains aboard *The Vixen.* The three ships sailed in close convoy, heading generally southeast in the direction of Lost Island.

Colin, Elizabeth, and Garcia, along with what Colin had taken to calling their war council, M'nondo and O'Reilly, they sat around the small table in Elizabeth's cabin. The mood, after Colin announced the signing of the peace treaty in Ghent, Netherlands, was mixed.

"It's good that the war is finally over," Colin said. "But, this means the English here in the Caribbean are now free to deploy ships and soldiers to hunt for us. Life just got very, very dangerous for us."

"What do we do?" Garcia asked. "They have always tried to find us, but I think this time will be different."

Colin nodded. "In that, you're correct. We must assume that before I . . . that Dangerfield told them about us, and my history with you, so now they will know who they are looking for."

"We should not have left that Brice fellow alive," M'nondo said.

"In hindsight, you're probably correct, but I don't like killing an unarmed man."

"It doesn't matter," Elizabeth said. "If Dangerfield gave this Brice information, we must assume that he shared it with others in the governor's office, or with the military. So, Colin, what do you think will happen now?"

"I'm just speculating, but I think it's a good bet that the forces not sent south will come after us, and as you know, Dangerfield came close to finding your base on Lost Island last time."

Elizabeth's face contorted in shock. "That means our families could be in danger."

"Precisely," Colin said. "Our first priority now is to protect them, and the people of Skull Island. Don't forget, they helped us embarrass Dangerfield, and I doubt if he forgot it, so it's likely he also told Brice about Skull Island."

"How do we protect both?" Garcia asked.

During the escape from Nassau, Colin had been thinking on just that problem. He had in mind a solution, but he knew it wouldn't be popular. Nonetheless, he had to offer it. "The only way is to move the people from both islands, to some other remote place where the English might not think to look."

"There are hundreds of small islands all over the Caribbean," Elizabeth said. "And, with three ships, we could move everyone."

"But, Chief Kojomo and his people will not want to move," M'nondo said. "Skull Island is their home."

"I thought of that," Colin said. "But, we have to make the offer."

"So, how do we do this?" Elizabeth asked.

"I think that M'nondo and I should take *Avenger* to Skull Island, since he knows Chief Kojomo best. You and *Hellhound* should go to Lost Island and begin preparing the folks there to leave."

She looked sad. "Lost Island has been our home for so long. Many of our people will be as reluctant to leave as the people on Skull Island."

"Home," M'nondo said. "Is where you are with people who love and care for you. As long as we keep together, it will not matter where we go. If they stay, though, they will surely die. I know this in my heart."

Elizabeth put a hand on his arm. "I should take you with us. That speech would surely convince any who are reluctant to leave."

"You do not give yourself enough credit, little sister. The people stay on Lost Island because of you. If you say leave, they will also leave."

"I hate to interrupt such a touching moment," Colin said. "But, we really need to get moving if we're to pull this off before the English are swarming all over the place."

Elizabeth stood. "You are right. Will you come to Lost Island after talking to the chief?"

"If he refuses to leave his island, yes. But, if we must evacuate his village, we should plan a rendezvous somewhere far away from here."

"South of Haiti, in the Turks and Caicos Islands is a small island we hid on once," she said. "You remember, M'nondo?"

"Yes, it was Seal Cays, one of the southernmost islands in that chain," he said. "Very isolated, and unlikely that the English will think to look there, at least not for many weeks, while they look for us up here."

"Good, then we meet there." She held out a hand to Colin. "Good luck and be safe . . . both of you."

He took her hand in both of his and gazed into her eyes. "You, too . . . all of you, and your families. Stay safe until we meet again."

Charles Ray

Chapter 46

February 1814, Seal Cays, Turks and Caicos Islands

It took M'nondo and Colin two days of nonstop argument to convince Kojomo and his people that it was time to leave their island paradise because it was about to be invaded by many serpents who would bring nothing but death and destruction. Many of the young warriors protested, still drunk on the excitement of defeating Macintosh's raiders, but M'nondo reminded them that Royal Marines supported by ships of the line were not something that warriors with spears and arrows could prevail against.

"Better to walk away, and live to fight another day," he said. "A warrior must be wise as well as brave."

Every young man on the island knew of M'nondo's bravery and prowess as a fighter, so for him to suggest such a thing must, they thought, be the wise thing to do. When their chief agreed with the two visitors, the die was cast.

That led to the logistical nightmare of transporting 150 men, women, and children, with twenty goats, dozens of chickens, and five pigs aboard *Avenger*. It was done, but the voyage south, with the fitful ocean breezes unable to move the stench of so many people and animals in such close quarters.

Fifty miles south of Skull Island, they were hailed by a British frigate. Colin ordered the sails trimmed to reduce speed and aloe the frigate to come alongside. Colin and M'nondo, on the off chance that Brice had given their descriptions to the navy, crouched low to avoid being seen, and Colin quietly instructed the helmsman in what to say. An officer at the rail of the frigate, speaking through a horn, ordered them to stand to and allow a boarding party to inspect their vessel, but when a stray breeze blew the noxious fumes from *Avenger*, he decided that the helmsman's explanation that he was taking a group of refugee American slaves south to Brazil was sufficient, and warned them to keep their smelly ship out of the main shipping lanes. After that incident, Colin no longer minded the smell so much.

Finally, on the fifth day of February, M'nondo, standing on the quarterdeck next to Colin, pointed off the southeast.

"The island we seek is there," he said.

Seal Cays was little but a dark speck against the bright blue sky for a long time. Little by little, that speck resolved itself into a small mountain, the tip of a long-dormant volcano, covered in palm trees and other lush jungle growth, and fronted by a pearly white beach. *The Vixen* and *Hellhound* were anchored in the deep water a hundred yards offshore, and he could see dozens of figures standing near the surf watching them approach.

They dropped anchor near where the other two ships were anchored and began shuttling people and livestock to shore. The first group to arrive set off a raucous welcome, and soon, the beach was covered with people and animal, bleating, crying, laughing, hugging, and running around like children at the last session of the last day of school.

Colin strode toward Elizabeth, who stood at the edge of the melee watching everything with a motherly gaze. When she saw him coming, her eyes lit up and her mouth curved into a smile.

When he reached her, she fell into his arms.

"I see you were successful convincing the people of Skull Island to leave," she murmured against his shirt, and then, she sniffed and drew back. "But, you smell awful."

"That's what you smell like when you've been cooped on a small ship for days with all that livestock," he said. "Is there somewhere I can wash the stench off?"

"Yes. There's a little lagoon beyond that line of trees, a secluded place, and the water is the perfect temperature." She looked into his eyes. "Would you like me to scrub your back?"

He held her shoulders and looked back into her dark, inviting eyes. "Only if you'll let me scrub yours."

Charles Ray

Chapter 47

East of Haiti

Colin informed Elizabeth that he had urgent business in Cap Haitien, but would return as soon as it was concluded, but she insisted on traveling with him. So, instead of going as captain of his own ship, *Avenger*, he sailed as a passenger on *The Vixen*, one of his most enjoyable voyages, with most of his time spent in the captain's cabin with Elizabeth while O'Reilly, under M'nondo's watchful eye, commanded the ship.

He didn't tell anyone the nature of his visit until they moored in Cap Haitien's harbor. His announcement left the deck crew speechless, M'nondo smiling knowingly, and Elizabeth smothering his neck with kisses.

"Come now," he said. "None of you should be particularly surprised that I've decided to resign from the navy."

"I know I am not," M'nondo said.

"You be one of the best pirate ship captains I know," O'Reilly said. "With the exception of Captain Parker here, of course."

"But, you will be giving up a career that you have worked your whole life to build," Elizabeth said. "Will you not miss being with your navy comrades?"

He kissed the top of her head. "Maybe a little at first, but I have new comrades now, and if I leave the lot of you, I think I will miss you more, and longer. Besides, I have a new career in mind."

"Oh, and what is that?"

"Why, I plan to be your first mate, Captain Parker."

"But, you are captain of your own ship, both here and in your navy. Why would you wish to give that up to become my first mate?"

"I do not think that is the *mate* position that he is referring to," M'nondo said. He chuckled.

"Then . . . you mean, mate, as in—"

Colin took her hand, bowed over it, and kissed it softly. "That is correct, my dear captain. I wish to be your mate for life, to go where you go, and to grow old with you."

Elizabeth blinked. Her cheeks reddened. Her mouth opened, and then closed.

"I believe, little sister," M'nondo said. "The correct answer to the question that my brother Colin so clumsily did not ask is, 'yes,' unless you do not wish to be mated to him."

"M-mated . . . as in married? You wish to b-be my husband? I . . . you . . . oh, yes, I suppose we should. But, know this, Colin Worth, I will not be a subservient little woman, jumping to your every whim."

"I would not expect that of you, dear lady."

"And, I will *not* change my name. Elizabeth Parker I was born, and Elizabeth Parker I will die."

"I would have it no other way."

"Then, the answer is yes."

M'nondo snorted. "I prefer the way Chief Kojomo and his people do it. A young man goes to the father or elder brother of the woman he wants, and presents him with a goat or two pigs, and she is sent to his hut. The two of you have taken twice as long to get to the point as they would."

"It's called courtship, my friend," Colin said.

"Hmph, I call it a waste of time. Everyone here, but the two of you knew this day was coming. It was plain to see in your eyes. I had feared that I would lose my little sister when she went back to America with you, but instead, I have gained a brother. So, if that is how you Americans and English do it, so be it. When you jump the broom?"

"What?" Colin and Elizabeth asked in unison.

"The slaves on the plantation I escaped from had a ceremony when a man and woman decided to marry. They held hands and jumped over a broom to symbolize the joining and entering into a new relationship."

"Aye, and it was common in England when a man wanted to marry a woman too young to marry legally in the church," O'Reilly said. "I think the bloody Normans might've brought the custom from France where couples running away to get married were said to be, how do they say it in that bloody frog language, *un marriage sur la croix de l'epee.*"

"My French is rusty," Colin said. "But, you just said, making a marriage on the cross of the sword. What the hell does that have to do with a broomstick?"

"Well, you know the English dinna know other languages, and they translated it as marriage by leaping over a broomstick."

"Hm, it does sound interesting," Elizabeth said.

"Well, my dear, will you jump the broom with me?"

"I will."

"In addition, I will have Mr. Hoskins, the American consul in Cap Haitien, perform a marriage ceremony, so we will be considered legally married even in places where they never heard of jumping over a broom."

"Can he do that?"

"I don't know, but I'm pretty sure I can get him to give us a nice legal sounding document saying we're man and wife. Since we won't be going to America, I doubt that anyone will question it."

She shook her head and smiled. "You, my dear husband-to-be, *are* a pirate deep down in your heart."

"Well, why don't we do the broom jumping right here on *The Vixen*," O'Reilly said. "We can use one of the swabs."

"And, we can have a big party as soon as we dock at Cap Haitien," Garcia added.

Chapter 48

Cap Haitien

And, it was thus taken completely out of the couple's hands. The three ships sailed side by side, close enough to toss bottles of ale back and forth, or swing by ropes from the yard arms, which many of the crew did in order to congratulate the new couple. And, rather than waiting until arriving in Haiti to have a party, they had a loud, drunken soiree as they sailed, arriving in port with hangovers, headaches, and hoarse throats from singing and cheering.

As soon as they docked, Colin and Elizabeth went straight to Hoskins' office. They found him seated behind his desk, his shirt open at the neck, with a half-empty bottle of whiskey at his elbow and a glass in his hand. His cheeks were covered in a dark stubble, and his eyes were bloodshot, but he grinned lopsidedly at them as they entered. He raised the glass.

"Here's to victory," he said. "A bittersweet mistress she is."

"If you're referring to the peace treaty, I guess I'd agree," Colin said. "All of that killing and destruction, and things are right back where they started."

"Hah, the treaty. The only good thing about that was it stopped the war. No, I was referring to Old Hickory's victory at New Orleans."

"Who is Old Hickory?" Elizabeth asked.

Hoskins squinted up at her, then he stood and bowed, almost falling over in the process. "Forgive me, my lady," he said. "I didn't see you behind this big galoot. You must be Captain Elizabeth Parker. I must say, you don't look like a demon from hell to me."

"Huh?" Her brow knitted and she frowned. "Who called me a demon from hell?"

"Why, that was how our English friends described you in the dispatches my spies managed to . . . borrow. To me, though, you look like an angel."

She blushed. "Why, thank you, kind sir. But, you did not answer my question. Who is this Old Hickory?"

"He's talking about Andrew Jackson," Colin said. "The army officer in command of American forces in the south. His job was to defend New Orleans."

"And, defend it he did," Hoskins said. "With a ragtag army of a few regulars, some militia boys from Alabama and Louisiana, pirates, shopkeepers, free men of color, and even slaves, less than 5,000 men overall, he defeated a British force three times his size. Sent General Pakenham and Admiral Cochrane running like scared rabbits."

"When did that happen?" Colin asked.

"Their first attack was on December 14, at Lake Borgne, and they overran the few gunboats we had there and set up a garrison on Pea Island, just 30 miles east of New Orleans. By December 23, 1,800 redcoats were nine miles south of New Orleans, but instead of attacking along the undefended road into the city, they set up camp. Old Hick-, er, General Jackson, heard about it, and that night he attacked their camp. He had to pull back, but the audacity of the attack caused the British commander to be too cautious, and it gave Jackson time to construct earthworks and set up artillery to defend the entry into the city. When the redcoats attacked, instead of the walkover they'd been told to expect, they met a wall of fire. Pakenham and his second in command were both killed early in the fighting, which went on until January 18 or 19, when the British finally gave up and withdrew. Of course, soon after that, everyone learned that the peace treaty had been signed, so the attack was a wasted effort. They wouldn't have been able to keep the city even if they'd won, but they didn't, so hundreds of their soldiers died in vain. But, old Jackson is now a hero, the winner of the Battle of New Orleans. I wouldn't be surprised if he doesn't use that to move himself right into the president's mansion in Washington City."

Colin looked at Elizabeth and nodded. "Well, we didn't stop the English attacking New Orleans, but I imagine they might have done better if the ships that were chasing us were supporting them in the Gulf."

"You got that right, son," Hoskins said. "You and this young lady here did the country a great service. I'm recommending you for a medal, and a letter of thanks for Captain Parker and her folks."

"Uh, that won't be necessary, sir," Colin said.

"But, why not? You deserve it. Besides, it'll help your navy career."

Colin took his resignation letter from his pocket. "About that," he said. "I have here a letter I'd like you to deliver to the secretary of the navy."

Hoskins took the letter and began reading, his eyes widening. He stopped reading and looked up at Colin.

"You're giving up your navy career? Why?"

"Let's just say that I've found a new calling. Besides, I am now a family man, and I don't think my new wife would like being married to a navy officer."

Hoskins' gaze shifted to Elizabeth. "And, who is your new wife?"

Elizabeth blushed. "I, sir, have that honor."

He looked back and forth, from one of them to the other, a lopsided grin on his face. "When the hell did you find time to get married?"

They explained the ceremony held shipboard enroute to Haiti. "What we'd really like," Colin said. "Is a marriage certificate from you just in case we make landfall somewhere they care about such things."

"Regrettably, we consuls aren't authorized to marry folks. I can, though, introduce you to a local priest who can do it all official like."

"Not one of those voodoo priests," Elizabeth said.

Hoskins shook his head. "No, not a voodoo priest, good lady. A lot of Haitians, though, are Catholic. You don't have any objection to being married by a papist, do you?"

"As long as it's legal and binding, he could even be a Mohammedan for all I care," said Colin.

"Well," Hoskins said. "Let's go find ourselves a priest. I want to give the bride away."

Chapter 49

March 1814, 200 miles east of the coast of Brazil

After accompanying Hoskins to a Catholic church, where, after Colin had given over five gold pieces, a wizened old priest performed the marriage vows, and gave them a certificate written in Latin and French, proclaiming them to be husband and wife in the eyes of God and man, they returned to Seal Cays.

As Colin had anticipated, Chief Kojomo and his people had found the island to their satisfaction, and decided to rebuild their village there, at the base of a small mountain with a panoramic view of the sea. Enough of Elizabeth's crew, including all of the men who had sailed with Macintosh, along with their wives and children, and the elderly, asked and were given permission to remain with them, that it was decided that *Hellhound* would remain with them, to be used in emergencies, and to make supply and trading trips to the other islands in the chain. Diego Garcia, torn between his loyalty to Elizabeth, and his friendship with Colin and M'nondo, took several hours to decide to remain behind to captain the ship, and serve jointly with Kojomo as chief of the new settlement.

With two full crews, along with several of the more adventurous wives, *The Vixen* and *Avenger* headed south.

The first eight days of the voyage were uneventful, with the occasional stop at a coastal island to replenish the fresh water supply, and trade for food.

They were 200 miles northeast of Sao Luis when they spotted the ship sailing toward them from the east, clearly on an intercept course. At the time, Colin was in command of *Avenger,* sailing an eighth of a mile astern of *The Vixen,* and it was his lookout that first spotted the ship. He adjusted the sails to increase speed and came alongside *The Vixen.*

"Signalman," he said. "Send to *Vixen,* ship following. Looks like British frigate."

The reply came back quickly. "She wants to know what you think we should do, cap'n," the signalman said.

"Let's give him a royal welcome," he said.

"She says, acknowledged. You take port, we have starboard."

There was no need to communicate further. The maneuver he knew she had in mind was similar to what they'd used on merchant ships. With a naval vessel as the target, though, it would have to be adjusted slightly, and unlike the merchants, who surrendered as soon as they saw pirate ships on both sides, the navy would fight, of this Colin was sure.

"Gunners prepare port and starboard cannons," he said. "Sharpshooters aloft. You have permission to fire at any target you see."

"Will we be boarding?" M'nondo, standing, as always, at his left.

"No, not this one. The objective is to do maximum damage, and then put as much distance between us and the British navy as quickly as we can."

"Aye, captain. So, the boarding parties will be assigned to help on the cannons or be extra sharpshooters."

"Good idea. Issue the muskets. They won't be needing their sabers on this one."

The two ships drifted apart until a half mile separated them, and then trimmed sails to slow their speed. Colin kept an eye on the frigate, which was closing on them rapidly.

Colin watched as the frigate adjusted her course, aiming at him, as he knew would happen. Of the two vessels, *Avenger* looked the easiest target, so he assumed the frigate captain would go for the softest target before tackling the more formidable looking *Vixen*. He had discussed this with the others, so he knew that Elizabeth, too, was watching and would make the appropriate adjustments to her course, which meant she would appear to be moving away from *Avenger*, giving the impression that she knew what the English captain was doing, and was taking the opportunity to get away while her weaker companion was being savaged.

As the frigate drew closer, Colin could see the cannon crews at their stations. The frigate, like his ship, had sharpshooters in the masts.

"Sharpshooters, your targets are their marksmen in the masts, starboard cannon crews, be prepared to fire as soon as they're alongside."

He looked forward and saw that Elizabeth was beginning to make her turn. The frigate skipper, apparently intent on what looked to be an easy target, had probably moved *The Vixen* to the back of his mind, prey for later pickings.

By the time the frigate was three ship lengths from *Avenger*, *The Vixen* had completed her turn, and now bore down on the frigate like a hawk swooping down on an unsuspecting rabbit. From the spray being thrown up by her bow as it cut through the water, Colin estimated that she would be nearly alongside the frigate at about the same time it pulled abreast of *Avenger*. He crossed his fingers that the plan would work.

The next half hour was a waiting game. Three ships dancing a deadly dance on the tossing sea, a dance that, if Colin's plan worked, the British frigate would not survive.

The British sharpshooters jumped the gun and began firing at *Avenger* as soon as they were in range of their muskets. The hot lead pellets made 'thunk' sounds as they slammed into the hull and deck, but the distance was too great for accuracy, and no one was hit. Colin's shooters had been trained to wait until a target was well within range, so they merely hunkered down, keeping as much of the mast and sails between them and the British shooters as possible.

When the bowsprit of the frigate was half a ship-length from *Avenger's* stern, Colin cupped his mouth with his hands and shouted up to the snipers, "Give the bastards a taste of some real shooting."

His command was relayed by men scattered about the deck, and a staccato 'crack' sounded from the masts. Colin turned in time to see two forms falling from the frigate's masts, and cannon crews on the ship's port side ducking as bullets slammed into the deck.

"Cannon crews, ready," he said. "You know the drill. When half of her bulk is within range, start from the aft cannon, and fire in succession. Port cannons, prepare your pieces."

His plan hinged on his assumption that the British captain would wait until he could bring all of his cannons to bear before firing in order to inflict maximum damage.

His assumption proved to be correct. As the first cannon abreast of the quarterdeck, Colin tensed, but the gun didn't fire. He could see the crews standing at the ready, waiting for the command to fire. His crews, on the other hand, already had their instructions, and as soon as the first British cannon crew was in range, his aft cannon fired. The six-pound iron ball slammed into the gunwale of the frigate, smashed into the cannon and its crew, sending pieces of wood, metal, and bodies flying across the deck, and causing adjacent crews to duck. The forward momentum of the frigate made it impossible to prevent what happened next.

As the ship slipped forward, *Avenger's* next cannon fired, and the next, and the next. Each ball hit the frigate, and while none of the other cannon crews were hit directly, men were felled by flying debris. At the same time, *The Vixen* had come alongside to the frigate's starboard, and turned slightly to port, firing all four of her cannons in an angled trajectory that would allow any balls that missed to fall behind *Avenger*. The starboard side of the frigate was soon a mangled mess of damaged cannons and fallen sailors.

On the quarterdeck of the frigate, realization of the trap they'd been drawn into caused panic. Colin could see a lot of arm waving and mouths moving but couldn't hear over the boom of cannons and the crack of muskets.

The encounter was over in ten minutes, ten minutes that must have seemed to the beleaguered British crew like a lifetime.

The frigate was damaged severely. Because the cannon shots had been aimed at the upper portion of the hull, it wasn't in danger of sinking, but the main mast had been smashed, and a large percentage of the crew killed or seriously injured. The ship would be able to limp to a port, but it was no longer a threat to *Avenger* or *The Vixen*.

Colin had *Avenger* turn, and thirty minutes later came alongside *The Vixen*. He signaled Elizabeth to turn east, and sail for fifty miles before turning south. *Avenger* would follow behind to keep lookout in case the frigate had friends in the area.

Charles Ray

Chapter 50

Mouth of the Amazon River, Brazil

On the off chance that another ship had come along and questioned the survivors of their attack, they sailed east and then north for an hour, before turning back south, their destination the southern tip of South America, and from there out into the wide Pacific Ocean and whatever awaited them.

They made their turn early in the afternoon, and for another two hours their journey was peaceful. Then, a lookout on *The Vixen* spotted six sets of sails in the distance behind them and gave the warning. Colin had known their feint was a long shot, but he hadn't figured on the English tumbling to it so quickly, and worse, correctly estimating their course. The two ships stood no chance against six British warships. Their only choice was to make a run for it.

Colin knew, though, that on the open ocean, they would eventually be caught. As nimble as their ships were, the British fleet had faster, more nimble vessels. No, they had to find a place to hide. He had a thought of just such a place. It would only require them to maintain their distance ahead of the pursuing ships until near nightfall.

He had his signalman send to *The Vixen,* 'Make for mouth of Amazon River. Will follow and keep eye on pursuers.'

Elizabeth signaled back, 'Should stay and help you fight.'

'No intention of fighting. Just make for Amazon at top speed. Rendezvous with you there.'

He alternated between watching the British ships, which didn't seem to be getting any closer, and *The Vixen*, which was becoming smaller and smaller as it increased speed, hoping that only *Avenger* had been sighted. That would enable him to lead the British away from their intended destination. He made a slight course change to the southeast and was rewarded minutes later when he noticed the six ships had also changed course.

"Rig sails for as much speed as we can get, M'nondo," he said. "Maintain this course for two hours, then change to southwest."

"Aye," the big man replied, and trotted off to carry out his instructions.

The spurt of speed widened the gap, but only momentarily, as the British also increased speed.

The chase continued for three hours, and when the bottom of the sun's disk was touching the water in the west, Colin changed course to due south.

Darkness at sea can sometimes be a gradual process, but at others, the interval between twilight and night is nil. One moment things can be dimly seen, and the next, the only thing you can see is the inky-black sky festooned with millions of twinkling lights.

Through his spyglass, Colin could see the soft glow of lanterns on the British ships. *Avenger*, however, was running dark, his men having had many months of experience operating the ship in total darkness as they sneaked up on unsuspecting targets at night.

Now was his time. He turned to M'nondo who stood silently at his side.

"Change course, make for the mouth of the Amazon."

The coast of Brazil was a dark, brooding shape against the only slightly lighter black sky at half past midnight when *Avenger* entered the mouth of the Amazon, the mightiest river in the known world. Flowing from the western side of the South American continent, it flowed over 4,000 miles through dense jungle and lush plain before emptying into the Atlantic. The mouth of the Amazon is over 100 miles wide, but Colin had heard old sailors talk about a navigable channel between the islands of Curua and Jurapan that was about nine miles wide, that would easily accommodate a ship the size of *The Vixen* or *Avenger*. His plan was for *The Vixen* to arrive and sail up river until she reached a point where the channel narrowed and was lined on both sides with thick jungle growth. She would then turn to face downriver, and anchor in the center of the channel, to await *Avenger.*

For his plan to succeed, Colin would have to get *Avenger* into the channel and past the islands before first light, before the pursuing English could see him.

He breathed a sigh of relief. They just might make it. But, he didn't relax until the ship slipped past Jurapan on her starboard.

The change from the ocean, which is never quiet: with the sound of the ship carving through the water, waves slapping against the hull, and the whisper of the wind, to the river, with the raucous call of jungle birds, the chatter of monkeys, and the splash of some water creature, was profound. But, the thing that affected Colin most was the smell. At sea, the tang of salty air is refreshing, but the river had a moldy, clinging, though not unpleasant, odor that hung in the air.

That was another thing that he noticed. At sea, even in periods of calm, when there's not enough wind to fill the sails, you can still feel the movement of air. But, here, surrounded on all sides by hulking, dark trees, the air was heavy and wrapped you like a wool blanket.

They found *The Vixen* after sailing only two miles upstream, a journey that took longer than it would have on the ocean because there wasn't t he same volume of wind, and they were sailing against the current.

The Vixen was anchored in the middle of the channel, her bow pointing southeast, giving her a shot with the port cannons, which were manned by nervous-looking men. In the dim moonlight, Colin could see Elizabeth pacing the quarterdeck. He decided that the prudent thing to do was identify himself early.

"Ahoy, *Vixen*, *Avenger* coming alongside."

Elizabeth stopped pacing and rushed to the rail.

"Colin, did you give them the slip without having to do battle?"

"Aye, that we did," he said. "I just thought of myself as a fox, and the English were fox hounds. The object is not to fight, but to get away. I doubt they'll be looking for us here."

"How long do we have to stay here?" He could hear a nervous tremor in her voice. "The sounds coming from the jungle around us unnerves me, and I've heard stories of cannibals living in these jungles."

"Not cannibals," M'nondo said quietly. "But, there are several warlike tribes, including a few that shrink the heads of their dead enemies."

Colin shuddered. "Cannibals or head shrinkers, not much difference if you're on the losing end."

"No, I suppose not. You had better give her an answer. This is the first time I have ever heard fear in her voice."

"Hm, I suppose you're right." Colin turned back to the rail. "I figure two days should give them time to realize that they've lost us, and that we probably slipped back north."

She sniffed. "Two days, then, and not a minute more."

"My goodness, you're right. She's scared. I never thought I would see that woman frightened of anything."

M'nondo looked around. "I was only a boy when the slave traders took me, but I remember my village in Africa. The white men called it jungle, but it was nothing like this. I must admit, this place makes *me* a bit edgy."

Colin shrugged and clapped a hand on his shoulder. "Every environment has its dangers, my friend. They differ only in nature, not in the damage they can do to you. In Philadelphia or Baltimore, two of our major cities, you are in danger of being run down by a horse cart. Dead is dead, and it does no good to dwell on it."

"Tell that to my little sister," M'nondo said.

Charles Ray

Chapter 51

Two days went by with the slowness of cold molasses, minutes seeming like hours, and hours too long to count, but finally, the second day came, and Elizabeth reminded Colin of his promise.

They hauled anchors up and owing to the width of the channel sailed side by side toward the mouth of the mighty river.

A shock awaited them where the Amazon poured its fresh water into the briny ocean. Two British frigates lurked a mile off shore.

Colin signaled. "I guess we didn't fool all of them. Care for a little fight."

Elizabeth signaled back. "After two days in that jungle, yes, I feel like fighting."

"Let's play with them a while," Colin signaled. "Butterfly."

Elizabeth signaled agreement.

Butterfly was a tactic Colin had been toying with in the event they came into contact with more than one British ship, as a way to confuse the enemy and make it difficult for them to use their traditional battle tactics. He thought it would work better with three ships but was willing to try it with two.

Avenger and *The Vixen* sailed side by side, on a heading directly at the two British warships, and then, when they were half a mile away from them, *Avenger* swung to port and *The Vixen* to starboard, forcing the

British ships to decide whether to split and go after both of them simultaneously, or go after one and ignore the other. News of what they'd done previously had obviously spread, because the two ships also changed course, one after each of them.

He watched them closely, waiting until they were a good half mile apart, then ordering a course change to rejoin *The Vixen*. The captain pursuing him didn't realize at first what was happening, and by the time he did, *Avenger* and *The Vixen* were closing a pincer around his comrade, angling their courses so any of their cannon balls missing their target—and, few did—wouldn't hit the other ship.

The first frigate was a smoldering wreck in minutes, and they turned to go after the other ship, which was slicing through the water at maximum speed, coming to his comrade's aid. But, when he was a quarter mile away, the unfortunate captain saw that not only was he too late, but he, too, had been pulled into a trap.

Frantic efforts to turn the frigate were wasted. By the time her bow was turned north, *Avenger* and *The Vixen* fell upon her like a hungry pack of wolves on a rabbit, their cannons splintering upper and lower sections of hull, smashing into masts and sending them tumbling, and completely destroying the quarterdeck and all who were unfortunate to be on it at the time.

They decided not to stay and finish the job. The two ships turned southwest and sailed away, leaving the two frigates dead in the water, sails useless, and hulls breached in a dozen places. These two wolves of the sea would not hunt again.

Colin signaled to *The Vixen,* 'Well done.'

The reply; 'That was fun. We must do it again sometime.'

"She has her sense of humor back," M'nondo said. "That is good."

Chapter 52

April 1815, Easter Island, 2,182 miles west of Chile

After a month of nothing to see but the boundless ocean, the first sight of Easter Island, a mere smudge on the western horizon, generated excitement on both ships.

After rounding the southern tip of the South American continent, they'd sailed northwest, stopping occasionally at islands along the coast to replenish supplies, and then west, aiming for the Polynesian island chain where they knew the long arm of the British navy was unlikely to find them.

The crews, antsy after so long without the sight of land, wanted to sail in and land, but Colin calmed his own crew, and signaled to *The Vixen* that they should discuss it before anyone set foot on the island. Bowing to her seniority as a pirate captain, he suggested that the senior officers meet on her ship.

Colin, Elizabeth, M'nondo, and O'Reilly gathered around the table in her cabin after they anchored the two ships a half mile off the shore. Colin cautioned the lookouts to be on special watch for any canoes or small boats coming toward them from the island, and when he arrived aboard *The Vixen* suggested that Elizabeth do the same.

"Why should we have to worry about the island natives?" she asked when everyone had settled down and poured a mug of rum.

"You need to understand the history of this place," Colin said. "The locals have no reason to trust outsiders, and they can be hostile." He took a sip of rum. "They'd been living on this island peacefully for hundreds of years before the first Europeans came. There were two different native groups, one at the north and west ends, and one at the east end of the island when a Dutchman, Jacob Roggeveen, stumbled across it while looking for another island, sort of like Christopher Columbus bumping into Haiti when he was looking for India. It was Roggeveen who gave it the name Easter Island, because he arrived on Easter Sunday, April 5, 1722. It's unclear what the natives themselves called it, or even if they had a name for it, but shortly after the white man's arrival, war started between the two tribal groups over control of the whole island, and from the reports I heard in 1812 before our war started, that fight goes on still."

Elizabeth shook her head. "Wouldn't do for us to drop in right in the middle of a local battle."

"Nor should we be seen as favoring one side over the other," Colin said. "Although, I would love to go ashore to see the statues I heard about."

"Statues," O'Reilly said. "What statues?"

"They have these huge stone heads carved from local rock. I believe they call them *moai*, or something like that. I was told that they represent ancestors, and that there are hundreds of them, sitting there, facing the sea, to bring good fortune and ward off bad fortune."

"Dinna sound like they worked too well," the Irishman said. "The bloody Europeans came anyway

300

and sounds to me like they brought a lot of misfortune."

"True. Apparently, there was some kind of confrontation with Roggeveen's group, resulting in the death of several natives. Anyway, I don't think a visit is wise. Maybe we can sail around close enough that we can see the statues, and then we sail on."

"What's our final destination?" Elizabeth asked.

"Who knows." Colin smiled around the table. "I thought we'd go first to Pitcairn. That's the island I hear the crew of the British ship, Bounty, settled on after their mutiny. I figure they'll be welcoming enough, considering our history with their former masters. After that . . . well, there's a wide world out there, and a lot of ocean to sail. I say we just aim our bow west and see if we can learn where the sun goes at night."

He lifted his mug in a toast.

"Yes," M'nondo said, lifting his mug. "Let us chase the sun."

Charles Ray

Books by this author:

Al Pennyback mysteries
Color Me Dead
Memorial to the Dead
Deadline
Dead, White, and Blue
A Good Day to Die
The Day the Music Died
Die, Sinner
Deadly Intentions
Death by Design
Till Death Do Us Part
Deadly Dose
Dead Man's Cove
Dead Men Don't Answer
Deadly Paradise
Kiss of Death
Death in White Satin
Death and Taxis
Deadbeat
A Deadly Wind Blows
Death Wish
Deadly Vendetta
A Time to Kill, A Time to Die
Dead Ringer
Death of Innocence
Dead Reckoning
Murder on the Menu
Over My Dead Body
Bad Girls Don't Die
A Deal to Die For

Ed Lazenby mysteries
Butterfly Effect
Coriolis Effect
The Cat in the Hatbox
Negative Side Effects

Murder is as Easy as ABC

Buffalo Soldier series
Buffalo Soldier: Trial by Fire
Buffalo Soldier: Homecoming
Buffalo Soldier: Incident at Cactus Junction
Buffalo Soldier: Peacekeepers
Buffalo Soldier: Renegade
Buffalo Soldier: Escort Duty
Buffalo Soldier: Battle at Dead Man's Gulch
Buffalo Soldier: Yosemite
Buffalo Soldier: Comanchero
Buffalo Soldier: Range War
Buffalo Soldier: Mob Justice
Buffalo Soldier: Chasing Ghosts
Buffalo Soldier: The Piano
Buffalo Soldier: Family Feud
Buffalo Soldier: The Lost Expedition

Other fiction
Angel on His Shoulder
She's No Angel
Child of the Flame
Pip's Revenge
Wallace in Underland
Further Adventures of Wallace in Underland
Dead Letter and Other Tales
The White Dragons
The Dragon's Lair
Dragon Slayer
The Last Gunfighters
The Culling
Frontier Justice: Bass Reeves, Deputy
  U.S. Marshal
Angel on His Shoulder-Revised Edition
Battle at the Galactic Junkyard
Mountain Man
Devil's Lake

Vixen
Wagons West: Daniel's Journey
Wagons West: Trinity
Awakening
Fatal Encounters: The Adventures of Bass
    Reeves, Deputy U.S. Marshal
The Marshal and the Madam: The Adventures
    of Bass Reeves, Deputy U.S. Marshal, Volume 2
Chase the Sun

Nonfiction

Things I Learned from My Grandmother About
    Leadership and Life
Taking Charge: Effective Leadership for the
    Twenty-first Century
Grab the Brass ring
African Places: A Photographic Journey
    Through Zimbabwe and southern Africa
A Portrait of Africa
There's Always a Plan B
In the Line of Fire: American Diplomats in
    the Trenches
Advice for the Insecure Writer
Looking at Life Through My Lens
Ethical Dilemmas and the Practice of Diplomacy
Making America Grate Again
DC Street Art
Dead Letters and Other Tales: Revised edition
Things I Learned from My Grandmother About
Leadership and
    Life, Second Edition
Feathers, Fur, and Flowers

Children's books

The Yak and the Yeti
Samantha and the Bully
Molly Learns to Share
Where is Teddy?

Catie and Mister Hop-Hop
Tommy Learns to Count
Catie Goes to School

About the Author

Charles Ray has been writing fiction since his teens. He won a Sunday school magazine writing contest when he was thirteen and having his byline on a short story published in a national publication forever hooked him on writing. During his time in the army (1962-1982) he often moonlighted as a newspaper or magazine journalist and was the editorial cartoonist for the Spring Lake (NC) News, a weekly newspaper, during the 1970s. In addition to his writing, he was an artist/cartoonist and photographer for a number of publications, including Ebony, Eagle and Swan, and Essence, and had a monthly cartoon feature and did several covers for Buffalo, a now-defunct magazine that was dedicated to showcasing the contributions of African-Americans to the country's military history.

After retiring from the army, he joined the U.S. Foreign Service, and served as a diplomat in posts in Asia and Africa until his retirement in 2012. He has worked and traveled throughout the world (Antarctica is the only continent he hasn't visited), and now, as a full-time writer, continues to globetrot looking for interesting things to write about, draw, or take pictures of.

A native of Texas, he now calls Maryland home. For more on his writing and other projects, check one of the following Web sites:

http://charlesaray.blogspot.com
http://charlieray45.wordpress.com
http://www.twitter.com/charlieray45
http://www.facebook.com/charlieray45
http://www.flickr.com/photos/charlesray45/
http://www.viewbug.com/member/charlesray

You can also order some of my books through my author's website: http://charlesray-author.com/

Authors write to be read, and that can only happen when readers are made aware of the books available. Reviews are one way this happens. If you liked this book, please leave a review, even if only a few words, on Amazon or Goodreads.